U0022546

Reading Power 系列

Intermediate

★ 108課綱、中級全民英檢必備

Intermediate Reading
新聞宅急通

C

三民英語編輯小組　彙編

ACKNOWLEDGEMENT

The articles in this publication are
adapted from the works by Theodore
J. Pigott and Jason W. Crockett.

三民書局

國家圖書館出版品預行編目資料

Intermediate Reading:新聞宅急通C／三民英語編輯小
組彙編.－－初版五刷.－－臺北市: 三民，2022
　　面；　公分.－－(Reading Power系列)
　含索引
　ISBN 978－957－14－5799－4 （平裝）
　1.新聞英文 2.讀本

805.18　　　　　　　　　　　　　　　102007698

Intermediate Reading: 新聞宅急通 C

彙　　　編	三民英語編輯小組
發 行 人	劉振強
出 版 者	三民書局股份有限公司
地　　　址	臺北市復興北路 386 號 (復北門市)
	臺北市重慶南路一段 61 號 (重南門市)
電　　　話	(02)25006600
網　　　址	三民網路書店 https://www.sanmin.com.tw
出版日期	初版一刷 2013 年 5 月
	初版五刷 2022 年 1 月
書籍編號	S809750
I S B N	978-957-14-5799-4

著作權所有，侵害必究
※ 本書如有缺頁、破損或裝訂錯誤，請寄回敝局更換。

三民書局

序

知識，就是希望；閱讀，就是力量。

在這個資訊爆炸的時代，應該如何選擇真正有用的資訊來吸收？
在考場如戰場的競爭壓力之下，應該如何儲備實力，漂亮地面對挑戰？
身為地球村的一分子，應該如何增進英語實力，與世界接軌？

學習英文的目的，就是要讓自己在這個資訊爆炸的時代之中，突破語言的藩籬，站在吸收新知的制高點之上，以閱讀獲得力量，以知識創造希望！

針對在英文閱讀中可能面對的挑戰，我們費心規劃 Reading Power 系列叢書，希望在學習英語的路上助你一臂之力，讓你輕鬆閱讀、快樂學習。

誠摯希望在學習英語的路上，這套 Reading Power 系列叢書將伴隨你找到閱讀的力量，發揮知識的光芒！

給讀者的話

誠如英語教學大師 H. Douglas Brown 所言：「閱讀」往往與聽、說、寫等語言能力培養有著密不可分的關係。閱讀通常被認為是學習語言的基本能力，這種能力的提升能夠幫助語言學習者更有效地學習。至於要如何加強閱讀能力呢？目前最為人所認同的理念包括「真實材料」(authentic material)、「由上而下的閱讀技巧」(top-down strategy) 以及「基模理論」(schema theory) 等。

「真實材料」指的是存在於真實情境中的語料，目的是為了使語言學習者能夠接觸到真實情境中使用到的語言，並進行更有意義的學習。本書的取材來自國內外的重要新聞，透過外籍作者的撰寫，設計出適合讀者程度的閱讀內容。「由上而下的閱讀技巧」簡而言之指的就是由整體到部分，這也正是本書的編排理念，從整篇文章的閱讀到文中的單字片語分析，讓讀者可以獲得更全面的了解。最後，「基模理論」是透過現有的想法和知識，納入新的概念，最後內化成自己的知識。讀者倘若對某篇文章內容有基本的認識與了解，必定會提高對這篇文章的興趣；在閱讀過程中，也可以快速掌握重點並理解內容。本書所蒐集的題材皆為近年來熱門話題，藉由讀者本身對該新聞事件的了解，產生共鳴進而提高閱讀效果。

在這樣的設計架構下，本書之新聞主題貼近生活，撰文亦力求符合讀者程度，並設計以下單元以增進讀者學習成效：

◆ Exercise：根據文章內容設計綜合測驗、文意選填和閱讀測驗，讓讀者透過這些練習，增加閱讀速度、加強字彙量以及對題型的熟練程度。

◆ Vocabulary：列出文章中關鍵字彙，並提供中文解釋與例句，讓讀者能夠正確使用詞彙。

◆ Idioms & Phrases：列出文章重要片語，並提供中文解釋及例句。

◆ Pop Quiz：針對字彙與片語的小測驗，有選擇、拼字、文意選填等多種題型，提供讀者自我評量的工具。

此外，本書附冊附有所有文章之全文翻譯，讓讀者對文章可以有更深入的理解；同時還有精闢的 Exercise 解析，提供實用的解題技巧。

本書之編寫力求完善，但難免有疏漏之處，希望讀者與各界賢達隨時賜教。

三民英語編輯小組　謹誌

Table of Contents

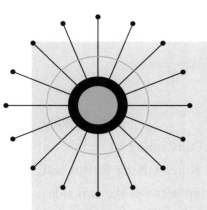

International Relation

國際關係

UNIT 01

North Korea at It Again

June, 2009

The world's attention turned to the Korean peninsula this spring as tensions between [1]North and South Korea began to rise. With North Korea talking tough and claiming that it ___1___ another nuclear bomb, the relationship between the two sides was at its lowest, and perhaps most dangerous, point in recent years.

Korea was a single country until the end of [2]World War II. Then, a brutal civil war broke ___2___. The North was supported by China, ___3___ the South was backed by the United States. The two sides fought until 1953, when a temporary peace agreement was signed. In the years that followed, ___4___ no further major military outbreaks, but the two sides kept a careful eye on one another. Even today, both North and South Korea still have troops located on the border that separates the two countries.

This spring, however, North Korea began to take actions that would threaten the peace between the two sides. In April, it launched a ___5___ missile. The rest of the world, ___6___ the [3]United Nations, condemned North Korea for this move. In response, North Korea announced on May 25 that it had successfully completed a second nuclear weapons test. The country's first test had ___7___ in 2006. It also stated that the temporary peace agreement that had stopped the Korean War in 1953 would no longer be followed.

Why is North Korea now acting in such an unpredictable and risky way? Some say that it is ___8___ South Korea recently joined a US-led effort to stop the spread of nuclear weapons. For years, the United States ___9___ to get North Korea to end its nuclear weapons program. Others say that North Korea's leader, the mysterious [4]Kim Jong-Il, is just looking for attention. Experts also say that North Korea ___10___ needs economic assistance, and these recent moves might be an attempt to bargain for help.

In any case, with its recent actions, North Korea is certainly threatening to upset more than fifty years of relative peace between North and South Korea.

Exercise

Choose the correct answers.

(   ) 1. (A) had tested   (B) tested   (C) tests   (D) has tested

(   ) 2. (A) out   (B) in   (C) up   (D) down

(   ) 3. (A) and   (B) while   (C) as   (D) so

(   ) 4. (A) it was   (B) these were   (C) there were   (D) there was

(   ) 5. (A) low-risk   (B) long-lived   (C) far-reaching   (D) long-range

(   ) 6. (A) inclusive   (B) includes   (C) included   (D) including

(   ) 7. (A) given away   (B) taken place   (C) come across   (D) carried out

(   ) 8. (A) so   (B) but   (C) when   (D) because

(   ) 9. (A) tries   (B) had tried   (C) has been trying   (D) tried

(   ) 10. (A) badly   (B) nearly   (C) hardly   (D) shortly

≫ Vocabulary

1. **peninsula** [pə`nɪnsələ] *n.* [C] 半島
   - A peninsula is a long piece of land, which has three sides surrounded by water and one side joined to a large piece of land.

2. **tension** [`tɛnʃən] *n.* [C] 緊張局勢；[U] 緊張
   - The country's growing social tensions caused the serious riot.
   - It is reported that exercise can help relieve tension.

3. **tough** [tʌf] *adv.* 堅定地
   - The tennis player can play tough when she meets her match.
   tough [tʌf] *adj.* 強硬的
   - It's time to get tough with drunken drivers.

4. **nuclear** [`njuklɪɚ] *adj.* 核子的
   - People in Taiwan were debating whether they should build another nuclear power plant or not.

5. **brutal** [`brutl̩] *adj.* 殘忍的
   - You are such a brutal man to abuse a dog like that. Don't pull its tail anymore!

6. **outbreak** [`aʊtˌbrek] *n.* [C] 爆發

- It was racial problems that led to the outbreaks of fighting.

7. **launch** [lɔntʃ] *vt.* 發射
   - Eumetsat (歐洲氣象衛星組織) will launch a weather satellite tomorrow.

8. **condemn** [kən`dɛm] *vt.* 譴責
   - The factory was condemned for discharging waste water into the river.

9. **unpredictable** [ˌʌnprɪ`dɪktəbl] *adj.* 無法預測的，出乎意料的
   - Spring weather can be unpredictable. It alternates between warm and cold.

10. **risky** [`rɪskɪ] *adj.* 冒險的，大膽的
    - It's far too risky to go to the beach when a typhoon comes.

11. **recently** [`risn̩tlɪ] *adv.* 最近，近來
    - I am reading Suzanne Collins's novel *The Hunger Games* recently. I am almost finishing it.

12. **mysterious** [mɪs`tɪrɪəs] *adj.* 神祕的
    - Several people reported that they had seen mysterious lights in the sky.

13. **assistance** [ə`sɪstəns] *n.* [U] 協助
    - The government should offer financial assistance to the students who cannot pay the tuition.

14. **bargain** [`bɑrgɪn] *vi.* 討價還價，談條件
    - Mr. Wang bargained with the real estate agent for a lower price.

15. **certainly** [`sɝtn̩lɪ] *adv.* 必定，一定
    - Frank works so hard that I believe he will certainly succeed in the future.

≫ Idioms & Phrases

1. **be at it again**　做某事 (表不贊同某人做的事)
   - Tess is at it again. Every time she gets angry, she yells at her boyfriend.

2. **keep an eye on...**　盯著 (某人)，注意 (某人的) 行動
   - You should keep an eye on your son. I found that he had skipped class last week.

≫ 補 充

1. **North Korea**　北韓
   首都平壤，南部與北部與中國、俄羅斯接壤，西臨黃海，東臨日本海。是一個典型的社會

主義國家。

South Korea　南韓

首都首爾。位於東北亞朝鮮半島南端，西南、東南和東邊分別面對黃海、朝鮮海峽與日本海。北面隔著三八線非軍事區與北韓相鄰。該國經濟發展繁榮，已於 2010 年躋身已開發國家之列。

2. World War II　第二次世界大戰

部份學者認為第二次世界大戰的起迄時間是從 1939 年 9 月 1 日德國入侵波蘭開始，到 1945 年 9 月 2 日日本向同盟國投降結束。戰火遍及全球，造成約 7 千 2 百多萬人死亡，為目前規模最大的全球性戰爭。交戰雙方為同盟國與軸心國，前者由中華民國、美國、英國、法國、蘇聯為主的政府組織組成，後者由納粹德國、日本帝國、義大利等軍國主義國家所組成，最後同盟國贏得勝利。

3. United Nations (UN)　聯合國

一個由主權國家組成的國際組織。1945 年 6 月 26 日，50 個創始會員國在美國加州舊金山簽定《聯合國憲章》。該憲章於 1945 年 10 月 24 日生效，聯合國正式成立。1946 年 1 月 10 日舉行第一次會員國大會，共有 51 個國家出席。到 2012 年為止，聯合國共有 193 個成員國。

4. Kim Jong-il　金正日 (1941～2011)

北韓第二代最高領導人，為建國者金日成的兒子。

 Pop Quiz

Fill in each blank with the correct word to complete the sentence. Make changes if necessary.

brutal	risky	certainly
launch	tension	condemn

1. The fighter aircraft _____ several missiles to shoot down enemy aircraft.
2. The restaurant's service was bad and so was its food. We will _____ never go there again.
3. Celine tried hard to relieve the _____ between her parents. They had stopped talking to each other for days.
4. Buying a foreclosed house (法拍屋) can be a _____ business.
5. The public _____ the cold−blooded murderer for killing those children.

UNIT 02

A Surprising Choice

November, 2009

In an unexpected announcement, the [1]Norwegian Nobel Committee awarded the 2009 Nobel Peace Prize to President Barack Obama. The decision __1__ many people because he has served in office for less than a year. Although the Nobel Committee explained that President Obama received the prize for "his extraordinary efforts to strengthen international diplomacy and cooperation between peoples," critics complained that they were simply rewarding him for his __2__ popularity.

When Swedish dynamite inventor [2]Alfred Nobel died in 1896, he provided money in his will for the establishment of prizes recognizing achievements in physics, chemistry, __3__, literature, and peace. The first prizes were awarded in 1901, and the winners, known as laureates, receive a diploma, a __4__, and approximately $1.4 million. Many people consider the Peace Prize to be the __5__ prestigious, as it is the final one to be awarded each year.

Although most of the Nobel Prizes award achievements over a long period of time, many recipients of the Peace Prize have been recognized for more recent accomplishments. This has often __6__ controversy, because many winners have been just as responsible for war as they have been for peace. For example, [3]Henry Kissinger, __7__ won the prize in 1973 for negotiating a peace agreement with Vietnam, had earlier helped to plan a secret bombing campaign in [4]Cambodia that killed thousands of civilians.

Even supporters of President Obama seemed to agree that it was perhaps __8__ early to recognize him with such a prestigious award. Many felt that winning the prize would only serve to put unnecessary pressure __9__ the president. Although some people __10__ that he should turn down the honor, President Obama decided to accept the award as "a call to action, a call for all nations to confront the challenges of the 21st century."

Exercise

Fill in each blank with the correct word or phrase.

(A) too	(B) worldwide	(C) led to	(D) who	(E) most
(F) on	(G) suggested	(H) surprised	(I) medicine	(J) medal

1. _____ 2. _____ 3. _____ 4. _____ 5. _____

6. _____ 7. _____ 8. _____ 9. _____ 10. _____

Vocabulary

1. **diplomacy** [dɪ`plɒməsɪ] *n.* [U] 外交
   - The U.S. Secretary of State stressed that the North Korea problem should be resolved through formal diplomacy.

2. **cooperation** [ko͵ɑpə`reʃən] *n.* [U] 合作
   - The Farmers' Market works in cooperation with local farmers and is open to the public on weekends.

3. **popularity** [͵pɑpjə`lærətɪ] *n.* [U] 受歡迎，流行
   - The social networking websites, such as Facebook and Twitter, have gained great popularity all around the world.

4. **dynamite** [`dɑɪnə͵mɑɪt] *n.* [U] 炸藥
   - To build the railway tunnel, the engineer decided to use sticks of dynamite to blast an opening through.

5. **will** [wɪl] *n.* [C] 遺囑
   - Mr. Johnson left his daughter the house in his will.

6. **laureate** [`lɔrɪɪt] *n.* [C] 獲獎者
   - Robert Frost, one of the most important modern American poets, was the United States Poet Laureate during 1958 to 1959.

7. **diploma** [dɪ`plomə] *n.* [C] 證書
   - After finishing four years of college education, Jane got a college diploma.

8. **prestigious** [prɛs`tidʒəs] *adj.* 有聲望的
   - Adele is a prestigious singer. She is highly admired by her fans all over the world.

9. **recipient** [rɪ`sɪpɪənt] *n.* [C] 得主，接受者
   - William Lawrence Bragg, the youngest recipient of Nobel Prize, was the winner in the area of physics at the age of 25.

10. **recognize** [`rɛkəg,naɪz] *vt.* 肯定，認同
    - Charles Chaplin is recognized as having a talent for acting.

11. **accomplishment** [ə`kɑmplɪʃmənt] *n.* [C] 成就
    - The invention of the Internet is considered one of the most important technological accomplishments in the 20th century.

12. **negotiate** [nɪ`goʃɪ,et] *vt.*; *vi.* 談判，商定
    - The phone company is negotiating a new contract with the union.
    - Though the company claimed the huge loss in the previous quarter, the union representatives still strove to negotiate for at least five percent pay raise.

13. **campaign** [kæm`pen] *n.* [C] 戰役
    - The US-led coalition launched the air campaign, *Operation Instant Thunder*, which led to the victory of Persian Gulf War.

14. **civilian** [sə`vɪljən] *n.* [C] 平民
    - Hundreds of innocent civilians were reported to be injured in the bomb blast last night.

15. **serve** [sɝv] *vi.* 用於 (產生…效果)；擔任…職務
    - The incident happened yesterday served to emphasize the importance of airport security.
    - Mr. William has served as a general manager at the car company since 2000.

≫ Idioms & Phrases

1. **in office**　擔任政府重要官職
   - Alan Greenspan, the former Chairman of the Federal Reserve, had been in office for 19 years.

2. **turn down**　回絕，拒絕
   - But for the final examination, I wouldn't have turned down your birthday party invitation.

1. **Norwegian Nobel Committee** 挪威諾貝爾委員會

   成立於 1897 年，為頒發諾貝爾和平獎的機構，由挪威議會任命的五名評審委員所組成。此委員會每年會收到上百位推薦人選，二月時會評選出五到二十個候選人，得獎者會在十月份由委員會公布，頒獎典禮則是在 12 月 10 日 (諾貝爾辭世之日) 舉行。

2. **Alfred Nobel** 阿爾弗雷德・諾貝爾 (1833～1896)

   為瑞典化學家、工程師、發明者及軍火製造商。諾貝爾原先製造液體炸藥硝化甘油，但在投產後不久的 1864 年，工廠發生爆炸，他最小的弟弟和另外 4 人被炸死。因為此種炸藥太危險，諾貝爾開始將硝化甘油和矽藻土原料混合，製成穩定性較高的黃色炸藥。由於大量炸藥被運用在戰爭之中，讓諾貝爾相當難過，所以在遺囑中特別將遺產作為創立諾貝爾獎的基金，分別表彰在物理、化學、生物醫學、文學及和平領域的傑出人士，1901 起開始頒獎。諾貝爾經濟學獎是在 1968 年瑞典國家銀行為紀念諾貝爾所設置的獎項，並於次年開始頒發。

3. **Henry Kissinger** 亨利・季辛吉 (1923～)

   美國前國務卿、政治家、外交官。在 1969 到 1977 年間扮演了美國外交政策的關鍵角色。期間先後擔任總統尼克森和福特的國務卿。1971 年與中國總理周恩來的兩次會談，為冷戰時期開啟了中美關係的新篇章。1973 年因促成結束越戰的巴黎和談，與越南的黎德壽共同獲得該年的諾貝爾和平獎，但因為他在 1968 年主導轟炸柬埔寨的軍事行動，也招致不少批評聲浪。

4. **Cambodia** 柬埔寨

   舊稱高棉，首都金邊，為中南半島國家之一，政治為君主立憲制。西與泰國接壤，東北與寮國，東與越南相鄰。境內有湄公河及東南亞最大的淡水湖洞里薩湖。人口約為一千四百多萬，其中大多信奉佛教。舉世聞名的世界遺產吳哥窟每年都吸引許多遊客前來朝聖。

Pop Quiz

Choose the best answer to each of the following sentences.

(   ) 1. My grandmother left me the pearl necklace in her _____ .

(A) recipient   (B) choice   (C) civilian   (D) will

(   ) 2. The country decided to lower the interest rates; this _____ to boost its economy.

(A) negotiated   (B) bargained   (C) served   (D) compared

(   ) 3. Jeff thought that the publication of his first novel was the greatest _____ of his life.

(A) will   (B) outbreak   (C) campaign   (D) accomplishment

(   ) 4. After graduating from a highly _____ university, Amy soon got a good job.

(A) risky   (B) prestigious   (C) various   (D) tough

(   ) 5. Kate _____ the job offer because the salary was too low.

(A) turned down   (B) broke out   (C) kept up   (D) led to

UNIT 03

End to Hunt for World's Biggest Terrorist

June, 2011

[1]Osama bin Laden, the world's most wanted terrorist, was perhaps best known as the founder of [2]al-Qaeda, a terrorist organization that carried out the September 11 attacks in the United States. Born into a devout [3]Muslim family in Saudi Arabia, bin Laden became very interested in religion while in college. Some believe that he dropped out of school and traveled to [4]Afghanistan in 1979 to fight the invading[5]Soviet army. After the defeat of the Soviets, he became interested in a radical form of [6]Islam, stating that the U.S. government was oppressing Muslims in the Middle East. As a result, bin Laden's al-Qaeda organization carried out a series of terrorist attacks around the world, including the 1993 [7]World Trade Center bombing in New York City, the killing of 19 U.S. soldiers in Saudi Arabia in 1996, bombings of American embassies in [8]Kenya and [9]Tanzania in 1998, and the September 11 attacks, which left more than 3,000 people dead.

After the September 11 attacks, the then U.S. President [10]George W. Bush vowed to get bin Laden "dead or alive." In December of 2001, bin Laden was almost captured in the [11]Tora Bora region of Afghanistan, but he managed to slip away. He then escaped capture for the next several years.

Bin Laden remained on the run for almost a decade. For years, the world wondered exactly where he was hiding. Then, on the evening of May 2, 2011, American President Barack Obama made a startling announcement: "Today, at my direction, the United States launched a targeted operation against compound in [12]Abbottabad, [13]Pakistan. A small team of Americans carried out the operation with extraordinary courage and capability. No Americans were harmed. They took care to avoid civilian casualties. After a firefight, they killed Osama bin Laden and took custody of his body."

News of Osama bin Laden's death brought joyful celebrations in some parts of America. However, some terrorist organizations in other parts of the world vowed to carry out **revenge** attacks for his death. Yet, many people expressed the hope that with the death of bin Laden, the U.S. will now be able to begin to **withdraw** its **troops** from Afghanistan and end the fighting there. Members of anti-war organizations have stated that now that the hunt for bin Laden is over, perhaps peace in this area can begin.

Exercise

Choose the best answers.

(   ) 1. What is the passage mainly about?
      (A) Osama bin Laden's death might bring hopes for peace in the Middle East.
      (B) Al-Qaeda organization carried out a series of terrorist attacks.
      (C) The September 11 attacks caused more than 3,000 people dead.
      (D) Information about Osama bin Laden's educational background.

(   ) 2. Choose the correct sequence of the following events of Osama bin Laden.
      a. Osama bin Laden became interested in a radical form of Islam.
      b. Osama bin Laden went to college.
      c. Osama bin Laden fought the invasion of Soviet army in Afghanistan.
      d. Al-Qaeda organization launched several terrorist attacks around the world.
      (A) abcd   (B) bcad   (C) dabc   (D) cbad

(   ) 3. Which of the following events does NOT occur after the death of Osama bin Laden?
      (A) There were joyful celebrations in some parts of America.
      (B) Terrorist organizations claimed to take revenge for his death.
      (C) People hope that his death would bring peace.
      (D) Al-Qaeda organization carried out World Trade Center bombing.

(   ) 4. U.S. President Obama mentioned in his announcement about Osama bin Laden's death that _____ .
      (A) some U.S. soldiers were shot dead
      (B) U.S. soldiers put Osama bin Laden in prison
      (C) they killed Osama bin Laden in Abbottabad, Pakistan
      (D) U.S. soldiers took care of the injured civilians

(　　) 5. The al-Qaeda organization _____ .

    (A) asked the U.S. to withdraw its troops from Afghanistan peacefully

    (B) fought the invasion of Soviet army in Afghanistan

    (C) was said to be responsible for the September 11 attacks

    (D) fought a war for Saudi Arabia with Afghanistan

≫ Vocabulary

1. **religion** [rɪ`lɪdʒən] *n.* [U] 宗教信仰；[C] 宗教教派
   - In Taiwan, everyone can enjoy freedom of religion.
   - "What religion do you practice? " "Buddhism."

2. **invade** [ɪn`ved] *vt.* 入侵，侵略
   - Japanese invaded and governed Taiwan for about half a century.

3. **defeat** [dɪ`fit] *n.* [U][C] 失敗，戰敗
   - The soccer team suffered defeat in the championship game.
   - The ruling party faced a great defeat in the local election.

4. **radical** [`rædɪkl̩] *adj.* 極端的，激進的
   - Ben's idea about religion is so radical that nobody can accept it.

5. **oppress** [ə`prɛs] *vt.* 壓迫，欺壓
   - The autocrat oppressed his people with guns to prevent them from going against him.

6. **embassy** [`ɛmbəsɪ] *n.* [C] 大使館
   - My uncle works at the American Embassy in London.

7. **vow** [vaʊ] *vt.* 發誓，立誓
   - Frank vowed that he would love his wife forever on their wedding.

8. **escape** [ə`skep] *vt.* 避開 (不好的事情)；*vi.* (從監禁中) 逃離
   - The baby boy narrowly escaped death in the terrible accident.
   - It was reported that two prisoners had escaped from prison by crawling through a drain.

9. **startling** [`startl̩ɪŋ] *adj.* 驚人的，令人驚訝的
   - It is startling to find out that there is water on Mars.

10. **announcement** [əˋnaʊnsmənt] *n.* [C] 宣布，宣告
   - On a TV show, the pitcher made an announcement about his retirement.
11. **compound** [ˋkɑmpaʊnd] *n.* [C] (有圍牆或籬笆等的) 建築群
   - This compound used to be a prison, but there are no prisoners in it now. It has changed into a tourist attraction.
12. **extraordinary** [ɪkˋstrɔrdn͵ɛrɪ] *adj.* 非凡的
   - The actress received the award because of her extraordinary achievements in acting.
13. **capability** [͵kepəˋbɪlətɪ] *n.* [C] 能力，才能
   - Fred has the capability to tackle the difficult problem.
14. **casualty** [ˋkæʒjʊəltɪ] *n.* [C] (車禍、事故的) 傷者，死者
   - The plane crash caused heavy casualties.
15. **custody** [ˋkʌstədɪ] *n.* [U] 扣押
   - The man's gun was held in the custody of the police as evidence in the murder case.
16. **revenge** [rɪˋvɛndʒ] *n.* [U] 報復
   - Hamlet killed his uncle in revenge for the murder of his father.
17. **withdraw** [wɪðˋdrɔ] *vt.* 撤退
   - Neither of the two countries agreed to withdraw its troops from that area.
18. **troop** [trup] *n. pl.* 軍隊
   - 20,000 troops were deployed in the war zone.

≫ Idioms & Phrases

1. **on the run**　在逃
   - The bank robber has been on the run for ten years.

≫ 補 充

1. **Osama bin Laden**　奧薩瑪・賓拉登 (1957～2011)
   沙烏地阿拉伯人，蓋達組織的首領。賓拉登被美國政府指控為 911 事件的幕後主使者，名列美國聯邦調查局十大通緝要犯之一。2011 年 5 月 2 日，美國總統歐巴馬聲稱賓拉登在巴基斯坦阿伯塔巴德的一座豪宅裡被美軍海豹部隊第六分隊突襲擊斃，其遺體於次日海葬於北阿拉伯海。

2. **al-Qaeda** 蓋達組織

   或譯為「基地組織」，是一個伊斯蘭教軍事組織，成立於 1989 年，被指控策劃了多起主要針對美國的恐怖攻擊。

3. **Muslim** 穆斯林

   信從伊斯蘭教真主阿拉的人，即伊斯蘭教徒。

4. **Afghanistan** 阿富汗

   阿富汗伊斯蘭共和國，簡稱阿富汗，首都喀布爾，是一個位於亞洲中南部的內陸國家。農業是主要的經濟支柱，但全國國土只有 12% 為可耕地，是世界上最貧窮的國家之一。

5. **Soviet** [ˋsovɪ͵ɛt] *adj.* 前蘇聯的

6. **Islam** 伊斯蘭教

   或稱回教，舊稱清真教，是以可蘭經和聖訓為教導的一神論宗教。可蘭經被伊斯蘭教信徒視為唯一真神阿拉逐字逐句的啟示，而聖訓為伊斯蘭教先知穆罕默德的言行錄。伊斯蘭教是世界第二大宗教，目前全球約有十多億名信徒。

7. **World Trade Center** 世界貿易中心

   又稱「世貿中心」、「紐約世貿」，是美國紐約曼哈頓一個建築群，由七座大樓組成，其中 110 層、樓高 417 和 415 公尺的世貿一、二期大樓，又被稱為北塔和南塔，合稱「世貿雙子星大樓」，自 1973 年啟用以來即為紐約市地標之一，高度超過帝國大廈，為當時世上最高的大樓。在 2001 年的 911 事件中，雙塔遭撞擊倒塌，目前部分區域已重建完成。

8. **Kenya** 肯亞

   肯亞共和國位於非洲東部，與衣索比亞、索馬利亞、南蘇丹、坦尚尼亞、烏干達接壤，人口約 410 餘萬人，首都奈洛比。肯亞是人類發源地之一，境內曾出土約 250 萬年前的人類頭蓋骨化石。肯亞於 1890 年淪為英國殖民地，直到 1963 年才宣告獨立。

9. **Tanzania** 坦尚尼亞

   坦尚尼亞聯合共和國是一個東非國家，位於赤道以南，本土地處維多利亞湖和印度洋之間，北鄰烏干達和肯亞，西與剛果民主共和國、盧安達和蒲隆地交界，南與馬拉威和莫三比克毗連，西南與尚比亞接壤。坦尚尼亞曾是英國殖民地，於 1964 年獨立。

10. **George W. Bush** 小布希 (1946～)

    美國第 43 任總統。任內遭逢 2001 年的 911 事件，因此發動了一連串所謂的「反恐戰爭」。在 2001 年 10 月布希總統發動阿富汗戰爭，藉以推翻塔利班政權和剷除蓋達組織勢力。接著又在 2003 年 3 月發動伊拉克戰爭，推翻了海珊政權。布希政府在反恐戰爭的正當性以及颶風卡崔娜救災工作的處置上遭到眾多非議，其執政民調認可度在 911 事件後逐漸下滑。

11. **Tora Bora region**　托拉波拉山區

　Tora Bora 為「漆黑洞窟」的意思，此地區位於東阿富汗的白山 (White Mountains)，接近阿富汗與巴基斯坦的邊界，是利用洞穴建造的居住設施，據傳為賓拉登藏匿的地點。

12. **Abbottabad**　阿伯塔巴德

　巴基斯坦西北邊境省的一個城市。

13. **Pakistan**　巴基斯坦

　全名為巴基斯坦伊斯蘭共和國，位於南亞，東與印度比鄰，南面是印度洋，西與伊朗接壤，西北和阿富汗相連，東北面可通往中國的新疆，首都伊斯蘭瑪巴德。1757 年，巴基斯坦成為英國殖民地，1947 年，巴基斯坦宣布獨立，成為英聯邦的自治領。

Pop Quiz

Choose the best answer to each of the following sentences.

(　　) 1. Learning that her best friend talked behind her back, Becky _____ never to speak to her again.

　(A) ordered　　(B) vowed　　(C) oppressed　　(D) served

(　　) 2. Albert Einstein, who developed the Theory of Relativity, is a truly _____ scientist.

　(A) predictable　(B) radical　　(C) risky　　(D) extraordinary

(　　) 3. The gifted poet has the _____ to compose a poem in a short time.

　(A) capability　(B) defeat　　(C) casualty　　(D) announcement

(　　) 4. African-American slaves had been _____ by white people in the U.S. for many years.

　(A) invaded　　(B) escaped　　(C) oppressed　　(D) withdrew

(　　) 5. Tess took _____ on her rival in love by spreading false rumors about her.

　(A) revenge　　(B) damage　　(C) custody　　(D) success

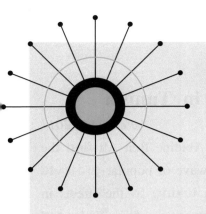

Politics

政　治

Politics

UNIT 04

[1]The Jasmine Revolution: Trouble in [2]Tunisia

February, 2011

After ruling Tunisia for 23 years, President [3]Zine el-Abidine Ben Ali fled the country on January 14, 2011 in response to a growing wave of popular protests against his government's oppressive rule. People began taking to the streets in December 2010 to voice their discontent with the government's unfair policies and corruption, ___1___ the country's poor economic conditions. The [4]interim government in Tunisia asked international authorities to arrest Mr. Ben Ali ___2___ is currently in [5]Saudi Arabia.

The revolution in Tunisia began when [6]Mohamed Bouazizi, a street vendor, set himself on fire to protest his country's injustice. His death later became a symbol around which others organized violent riots, ___3___ dozens of deaths. ___4___, the regime was unable to contain the big change. Growing numbers of protesters were angry over the luxurious lifestyles that their leaders enjoyed, while ordinary people could not find jobs nor afford basic living expenses. Mr. Ben Ali's promise to hold open elections was not enough to calm the uprising, and his [7]ouster led to the formation of an interim unity government ___5___ by Tunisia's prime minister, [8]Mohamed Ghannouchi.

One of Mr. Ghannouchi's first acts was to release 1,800 political prisoners on January 20, but demonstrations continued ___6___ many of Mr. Ben Ali's men remained involved in key positions. The interim government issued the [9]warrant for Mr. Ben Ali's arrest on charges of financial corruption, and also ___7___ international authorities to [10]detain members of the former president's family. A Tunisian journalist named Tunisia's political upheaval the "Jasmine Revolution." ___8___ the help of social networks, some observers even called it "Twitter Revolution." ___9___ Tunisians had done in this revolution was credited with inspiring similar calls for political change in other countries throughout [11]North Africa and [12]the Middle East. President Obama and other EU leaders have voiced their support for the protesters in Tunisia but ___10___ any involvement in spurring the revolution.

Exercise

Choose the correct answers.

(   ) 1. (A) in addition to   (B) as for   (C) instead of   (D) as well as

(   ) 2. (A) whom   (B) who   (C) , who   (D) , that

(   ) 3. (A) caused   (B) causing   (C) to cause   (D) cause

(   ) 4. (A) Thus   (B) However   (C) Moreover   (D) Then

(   ) 5. (A) led   (B) leading   (C) lead   (D) to lead

(   ) 6. (A) whether   (B) and   (C) as   (D) if

(   ) 7. (A) came to   (B) took off   (C) got over   (D) called on

(   ) 8. (A) Against   (B) To   (C) In   (D) With

(   ) 9. (A) Who   (B) Which   (C) What   (D) How

(   ) 10. (A) contain   (B) deny   (C) fail   (D) serve

≫ Vocabulary

1. **flee** [fli] *vt.*; *vi.* (flee, fled, fled) 逃跑，逃離
   - The political prisoner was caught before fleeing the country.
   - The writer fled to America during the Cultural Revolution.

2. **protest** [`prɔtɛst] *n.* [C] 抗議，示威
   - About 5,000 factory workers held a protest against the unfair welfare system in front of the President's Office.

   protester [prə`tɛstɚ] *n.* [C] 抗議者，反對者
   - Anti-government protesters gathered and then clashed with the police outside the Legislative Yuan.

3. **oppressive** [ə`prɛsɪv] *adj.* 壓迫的
   - People in North Korea have been living under the military oppressive rule since 1948.

4. **voice** [vɔɪs] *vt.* 表達 (意見)
   - A number of teachers and students have voiced their doubts about the educational reform.

5. **discontent** [͵dɪskən`tɛnt] *n.* [U] 不滿
   - The latest poll revealed public discontent with the current government.

6. **corruption** [kə`rʌpʃən] *n.* [U] 腐敗，貪污
   - The new prime minster vowed to root out long-standing political corruption.

7. **riot** [`raɪət] *n.* [C] 暴動，騷亂
   - A riot broke out after the union leader was assassinated.

8. **contain** [kən`ten] *vt.* 控制…以避免蔓延、惡化
   - The government failed to contain social unrest in the south of the country.

9. **luxurious** [lʌg`ʒʊrɪəs] *adj.* 奢侈的，奢華的
   - A billionaire sent his son a luxurious sports car as an 20-year-old birthday gift.

10. **expense** [ɪk`spɛns] *n.* [C] 花費，費用
    - As the prices keep going up, more and more people find it hard to cover their basic living expenses.

11. **formation** [fɔr`meʃən] *n.* [U] 組成，形成
    - This medical research explains some important factors that result in the formation of breast cancer.

12. **demonstration** [͵dɛmən`streʃən] *n.* [C] 遊行示威
    - The opposition party managed to hold a demonstration against the new tax policy.

13. **credit** [`krɛdɪt] *vi.* 把…歸於
    - The success of the social network is credited to the Facebook.
      → The Facebook is credited with the success of the social network.

14. **spur** [spɝ] *vt.* 激勵，促進
    - It is believed that the tax reform bill will spur more foreign investment and help our country maintain its competitive edge.

>> Idioms & Phrases

1. **in response to** 作為…的回應
   - The development plan was changed in response to the public outcry.

2. **take to** 湧入至、逃竄至 (某地)
   - Unruly mobs took to the streets in Paris, damaging shops and cars.

≫補 充

1. **Jasmine Revolution** 茉莉花革命

   指發生在突尼西亞的反政府示威事件，因茉莉花為其國花而得名。2010 年 12 月 17 日，一名 26 歲青年穆罕默德・布瓦吉吉自焚，引起大規模的街頭示威遊行，藉以爭取民主自由。事件導致當時總統班・阿里的專制政權一夜垮臺，成為阿拉伯國家中第一個因人民起義而推翻政權的革命。

   這原先是由突尼西亞記者齊德・艾爾海尼所創的詞彙，並用在 2011 年 1 月 13 日部落格的貼文上。在臉書及推特的推波助瀾下，之後西方媒體就將 2010 年 12 月 17 日開始的突尼西亞反政府示威運動，稱為「茉莉花革命」。

2. **Tunisia** 突尼西亞共和國

   位於北非，北鄰地中海，位於阿爾及利亞及利比亞間，人口約 1 千多萬人，面積約 16 萬平方公里，首都突尼斯。19 世紀中開始受到法國的殖民統治，直到 1956 才正式獨立。官方語言為阿拉伯文和法文。

3. **Zine el-Abidine Ben Ali** 扎因・阿比丁・班・阿里 (1936～)

   前突尼西亞總統，從 1987 年發動政變開始執政到 2011 年被抗議的群眾們逼迫下臺，結束他長達 23 年的執政，流亡於海外。

4. **interim** [ˋɪntərɪm] *adj.* 暫時的，過渡的

5. **Saudi Arabia** 沙烏地阿拉伯王國

   是阿拉伯半島上面積最大的國家，官方語言為阿拉伯文，人口約 2 千多萬。首都利雅德，北與約旦及伊拉克、東與科威特及阿拉伯聯合大公國、南與阿曼及葉門相鄰。東北岸有波斯灣，西有紅海的環繞。國境內有麥加及麥地那兩個伊斯蘭教的聖地。沙烏地阿拉伯是世界最大的石油輸出國，石油產業的收入佔全國總收入的 75%。

6. **Mohamed Bouazizi** 穆罕默德・布瓦吉吉 (1984～2011)

   是一名突尼西亞的水果小販。在 2011 年 1 月 17 日，為了抗議自己的生財工具遭到警察沒收且受到侮辱而自焚身亡。他的死引發了抗議浪潮，進而導致總統班・阿里下臺。

7. **ouster** [ˋaʊstə] *n.* [U] 罷免，廢黜

8. **Mohamed Ghannouchi** 穆罕默德・甘努奇 (1941～)

   爆發茉莉花革命時為突尼西亞總理，依據該國憲法自 2011 年 1 月 14 日起接任臨時代理總統，但由於他是前總統班・阿里的政府成員，突尼斯從 2 月 25 日開始再次爆發大規模遊行示威，要求他立即辭職下臺。迫於壓力，甘努奇於 2 月 27 日辭職。

9. **warrant** [`wɔrənt] *n.* [C] 逮捕令，授權執行令
   - authorize/issue a warrant 授權 / 發出逮捕令
10. **detain** [dɪ`ten] *vt.* 拘留，扣留
   - be detained in custody/hospital 遭到拘留羈押 / 住院治療
11. **North Africa** 北非
   以撒哈拉沙漠為分界的非洲大陸北部區域，包含西撒哈拉、摩洛哥、阿爾及利亞、突尼西亞、利比亞、埃及及蘇丹等國家或地區。此區域保有早期羅馬帝國及阿拉伯帝國殖民的遺跡，主要以阿拉伯語為通用語言，信仰以伊斯蘭教為主。
12. **the Middle East** 中東
   廣義的中東地區是指西亞與北非的國家，但傳統概念則侷限於阿拉伯半島及其周邊的國家 (敘利亞、約旦、以色列、黎巴嫩、伊拉克、沙烏地阿拉伯、科威特、巴林、卡達、阿曼、葉門及阿拉伯聯合大公國等) 和埃及、伊朗、土耳其。此地區位於歐亞非三洲的交界之處，氣候乾燥炎熱，相當缺乏水資源，但以石油礦產成為影響世界經濟發展的重要地區。此地區國家多以伊斯蘭教立國，又被稱為伊斯蘭世界。

Pop Quiz

Fill in each blank with the correct word to complete the sentence. Make changes if necessary.

flee	oppressive	voice	formation
protest	spur	expense	luxurious

1. Nick Vujicic's inspiring story _____ me on to success.
2. Due to Great Famine, many Irish _____ to America in the 1840s.
3. I can't afford to spend a night at the five-star _____ hotel. It costs me an arm and a leg.
4. Susan _____ complaints about her bossy employer; he orders her around and yells at her all the time.
5. Several anti-war organizations held a _____ against the War in Afghanistan.

UNIT 05

Widespread Riots in the UK

September, 2011

A series of riots erupted in [1]the United Kingdom after a man was shot dead by police in the city of [2]Tottenham. [3]Mark Duggan, 29, died after an alleged exchange of gunfire with police on August 4. Two days later, hundreds of __1__ gathered at the city's police station to demand justice for what they __2__ excessive force. The rioting began after some members of the crowd threw bottles at police cars and set one on fire. Over the next several days, violence __3__ in many of the country's major cities, including [4]Manchester, [5]Birmingham, [6]Liverpool, and [7]London. By the time the riots began to subside, more than 3,000 people had been arrested throughout the United Kingdom.

The __4__ riots affected everyday activity throughout the country as shops were burned and stolen. On August 11, Prime Minister [8]David Cameron addressed the parliament about the riots, __5__ them "criminality, pure and simple." The government reacted __6__ to the unrest, deploying more than 10,000 police officers to restore order in London alone. One of the government's most controversial actions was to set harsh [9]sentencing guidelines for those convicted for taking part in the violence. Courts held speedy trials and handed out tough sentences for people with no criminal records, leading to criticism that the government was more __7__ in setting an example than administering justice.

Politicians and other officials struggled to understand what caused such serious disorder. To prevent such riots in the future, Prime Minister Cameron ordered a review to investigate __8__ changes could be made to government policy. Although the government contends that the riots were the __9__ of a moral crisis in the country, others contend that many of the rioters came from impoverished neighborhoods and that anger over social inequality __10__ a major role in the unrest.

Exercise

Fill in each blank with the correct word or phrase.

(A) protesters	(B) widespread	(C) calling	(D) strongly	(E) viewed as
(F) interested	(G) result	(H) broke out	(I) what	(J) played

1. _____ 2. _____ 3. _____ 4. _____ 5. _____

6. _____ 7. _____ 8. _____ 9. _____ 10. _____

≫ Vocabulary

1. **erupt** [ɪˋrʌpt] *vi.* 突然爆發、發生 (動亂、暴動)
   - A bitter international dispute erupted among the countries around the Diaoyu Islands.
2. **alleged** [əˋlɛdʒd] *adj.* 涉嫌的
   - The police arrested the alleged killer for murder.
3. **demand** [dɪˋmænd] *vt.* 要求
   - The victim's family members demanded to see the police chief.
4. **excessive** [ɪkˋsɛsɪv] *adj.* 過度的，過多的
   - Excessive consumption of caffeine can damage your health.
5. **unrest** [ʌnˋrɛst] *n.* [U] 動盪
   - Due to recession, there is growing civil unrest in the country.
6. **deploy** [dɪˋplɔɪ] *vt.* 調動 (軍隊、武器等)
   - The general deployed his forces along the border.
7. **restore** [rɪˋstor] *vt.* 恢復 (某種情況、感受)
   - After the flood, all residents tried their best to restore the city town as soon as possible.
8. **controversial** [͵kɑntrəˋvɝʃəl] *adj.* 有爭議的
   - The Suao-Hualien freeway project is a highly controversial issue.
9. **harsh** [hɑrʃ] *adj.* 嚴厲的
   - In this country, the person who commits adultery would receive harsh punishment. He or she will be stoned to death.

10. guideline [ˋgaɪd͵laɪn] *n.* [C] 準則
    - The Department of Health recently has drawn up new guidelines on healthy and balanced diet for schoolchildren.
11. convict [ˋkənvɪkt] *vt.* 宣判⋯有罪 .
    - The notorious gangster was arrested and finally convicted of drug smuggling and armed robbery.
12. criticism [ˋkrɪtə͵sɪzəm] *n.* [U] 批評
    - The new educational reform has attracted strong criticism.
13. administer [ədˋmɪnəstɚ] *vt.* 執行 (法律)
    - The police are authorized to administer justice to keep social order.
14. contend [kənˋtɛnd] *vt.* 聲稱，主張
    - The police contended that they knew the whereabouts of the suspect.
15. impoverished [ɪmˋpɑvərɪʃt] *adj.* 貧窮的
    - Some volunteers are teaching children English in this impoverished area.

≫Idioms & Phrases

1. take part (in)　參與⋯
    - Jason took part in the speech contest voluntarily.
2. hand out　給予 (懲罰、建議等)
    - Ms. Ferguson always hands out advice to her students in class.

≫補　充

1. the United Kingdom　英國
   全名為大不列顛及北愛爾蘭聯合王國，簡稱「不列顛」或「聯合王國」，由英格蘭、蘇格蘭、威爾斯以及北愛爾蘭所組成，首都倫敦。英國為君主立憲國家。在國家最強盛時期連同其海外殖民地被稱為大英帝國，該帝國在 1922 年時達到巔峰，擁有全世界四分之一的陸地，是有史以來世界上面積最大的國家，因其控制的土地幅員廣闊，太陽無論何時都能照到英屬領土，故號稱「日不落帝國」。雖然在經歷兩次世界大戰後，英國國力減退，但仍是一個政治、經濟、文化和軍事強國。

2. **Tottenham**　托登罕

英國英格蘭倫敦北部「哈林蓋倫敦自治市」中的一區。現為非洲、哥倫比亞、阿爾巴尼亞、土耳其、愛爾蘭、葡萄牙等多元種族移民居住的地區。近年來治安差，儼然成為犯罪的溫床。

3. **Mark Duggan**　馬克・杜根

29 歲的牙買加裔黑人。2011 年 8 月 4 日他被警方懷疑預謀殺害自己的表兄弟，在追捕他的過程中將其槍殺。此事件導致家屬不滿，原為托登罕地區的一般示威活動，最後演變成蔓延到英國各大城市的大規模暴動。

4. **Manchester**　曼徹斯特

英國英格蘭西北大城，建城於 1 世紀。18 世紀工業革命使曼徹斯特成為工業城市，大量紡織廠在此設立。世界上第一條客運鐵路 (利物浦至曼徹斯特) 的啟用，也加速了這城市的發展。

5. **Birmingham**　伯明罕

英國英格蘭中部工業城，建城於 7 世紀，為倫敦以外最大的都會區。為英國文化最多元的城市，約有近 30% 人口為非白種人，有許多來自加勒比海、印度、愛爾蘭及亞洲等各地的移民定居。

6. **Liverpool**　利物浦

英國英格蘭西北部港口城市，建城於 1207 年，過去為英國主要的製造業城市。城內有多處古蹟被列為聯合國世界遺產，曾在 2008 年獲選為歐洲文化之都。

7. **London**　倫敦

英國首都，由古羅馬人建於西元 43 年。自大英帝國在世界各地的影響開始，就是全球化的政治、經濟及文化城市。與紐約市並列為世界金融中心，許多大型企業均在倫敦設立總部，也是歐洲最大的經濟中心。倫敦分別於 1908、1948 和 2012 年舉辦奧運，成為第一個舉辦過三次夏季奧運會的城市。

8. **David Cameron**　大衛・卡麥隆 (1966～)

事發當時的英國首相，英國保守黨領袖。在 2010 年大選擊敗首相戈登・布朗所領導的工黨，組成以保守黨為主體的聯合政府，正式接任首相。

9. **sentencing guideline**　量刑準則

於審訊後被判有罪或被告人自己認罪，法官便會依其罪判刑。除考慮到律師為被告人的請求陳詞外，法官亦須考慮以往同類案件的判刑，稱為量刑準則，判刑的刑度完全由法官決定。

Pop Quiz

Choose the best answer to each of the following sentences.

(   ) 1. Mr. Huang was _____ of fraud because he had cheated many people out of their fortune.

      (A) convinced   (B) convicted   (C) controlled   (D) contended

(   ) 2. Those black slaves received _____ treatment. Farmers of plantations had them work day and night.

      (A) alleged   (B) equal   (C) harsh   (D) widespread

(   ) 3. The environmental organization _____ that the government should introduce strict environmental laws.

      (A) oppressed   (B) spurred   (C) demanded   (D) administered

(   ) 4. Though Ben says that he is open to _____, he finds it hard to take it calmly.

      (A) criticism   (B) popularity   (C) corruption   (D) unrest

(   ) 5. The judge decided to _____ severe punishment for murder.

      (A) take part in   (B) find out   (C) take to   (D) hand out

UNIT 06

Free at Last

December, 2010

After holding her prisoner for nearly two decades, the government of [1]Myanmar (formerly known as [2]Burma) eventually released the pro-democracy opposition leader [3]Aung San Suu Kyi on November 13, 2010. Suu Kyi had remained under house arrest for almost 15 years since she began her political career. During her time as a political prisoner, she was once offered freedom as long as she left Myanmar, but she refused. That may explain why Aung San Suu Kyi becomes a symbol of courage and hope for pro-democracy activists around the world.

Aung San Suu Kyi was the third child and only daughter of Myanmar's independence hero, General [4]Aung San, who was assassinated in 1947. After years of studying and living abroad, she returned to Myanmar in 1988 to care for her sick mother. By coincidence, General [5]Ne Win, the head of the ruling party, stepped down that time. Suu Kyi called for a democratic government and helped establish the [6]National League for Democracy (NLD). She soon became a key figure in Myanmar's pro-democracy movement and led the NLD to a landslide election victory in 1990. However, the military [7]dictatorship that had ruled Myanmar since 1962 refused to honor the election results and retained power while confining Aung San Suu Kyi. Even when Suu Kyi was placed under house arrest, she continued to serve as the leader of the NLD. In response to her efforts to bring democracy to military-ruled Myanmar, Aung San Suu Kyi was awarded the Nobel Peace Prize in 1991 during her arrest.

The National League for Democracy was formally dissolved in May 2010 as an act of **defiance** against another round of unfair elections organized by the military government. Although Aung San Suu Kyi was no longer the leader of an official party, she has stated that she would continue her efforts to support a peaceful political revolution in Myanmar. Suu Kyi also expressed her willingness to work with the military government to bring about a peaceful transition from dictatorship to democracy for Myanmar.

Choose the best answers.

(   ) 1. The article is mainly about _____ .

       (A) the release of Aung San from his long house arrest

       (B) the development of the National League for Democracy

       (C) Myanmar's transition from dictatorship to democracy

       (D) Aung San Suu Kyi's efforts to bring democracy to Myanmar

(   ) 2. According to the article, the military dictatorship had ruled Myanmar for about _____ decades.

       (A) fifteen   (B) five   (C) twenty   (D) ten

(   ) 3. Which of the following statements about the National League for Democracy is true?

       (A) It was established by Aung San in 1947.

       (B) It put Aung San Suu Kyi under house arrest.

       (C) It was a pro-democracy political party that was dissolved in 2010.

       (D) It became Myanmar's ruling party since the election victory in 1990.

(   ) 4. The word "defiance" in the third paragraph is closest in meaning to "_____."

       (A) willingness   (B) independence   (C) popularity   (D) opposition

(   ) 5. Aung San Suu Kyi _____ .

       (A) was involved in politics because of her father's will

       (B) was awarded the Nobel Peace Prize due to her effort

       (C) was unwilling to work with the military government

       (D) became the leader of Myanmar's ruling party

>> Vocabulary

1. **decade** [ˋdɛked] *n.* [C] 十年
   - It is reported that the cost of living has soared greatly during the past decade.
2. **democracy** [dɪˋmɑkrəsɪ] *n.* [U] 民主
   - The practice of democracy means not only enjoying individual freedom but also working out a compromise among various parties.

democratic [ˌdɛməˈkrætɪk] *adj.* 民主的
- In some democratic countries like Taiwan, people over 20 can vote to elect the president.

3. **opposition** [ˌɑpəˈzɪʃən] *n.* [U] (*usu.* the O~) 反對黨
- The leader of the Opposition strongly questioned the new tax plans.

4. **assassinate** [əˈsesɪnˌet] *vt.* 暗殺
- Martin Luther King, Jr. was assassinated in 1968 at the age of 39.

5. **coincidence** [koˈɪnsədəns] *n.* [U] 巧合
- By coincidence, I met my long-lost friend on my way home.

6. **establish** [əˈstæblɪʃ] *vt.* 建立，創辦
- After having worked in a big company for five years, Amy quit and set out to establish her own business.

7. **election** [ɪˈlɛkʃən] *n.* [C] 選舉
- Ma Ying-jeou won the presidential election in 2012 and became the 13th President of Taiwan.

8. **retain** [rɪˈten] *vt.* 保留，保持
- The golfer must win the game if he wants to retain his No. 1 world golf ranking.

9. **confine** [kənˈfaɪn] *vt.* 監禁，禁閉
- The poor boy has been confined in a dark room for half a year.

10. **award** [əˈwɔrd] *vt.* 授予，給予
- The Nobel Prize in Literature was awarded to Albert Camus in 1957.

11. **dissolve** [dɪˈzɑlv] *vt.* 解散
- The couple's marriage was dissolved in 2012.

12. **defiance** *n.* [U] 違抗，反抗
- The teacher thought that talking back was an act of defiance against him.

13. **revolution** [ˌrɛvəˈluʃən] *n.* [C] 改革，變革
- The invention of the cell phone has caused a revolution in human communication.

14. **willingness** [ˈwɪlɪŋnɪs] *n.* [U] 樂意，願意
- Fred showed willingness to give us a ride back to town.

15. **transition** [trænˈzɪʃən] *n.* [C][U] 過渡時期
- The peace talk helped make a peaceful transition of power in the country.

- The transition from school life to full-time work is a hard time for me.

>> Idioms & Phrases

1. **care for sb.** 照顧某人
   - Larry stayed at home to care for his little brother.
2. **step down** (從職位、工作) 卸任，辭職
   - Due to a financial scandal, the CEO of the company was forced to step down.
3. **call for** 公開呼籲
   - Some child welfare workers launched a campaign to call for public attention to the issue of child abuse.

>> 補 充

1. **Myanmar** 緬甸聯邦共和國

   在 2011 年以前，緬甸是一個軍政府國家，在此不允許有政黨政治，因此多數政黨皆列為非法組織。緬甸民族團結黨代表軍隊，是由一個名為緬甸聯邦鞏固和發展協會的組織所支持。緬甸有非常嚴重的人權問題，例如，沒有獨立的司法部門，也不允許有與軍政府不同的政治意見，政府管制了網際網路，封鎖與軍政府言論相左的網頁，其中包括大多數反對黨和民主黨派的網頁。

   2010 年 10 月 21 日，緬甸國家和平與發展委員會頒布法令，正式啟用《緬甸聯邦共和國憲法》所確定的新國旗、新國徽。11 月 7 日，緬甸宣稱依據新憲法舉行多黨制全國大選，但禁止多數外國記者入境報導，且選舉結果一面倒向由軍政府所主導的政黨。被認為這是一場完全不公平且不自由的選舉，目的只是為了讓軍政府的執政有所謂的民意依據。雖然緬甸政府稍後釋放翁山蘇姬，並讓她參選成為國會議員，但距離真正的民主還有很長一段路要走。

2. **Burma** 緬甸 (舊稱)

   Burma 是緬甸英屬殖民地時的舊稱，1989 年時由緬甸軍政府改為 Myanmar。緬甸國內的民運人士不使用新稱 Myanmar，因為他們不接受一個未經選舉獲得政權的政府，擅自更改國名。雖然國際間對於 Burma 及 Myanmar 兩種名稱皆是認可的，但一般認為使用 Myanmar 的國家及媒體比較親近軍政府，而使用 Burma 的則支持緬甸的民主運動。

3. **Aung San Suu Kyi** 翁山蘇姬 (1945～)

生於緬甸仰光，是緬甸非暴力提倡民主的政治家。她也常常被稱為 Daw Aung San Suu Kyi，Daw 在緬甸語中是一種對年長女性的敬稱，即女士。1988 年，翁山蘇姬回到緬甸照顧生病的母親。同年，長期執政的社會主義綱領黨領袖吳奈溫將軍下台，緬甸爆發大規模的民主遊行，但遭到血腥鎮壓，新的軍政府隨後掌權。深受聖雄甘地的非暴力理論影響，翁山蘇姬開始參與政治，並致力於推行民選制度。1989 年遭到軟禁，她拒絕了將她驅逐出境以獲得自由的條件。1990 年帶領全國民主聯盟贏得大選的勝利，但選舉結果被軍政府作廢。其後她被斷斷續續軟禁於其寓所中長達 15 年，軍政府對於她人身的控制與監視一直沒有停止過。直到 2010 年 11 月 13 日終於獲釋。2012 年 4 月 1 日，翁山蘇姬在補選中當選國會議員，正式走向體制內的民主改革。

4. **Aung San** 翁山 (1915～1947)

翁山是帶領緬甸獨立的領袖。1942 年，翁山接受日本的援助，協助日本攻打緬甸，以結束英國的殖民統治。不久，翁山懷疑日本是否會讓緬甸獨立，於是改為與盟軍合作。第二次世界大戰後，翁山成為緬甸的總理，與英國展開有關緬甸獨立的談判。但在緬甸獨立前，他被暗殺身亡。翁山被緬甸人民尊稱為國父，他的女兒是緬甸民主運動領導人翁山蘇姬。

5. **Ne Win** 吳奈溫 (1911～2002)

於 1949 年 1 月 31 日出任緬甸軍隊參謀長，1962 年 3 月 2 日，吳奈溫發動政變奪取政權，推翻吳努，任命自己為緬甸聯邦革命委員會主席。1988 年 7 月，緬甸全國爆發大規模遊行示威，他被迫下台，政治影響力逐漸減退。

6. **National League for Democracy (NLD)** 全國民主聯盟

全國民主聯盟是一個緬甸政黨，成立於 1988 年 9 月 27 日，創辦人包括前緬甸陸軍副總參謀長昂季、緬甸國防部部長丁吳以及翁山將軍的女兒翁山蘇姬。自成立以來，該黨就在軍政府執政的環境下從事非暴力運動，並爭取緬甸早日實現向多黨民主制的轉變。

在 1990 年的國會選舉中，全國民主聯盟在 492 個議席中贏得 392 席，約佔 80%，但軍政府不承認選舉結果，拒絕交出權力。在 2001 年，緬甸政府容許全國民主聯盟重開國內所有的辦公室，到了 2004 年又被強行關閉。2010 初，軍政府以全國民主聯盟未根據新的政黨註冊法登記為理由，下令將其解散。2011 年 12 月，全國民主聯盟才被允許重新登記註冊並參與選舉。

7. **dictatorship** [dɪkˋtetɚˌʃɪp] *n.* [C][U] 獨裁政權

Pop Quiz

Fill in each blank with the correct word or phrase to complete the sentence. Make changes if necessary.

coincidence	decade	establish	step down
revolution	care for	award	election

1. Mrs. Simpson decided to quit her job to _____ her newborn baby.
2. The United Nations was _____ in 1945.
3. Due to a corruption scandal, the finance minister was forced to _____ from his post.
4. By _____ , my sister and I worked at the same company.
5. Dr. Lin will fight state _____ next year.

Note

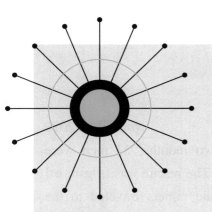

Society

社會

Miner Miracle

November, 2010

After being trapped underground for more than two months, 33 men were rescued from a collapsed mine in [1]Chile on October 13. The rescue was televised live, and people around the world watched as each of the miners traveled to the surface 在一 small [2]capsule. Chile's government earned praise for its handling of the operation ___1___ led to celebrations of national pride throughout the country. Although the miners emerged with relatively few physical problems, health officials ___2___ that the psychological consequences of their ordeal could affect them for some time.

The miners became trapped on August 5 when the gold and [3]copper mine ___3___ they were working collapsed. No one on the surface heard from the miners for 17 days, when a small probe hole reached the miners and they sent up a note ___4___ that they were all alive. Officials then used the small hole to send food, notes from family members, and entertainment down to the miners. ___5___, teams of engineers, doctors, and psychologists from around the world worked together to develop a plan to drill a larger rescue hole and maintain the miners' physical and mental health while they waited ___6___.

Family members, journalists, and government officials joined the rescuers outside the entrance of the mine to form a makeshift village called [4]Camp Hope while the rescue operation ___7___. Doctors made sure that the miners were healthy enough to make the trip to the surface and had them ___8___ special sunglasses to shield their eyes from the sunlight. [5]Sebastián Piñera, the Chilean president, joined family members in greeting the miners ___9___ they emerged from the rescue capsule. Since their rescue, the miners have agreed to keep the details of their story a ___10___ until they can sign book and movie contracts that will benefit all of them.

Choose the correct answers.

(   ) 1. (A) which   (B) , which   (C) , that   (D) whom

(   ) 2. (A) warmed   (B) showed   (C) ordered   (D) hoped

(   ) 3. (A) who   (B) when   (C) where   (D) which

(   ) 4. (A) say   (B) to say   (C) saying   (D) said

(   ) 5. (A) However   (B) Instead   (C) Therefore   (D) Moreover

(   ) 6. (A) inward   (B) straight   (C) nowhere   (D) underground

(   ) 7. (A) kept an eye   (B) took place   (C) handed out   (D) took part

(   ) 8. (A) wear   (B) wearing   (C) to wear   (D) worn

(   ) 9. (A) but   (B) if   (C) as   (D) and

(   ) 10. (A) will   (B) shift   (C) choice   (D) secret

» Vocabulary

1. **miner** [ˋmaɪnɚ] *n.* [C] 礦工
   - Miners work in dark tunnels underground, digging up valuable minerals such as gold and coal.

   mine [maɪn] *n.* [C] 礦坑
   - It is said that there are gold mines in Jinguashi.

2. **trap** [træp] *vt.* 困住
   - About ten people were reported to be trapped in the burning building.

3. **rescue** [ˋrɛskju] *vt.* 營救，救援
   - The police took immediate action to rescue these hostages.

4. **televise** [ˋtɛləˌvaɪz] *vt.* 電視轉播
   - The Emmy Awards ceremony will be televised live on Sunday night.

5. **surface** [ˋsɝfɪs] *n.* [C] 水面，地面
   - About 70 percent of the Earth's surface is covered by water.

6. **emerge** [ɪˋmɝdʒ] *vi.* (問題) 出現、發生
   - As time goes by, leaking pipes and peeling paints gradually emerge in this old building.

7. **relatively** [ˋrɛlətɪvlɪ] *adv.* 相對地，相當地
   - I think that a full-time job is relatively steady.

8. **consequence** [ˋkɑnsəˌkwɛns] *n.* [C] 結果，後果
   - Mark decided to quit his job, and now he must face the consequences of his decision.

9. **ordeal** [ɔrˋdiəl] *n.* [C] 苦難，折磨
   - The cancer victim began to wonder if he could go through the ordeal.

10. **collapse** [kəˋlæps] *vi.* (建築物) 倒塌
    - Due to the earthquake, the temple collapsed.

11. **probe** [prob] *n.* [C] (搜索用) 探測鑽孔
    - The latest probe cameras with high-definition lens are used in the mine rescue.

12. **entertainment** [ˌɛntɚˋtenmənt] *n.* [U] 娛樂
    - The magic show gives good entertainment value.

13. **drill** [drɪl] *vi.* 鑽孔
    - The construction worker drilled into a water pipe by mistake.

14. **makeshift** [ˋmekˌʃɪft] *adj.* 臨時替代的
    - The girl took a large paper box with a sheet as a makeshift bed for the poor kitten.

15. **shield** [ʃild] *vt.* 保護某人或某物
    - Maggie wore dark sunglasses to shield her eyes from the bright sun.

≫補充

1. **Chile** 智利

   智利共和國位於南美洲西南方，東與阿根廷、玻利維亞為鄰，北靠秘魯，西面向太平洋。國土南北狹長約有 4300 多公里，最寬處大約 400 多公里，有安地斯山脈貫穿全國，為世界上最狹長的國家。首都聖地牙哥，官方語言為西班牙語。智利的礦藏和森林資源相當豐富，是世界第一大銅礦產國，有「銅之王國」的美稱。

2. **capsule** [ˋkæpsḷ] *n.* [C] (膠囊狀) 密閉艙

3. **copper** 銅

   銅是一種呈現棕紅色、延展性和導電導熱性佳的金屬，化學符號為 Cu。

4. **Camp Hope** 希望營

   智利政府特別為了 33 名礦工的家屬，在發生意外的礦場附近搭建臨時營地。經過兩個多月

的漫長等待後，這營地變成一座住有一千多人的帳篷城。由於家屬堅定地抱持希望，才讓智利政府積極展開救援行動，才有礦坑奇蹟的出現。

5. **Sebastián Piñera** 薩巴斯提安・皮涅拉 (1949～)

為智利共和國第 47 任總統。出生於聖地亞哥，1971 年於智利天主教大學取得經濟學學士，並在 1976 年取得哈佛大學經濟學博士，先後在智利大學、天主教大學等大學任教。曾任智利參議院議員、駐比利時和聯合國大使。皮涅拉於 2005 年參加智利總統選舉，以些微差距落敗。但在 2010 年的總統選舉第二輪投票中勝出，終於贏得大選。

Pop Quiz

Fill in each blank with the correct word to complete the sentence. Make changes if necessary.

surface	rescue	ordeal	emerge
collapse	consequence	makeshift	relatively

1. The memoirs talked about the terrible _____ that the writer had been through.
2. It was the pouring rain that caused the bridge to _____ .
3. Compared with lemon, mango is _____ sweeter.
4. The firefighter _____ the woman from the burning flat last night.
5. If you are going to do something risky, you should be prepared to face the _____ .

UNIT 08

[1]Foxconn Suicides Highlight Growing Labor Problem in China

July, 2010

Up until a few months ago, many people had never heard of a company called Foxconn. But when twelve Foxconn workers tried to kill themselves over the course of just a few months, the whole world's __1__ promptly turned to Foxconn's China operations, where these suicides had occurred.

The first Foxconn employee to take his own life was Ma Xiangqian, who jumped to his death from his __2__ company dormitory on January 23, 2010. Ma had only been working at Foxconn Technology since November of 2009; he usually worked seven nights a week on an eleven-hour overnight shift. The month before he died, Ma had worked 286 hours, including more than 110 hours of overtime. Despite all of this work, Ma __3__ only about US$1 an hour.

During the first five months of 2010, a __4__ of eight men and four women committed suicide, or attempted to do so, at two Foxconn locations in [2]Shenzhen. Most of them were between the ages of 18 to 24 and had only been working at Foxconn for a short time.

Foxconn was __5__ by the Taiwanese businessman [3]Terry Gou. His factories in Shenzhen produce products for international companies like [4]Apple and [5]Dell. In response to the suicides, Foxconn raised salaries significantly for its workers, in some cases doubling the basic salaries of its laborers in China. Gou himself visited the factories in Shenzhen and made a __6__ apology.

Some experts say that the suicides represent a trend in China—when low wages and poor working conditions are still common throughout China, this new generation of workers, __7__ migrant workers from China's inland provinces, will no longer tolerate such conditions. A growing number have __8__ quit working in these types of factories. In other cases, such as at a [6]Honda plant in southern China, some workers have gone on strike to demand higher pay.

Even though some others point out that Foxconn's suicide rate is ___9___ below the China average, which is believed to be up to 20–30 per 100,000 people, the suicides at Foxconn were certainly tragic. It can only be hoped that they will lead to better working conditions and higher pay for workers at Foxconn and throughout the ___10___ of China.

Exercise

Fill in each blank with the correct word or phrase.

(A) total	(B) public	(C) established	(D) earned	(E) attention
(F) especially	(G) rest	(H) far	(I) high-rise	(J) simply

1. _____   2. _____   3. _____   4. _____   5. _____
6. _____   7. _____   8. _____   9. _____   10. _____

» Vocabulary

1. **labor** [ˋlebɚ] *n.* [U] 勞工，勞動力
   - In developing countries like Pakistan and India, many employers use children as cheap labor.

   laborer [ˋlebərɚ] *n.* [C] (體力勞動的) 勞工
   - An increase in illegal foreign laborers has a great impact on the job market.

2. **promptly** [ˋprɑmptlɪ] *adv.* 立即，馬上
   - Learning the bad news, Buck promptly burst into tears.

3. **operation** [ˌɑpəˋreʃən] *n.* [C] 企業，公司
   - The multinational operation's head office is located in Paris.

4. **dormitory** [ˋdɔrməˌtɔrɪ] *n.* [C] 宿舍
   - All freshmen are asked to live in the school's dormitory.

5. **shift** [ʃɪft] *n.* [C] 輪班
   - Most employees in this phone company work an eight-hour shift.

6. **overtime** [ˋovɚˌtaɪm] *n.* [U] 加班，加班時間
   - Mr. Huang has a very busy schedule; he always works overtime.

7. **significantly** [sɪg`nɪfəkəntlɪ] *adv.* 顯著地，明顯地
   - Because of an effective marketing strategy, the company's profits have increased significantly.
8. **apology** [ə`pɑlədʒɪ] *n.* [C] 道歉
   - The singer issued an apology for her rude remarks.
9. **generation** [ˌdʒɛnə`reʃən] *n.* [C] 世代
   - The ancient tradition has been handed down from generation to generation.
10. **migrant** [`maɪgrənt] *n.* [C] 移民者，移民
    - In Hong Kong, there are many migrant workers from China, and many of them are illegal.
11. **inland** [`ɪnˌlænd] *adj.* 內陸的
    - The Caspian Sea is the biggest inland lake.
12. **tolerate** [`tɑləˌret] *vt.* 忍受
    - I can't tolerate the loud noise any more.
13. **strike** [straɪk] *n.* [U] 罷工
    - Workers went on strike last Saturday to ask for a pay raise.
14. **tragic** [`trædʒɪk] *adj.* 悲慘的，悲劇的
    - A tragic car accident happened right here last Monday, killing two people.

≫Idioms & Phrases

1. **up to** 多達，高達
   - This conference room can seat up to five hundred people.

≫補 充

1. **Foxconn** 富士康國際控股有限公司
   由臺灣企業家郭台銘所創辦的企業集團，相當於鴻海科技集團的跨國營運主體，總公司位於新北市土城區，而主要生產基地位於中國。主營業務為手機代工，客戶包括蘋果公司、三星電子、LG、索尼 (Sony) 等。
2. **Shenzhen** 深圳
   位於中國廣東省鄰近舊香港英國租界區的城市，是中國第一個經濟特區。原是一個農村小鎮，近年來已發展成規模相當大的工商業城市，都會區總人口達一千多萬人。

3. **Terry Gou**　郭台銘 (1950～)

臺灣著名企業家，1974 年從一間小型塑膠公司起家，發展出鴻海科技集團，成為臺灣最大企業，個人財富在臺灣近年來皆名列前茅。

4. **Apple**　蘋果公司

創立於 1976 年的美國電子科技公司，以電腦、多媒體播放器、手機為主要產品，憑藉其領導創新的品牌風格，在業界佔有重要的地位。蘋果近年來陸續所推出的 iMac、iPod、iPhone、iPad 等，都獲得許多愛好者的支持。

5. **Dell**　戴爾公司

創立於 1984 年的美國資訊科技公司，主要產品為電腦及其週邊設備，在美國擁有很高的 PC 市占率，在全球亦名列前茅。

6. **Honda**　本田技研工業

創立於 1937 年，生產各式車輛、世界知名的日本汽車製造商，通稱本田汽車。

Pop Quiz

Choose the best answer to each of the following sentences.

(　　) 1. These workers were not satisfied with their salaries, so they decided to go on _____ .

(A) overtime　　(B) revenge　　(C) strike　　(D) corruption

(　　) 2. It would be _____ if the gifted singer couldn't win the talent show.

(A) tragic　　(B) risky　　(C) inland　　(D) prestigious

(　　) 3. Peter got a call from his mother and _____ rushed to pack his suitcase. Then, he went home immediately.

(A) exactly　　(B) significantly　　(C) promptly　　(D) certainly

(　　) 4. How could you _____ the bad smell? It smelled disgusting.

(A) serve　　(B) oppress　　(C) deploy　　(D) tolerate

(　　) 5. I made an _____ for the wrong decision.

(A) outbreak　　(B) operation　　(C) expense　　(D) apology

UNIT 09

Are Chinese Mothers Really Superior?

March, 2011

It was the article that filled the Internet with comments, links, and blog posts. Entitled "Why Chinese Mothers Are Superior," this short article in both the print and online versions of [1]*the Wall Street Journal* certainly caused quite a controversy in January. Even the article's title rubbed some the wrong way, and many were more disturbed by the article's content.

Written by [2]Amy Chua, a [3]second-generation Chinese-American and law professor at Yale University, the article attempted to explain how Chinese mothers in America are able to raise so many stereotypically successful children. She began by listing all of the things that most American kids could do, but that her two daughters were never allowed to do, when growing up: no [4]sleepovers, no [5]play dates, no TV, no computer games, and no grade below an A. In addition, the two had to learn to play a musical instrument, and it had to be the piano or the violin.

Chua's parents were of Chinese descent, and they immigrated to the United States from the Philippines. Raised in a strict fashion in the United States, Chua **excelled** academically and ended up with degrees from Harvard. When Chua became a parent, she was determined that her children, third-generation Chinese-Americans, would not be raised like most other American kids. She wanted to raise them, in her words, as a "Chinese mother"—strict, demanding, and unyielding.

Reactions to the article, and Chua's parenting techniques, have been varied. Some say that some of her actions border on child abuse, including calling one daughter "garbage" and not allowing the other to eat dinner or go to the bathroom until a piano piece had been learned. Others point out that the article was published a few days before the release of Chua's book, *Battle Hymn of the Tiger Mother,* and was deliberately controversial in order to boost sales.

One thing is certain: the article has certainly raised questions in America—and around the world—about which style of parenting is the best. Is a more permissive

Western style better? Or is a more demanding Eastern style ideal? Or could it be a combination of the two?

Exercise

Choose the best answers.

(　　) 1. What is the passage mainly about?

　　　　(A) Amy Chua's strict parenting style.

　　　　(B) Parents want their children to take up a useful hobby.

　　　　(C) The definition of third-generation Chinese-Americans.

　　　　(D) A combination of the Western and Eastern parenting style.

(　　) 2. Where were Amy Chua's two daughters born?

　　　　(A) Taiwan.　　　　(B) China.　　　　(C) The Philippines. (D) The U.S.

(　　) 3. Amy Chua's daughters are not allowed to _____.

　　　　(A) get a grade less than an A　　　(B) watch too much TV

　　　　(C) call their friends "garbage"　　　(D) play a musical instrument

(　　) 4. The word "excel" in the third paragraph is closest in meaning to "_____."

　　　　(A) educate　　　(B) immigrate　　　(C) be good at　　　(D) allow

(　　) 5. According to Amy Chua, which of the following words is NOT used to describe a "Chinese mother"?

　　　　(A) Strict.　　　(B) Permissive.　　　(C) Demanding.　　　(D) Unyielding.

≫ Vocabulary

1. superior [sə`pɪrɪə] *adj.* 更好的，更勝一籌的
   - Your new smartphone is far superior to mine.
2. entitle [ɪn`taɪtl] *vt.* 給…命名
   - Amber is reading a novel entitled *the Hunger Games*.
3. controversy [`kɑntrə,vɝsɪ] *n.* [U] 爭議
   - The school's rule about hairstyles caused controversy among the students. They expressed strong disagreements about it.
4. disturb [dɪs`tɝb] *vt.* 使煩惱，使不安
   - I was disturbed by the loud barking sound last night.

5. content [ˋkɑntɛnt] *n.* [U] 內容
   - I don't like the picture book because its content is not interesting.
6. attempt [əˋtɛmpt] *vt.* 試圖，嘗試
   - Teresa once attempted to lose some weight, but failed.
7. stereotypically [ˌstɛrɪəˋtɪpɪklɪ] *adv.* 典型地
   - Some people think that the Greeks are stereotypically lazy and hedonistic.
8. instrument [ˋɪnstrəmənt] *n.* [C] 樂器
   - Jay started learning to play a stringed instrument when he was little.
9. descent [dɪˋsɛnt] *n.* [U] 血統，世系
   - Bruno is of Italian descent. His family came from Italy.
10. immigrate [ˋɪməˏgret] *vi.* 移民 (移入)
    - Iris immigrated to Canada with her family when she was a child. She grew up and received education here.
11. determined [dɪˋtɝmɪnd] *adj.* 堅決的，堅定的
    - Cathy is a determined woman. She never gives up until she reaches her goal.
12. demanding [dɪˋmændɪŋ] *adj.* 苛求的
    - Mr. Wang is a demanding boss. He is not easily satisfied with his employees' performance.
13. technique [tɛkˋnik] *n.* [C] 技巧
    - With useful teaching techniques, the teacher made his students learn better.
14. abuse [əˋbjus] *n.* [U] 虐待
    - The organization aims to help women who suffer domestic abuse.
15. hymn [hɪm] *n.* [C] 聖歌，讚美詩
    - Christians sing hymns and praise God in churches on Sundays.
16. deliberately [dɪˋlɪbərɪtlɪ] *adv.* 故意，蓄意
    - Ken has been deliberately giving his wife the cold shoulder.
17. boost [bust] *vt.* 促進
    - Winning the first game in the tournament boosted the tennis player's confidence.
18. combination [ˌkɑmbəˋneʃən] *n.* [C] 結合
    - The artist's latest work is a combination of Eastern and Western styles.

19. permissive [pɚˋmɪsɪv] *adj.* 寬容的
   • Jean is a spoilt brat because her parents are too permissive.

1. **rub sb. the wrong way**　惹某人生氣
   • Tom and I didn't get along well. We rubbed each other the wrong way every time we met.
2. **in a ⋯ fashion**　以⋯方式
   • Mrs. Miller does everything in an orderly fashion. She keeps her house neat and clean.
3. **border on**　近乎，瀕於
   • Lucy's shyness bordered on low self-esteem.

>> 補 充

1. **The Wall Street Journal**　《華爾街日報》
   創辦於 1889 年，是美國影響力最大的日報，也發行國際版本，報導內容側重金融及商業領域。該報以深度報導著稱，題材選擇謹慎嚴肅。
2. **Amy Chua**　蔡美兒 (1962～)
   出生於美國伊利諾伊州，畢業於哈佛大學法學院，先後任教於杜克大學、耶魯大學。2011 年 1 月 8 日在《華爾街日報》上發表《為什麼中國媽媽更勝一籌？》一文，回顧自己教育女兒的方式，並描述她所認為的中美教育差異。此文一出，一時成為國際社會熱門的討論話題。
3. **second-generation Chinese-American**　第二代華裔美人
   指的是在美國出生的華人，父母為移民到美國的華裔人士，也稱第二代移民、美國華人第二代。因為在美國出生並接受教育，故較能適應美國主流文化。
4. **sleepover**　小孩在朋友家過夜的派對
5. **play date**　小孩一起玩的聚會
   指孩子們的父母安排時間，讓小孩到別人家跟其他小孩玩，或者一起到博物館、公園、遊樂場等場所遊玩的聚會。

Pop Quiz

Choose the best answer to each of the following sentences.

(　　) 1. The government set up an industrial park to help _____ its economy.

      (A) oppress   (B) boost   (C) televise   (D) entitle

(　　) 2. The rich man is such a _____ person. He is not easy to please.

      (A) determined   (B) prestigious   (C) oppressive   (D) demanding

(　　) 3. The hostage _____ to escape, but in vain.

      (A) disturbed   (B) spurred   (C) dissolved   (D) attempted

(　　) 4. The businessman used some new marketing _____ in order to reach out to new customers.

      (A) shifts   (B) hymns   (C) techniques   (D) ordeals

(　　) 5. Ted felt a sense of frustration _____ desperation.

      (A) taking to   (B) bordering on   (C) caring for   (D) calling for

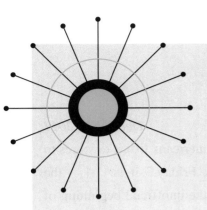

Economy

經濟

UNIT 10

Shop 'til You Drop

December, 2011

Every year on the day after Thanksgiving, millions of Americans flock to stores to take advantage of discounted prices. Known as "[1]Black Friday," it is ___1___ the busiest shopping day of the year in the United States ___1___ the unofficial beginning of the Christmas season. In the past, many stores would open at 6 in the morning, with shoppers ___2___ hours earlier to be the first in line when the doors opened. In 2011, some retail chains opened their stores at midnight for the first time ___3___ caused a backlash among those who believed that a shopping event should not intrude on the Thanksgiving holiday.

The term "Black Friday" was first used in [2]Philadelphia in the mid-1960s to describe the heavy traffic that became common ___4___ the day after Thanksgiving. In time, the term ___5___ to other areas of the country, and some people came to believe that it symbolized the time of year that most stores begin to make a profit, or be "in the black." Shoppers today must plan ___6___ to deal with the extreme competition to find the best deals in stores. Many people start searching online stores weeks in advance to find which ones will have the biggest sales, and people will arrive ___7___ 10 hours early to get a good place in line.

Critics of Black Friday complain that it promotes unrestrained [3]consumerism and can lead to ___8___. In 2008, a [4]Walmart employee was trampled to death by shoppers ___9___ they pushed their way inside the store. This year, one woman used pepper spray on her fellow customers as she was competed with them to buy a video game system. Black Friday sales have been slower than usual in recent years ___10___ the bad economy, but stores reported a strong turnout this year as people begin to spend more on Christmas gifts.

Choose the correct answers.

(   ) 1. (A) not...but   (B) neither...nor

            (C) not only...but also   (D) too...to

(   ) 2. (A) arrived   (B) who arriving   (C) arriving   (D) arrive

(   ) 3. (A) that   (B) , who   (C) whom   (D) , which

(   ) 4. (A) by   (B) on   (C) at   (D) in

(   ) 5. (A) spread   (B) took   (C) agreed   (D) fled

(   ) 6. (A) ahead   (B) nearby   (C) inward   (D) aside

(   ) 7. (A) as to   (B) in all   (C) or else   (D) up to

(   ) 8. (A) popularity   (B) revolution   (C) riot   (D) peace

(   ) 9. (A) and   (B) when   (C) if   (D) but

(   ) 10. (A) because   (B) because of   (C) in spite of   (D) in order to

≫ Vocabulary

1. **drop** [drɑp] *vi.* 累倒
   - After working over 20 hours, Tess was so exhausted that she felt ready to drop.

2. **flock** [flɑk] *vi.* 蜂擁，聚集
   - Thousands of people flocked to the new shopping mall on its opening day.

3. **discounted** [`dɪskaʊntɪd] *adj.* 折扣的
   - Wendy was so lucky to get the latest digital camera at a discounted price.

4. **retail** [`ritel] *n.* [U] 零售
   - This leather jacket is a real bargain—only 50 percent off the suggested retail price.

5. **chain** [tʃen] *n.* [C] 連鎖商店
   - Local grocery stores have been largely replaced by a chain of convenience stores in this city.

6. **backlash** [`bæk͵læʃ] *n.* [C] (對政治或社會變化) 強烈反對
   - The new tax policy provoked a furious backlash from the middle classes.

7. **intrude** [ɪn`trud] *vi.* 擾亂，侵擾
   - It is tourism that intrudes on this Mediterranean country.
8. **symbolize** [`sɪmbḷ͵aɪz] *vt.* 象徵，代表
   - In the West, the number 666 symbolizes the devil.
9. **profit** [`prɑfɪt] *n.* [C] 利潤，收益
   - The couple sold their apartment at a huge profit.
10. **competition** [͵kɑmpə`tɪʃən] *n.* [U] 競爭
    - There is stiff competition among department stores to attract customers.
    compete [kəm`pit] *vi.* 競爭
    - More than five thousands of applicants are competing for ten vacancies in this multinational company.
11. **unrestrained** [͵ʌnrɪ`strend] *adj.* 無節制的，放縱的
    - Unrestrained exploitation would lead to the exhaustion of natural resources.
12. **trample** [`træmpḷ] *vi.* 踐踏，踩踏
    - A man was trampled underfoot by crowds of shoppers who were escaping from the burning mall.
13. **fellow** [`fɛlo] *adj.* 同類的
    - Ms. Lin asked me to work on the science project with my fellow students.
14. **turnout** [`tɝn͵aʊt] *n.* [C] 到場人數
    - The Carnival in Rio de Janeiro always attracts a large turnout.

≫ Idioms & Phrases

1. **in line** 排隊
   - From a week ago, hundreds of fans have been in line for the concert tickets.
2. **in time** 經過一段時間之後
   - In time, people will forget who's to blame for the corruption scandal.
3. **come to** 開始有 (感覺或意見)
   - Mr. Chen comes to think that family comes first.
4. **be in the black** 有盈餘，有結餘
   - The popular cell phone game makes this new Internet start-up in the black.
5. **in advance** 事先，預先
   - You'd better book train tickets in advance.

 **補充**

1. **Black Friday**　黑色星期五

   指美國感恩節隔天的大拍賣活動日，是一年中最為熱絡的購物日，也被視為耶誕購物季的開始。稱此天為黑色星期五，據說是源自於美國費城，用以形容當天上街購物的人潮與車流。後來另有一說是店家因為大拍賣而大發利市，帳本上為「黑字」，就是有盈餘之意。

2. **Philadelphia**　費城

   是美國賓夕法尼亞州面積最大、人口最多的城市。費城於 1682 年在德拉瓦河谷區建城，是美國最具歷史意義的城市之一。在十八世紀時，費城的政治與社會的重要性超過紐約及波士頓，《獨立宣言》與《美國憲法》都是在此起草跟簽署的。該市現在亦是美國東北部商業、歷史文化、教育的重要城市。

3. **consumerism** [kən`sumə͵rɪzəm] *n.* [U] 消費主義

   消費主義強調創造需求，是一種社會及經濟上的秩序及信念，也是一種生活態度與意識形態，導向購買與獲得。

4. **Walmart**　沃爾瑪

   1962 年，山姆‧沃爾頓於美國阿肯色州羅傑斯城所創立的百貨商店。由於堅持低價策略，沃爾瑪一開始就獲得很大的成功，1990 年成為美國最大的零售商，1993 年成立國際部，1999 年成為世界最大的私人公司。目前全球約有八千多家店面，是世界最大的零售商。

Pop Quiz

Fill in each blank with the correct word or phrase to complete the sentence. Make changes if necessary.

in advance	flock	retail	in time
compete	symbolize	profit	fellow

1. Thanks to this best-selling tablet computer, the online retailer made a healthy _____ in this back-to-school sale.

2. In Western culture, the color black _____ death.

3. Susan and Fiona are my _____ members. We work on a science project.

4. The small company cannot _____ against the large multinational one.

5. The Mexican restaurant is so popular. You should book a table _____ .

UNIT 11

Taiwan Government to People: Go Shopping!

February, 2009

Without a doubt, the world is currently experiencing one of the most serious financial downturns in modern history. As a result of this crisis, many countries have had to come up with innovative solutions for their economies, and Taiwan is no exception. On January 18, government officials in Taiwan began to distribute special shopping vouchers, worth NT$3,600, to eligible residents in an effort to help __1__ the nation's economy.

Anticipation for the vouchers was __2__ , and eager residents began to form long lines at distribution centers early on the Sunday morning that the vouchers first became available. Altogether, more than 23 million people, including children and even foreign spouses, qualified for the money. At the end of the day, more than 90 percent of those eligible to receive the vouchers had picked them up, __3__ government officials.

"Voucher-mania" seemed to sweep Taiwan that same Sunday. Although the voucher is to be used before September, many residents immediately spent their "free money" in shopping malls and supermarkets on the __4__ day they got it. Television news reports showed shoppers using their vouchers in traditional markets, restaurants, and electronics stores. However, many shoppers claimed that they would __5__ use their vouchers to buy everyday items, such as groceries. Others said they planned to use the vouchers to prepare for the Chinese New Year holiday.

Eager to cash in on the voucher craze, many businesses offered special deals for __6__ using vouchers. Some stores __7__ special lotteries while others offered limited discounts. Several airlines, including EVA and China Airlines, also offered special deals for customers who used their vouchers to buy tickets. A few universities even said that they would __8__ students to pay their fees with the vouchers.

Taiwan's government set aside NT$86 billion for the voucher program, hoping to pump up Taiwan's economy. Not everyone, however, is pleased. Some call the vouchers a ___9___ of money, and a few critics have pointed out that the government has actually had to borrow money to finance this project.

One thing is clear, though: Whether they like these vouchers or not, residents in Taiwan have definitely claimed theirs and are certainly using them. What remains to be seen, however, is how much of an ___10___ these vouchers will have on Taiwan's economy.

 **Exercise**

Fill in each blank with the correct word or phrase.

(A) those	(B) according to	(C) allow	(D) actually	(E) high
(F) waste	(G) effect	(H) very	(I) boost	(J) set up

1. _____ 2. _____ 3. _____ 4. _____ 5. _____
6. _____ 7. _____ 8. _____ 9. _____ 10. _____

>> **Vocabulary**

1. currently [`kɝəntlɪ] *adv.* 現在
   • Mr. Smith is currently working as an editor of the China Post.
2. financial [faɪ`nænʃəl] *adj.* 財務的，金融的
   • Due to the economic recession, many companies faced severe financial difficulties.
3. downturn [`daʊntɝn] *n.* [C] (經濟的) 衰退
   • Because of the soaring oil price, the automobile industry is facing a downturn.
4. innovative [`ɪnəˌvetɪv] *adj.* 創新的，革新的
   • Our teacher came up with some innovative teaching methods to help us learn better.
5. economy [i`kɑnəmɪ] *n.* [C] 經濟
   • The government adopted a new tax policy to help stimulate its domestic economy.
6. exception [ɪk`sɛpʃən] *n.* [C][U] 例外
   • It has been raining these days, but today is an exception. It's sunny outside.

- Everyone was awed by the splendor of the scenery, and I was no exception.

7. **distribute** [dɪˋstrɪbjʊt] *vt.* 分發，分配
   - After the big earthquake, food and medical supplies were quickly distributed to the disaster area.

   distribution [͵dɪstrəˋbjuʃən] *n.* [U] 分銷，經銷
   - There is a big distribution center in the industrial suburb.

8. **voucher** [ˋvaʊtʃɚ] *n.* [C] 抵用券
   - The discount voucher can be used at every convenience store.

9. **eligible** [ˋɛlɪdʒəbl] *adj.* 有資格的
   - In Taiwan, anyone over twenty is eligible to vote.

10. **resident** [ˋrɛzədənt] *n.* [C] 居民
    - The foreign visitor got lost and asked a local resident for directions.

11. **anticipation** [æn͵tɪsəˋpeʃən] *n.* [U] 期望
    - Thousands of fans went into the hall in anticipation of seeing Lady Gaga.

12. **spouse** [spaʊz] *n.* [C] 配偶
    - "Spouse" is a formal term which people use to mean a wife or a husband.

13. **qualify** [ˋkwɑlə͵faɪ] *vi.* 使具有資格
    - A person who is involuntarily unemployed is qualified for unemployment benefits.

14. **percent** [pɚˋsɛnt] *n.* [C] 百分之一
    - 80 percent of the fifty students passed the exam. That is, ten students failed it.

15. **mania** [ˋmenɪə] *n.* [U] 狂熱
    - Bicycle mania is sweeping Taiwan. Many people ride their bicycles on weekends.

16. **immediately** [ɪˋmidɪɪtlɪ] *adv.* 立即，馬上
    - As soon as Johnson put the phone down, he immediately ran out.

17. **electronics** [ɪlɛkˋtrɑnɪks] *n.* [C] 電子用品
    - Taiwanese homes are filled with personal computers, TV sets, and other electronics.

18. **craze** [krez] *n.* [C] 狂熱
    - May started a craze for Korean soap operas.

19. lottery [`lɑtərɪ] *n.* [C] 抽獎，獎券
   - Frank won the lottery and became rich overnight.
20. critic [`krɪtɪk] *n.* [C] 批評者
   - The government's new construction project, which is heavily attacked by critics, is now put on hold.
21. finance [`faɪnæns] *vt.* 為…提供資金，資助
   - The museum was financed by the local government.
22. definitely [`dɛfənɪtlɪ] *adv.* 毫無疑問地，確定地
   - *Avatar* is definitely the best movie I have ever seen.

≫Idioms & Phrases

1. as a result (of sth.)　由於…
   - As a result of his broken leg, Andy has been confined to a wheelchair for two weeks.
2. come up with　想出，提出 (計畫、答案等)
   - We have discussed the problem for two hours but still couldn't come up with a good solution.
3. in an effort to　為了…
   - The single father had two part-time jobs in an effort to make more money.
4. cash in on　利用…賺錢
   - The publishing house tried to cash in on the writer's death by publishing his past works.
5. pump up　提高，增加
   - Our company worked with the local stores to pump up the sales of the new product.

Pop Quiz

Choose the best answer to each of the following sentences.

(   ) 1. It is reported that over 20 _____ of adults in Taiwan are overweight.

      (A) spouse   (B) percent   (C) resident   (D) outbreak

(   ) 2. _____ , Karen is on a diet. She eats a limited amount of food now.

      (A) Currently   (B) Significantly   (C) Immediately   (D) Relatively

(   ) 3. All the students, without _____ , have to attend the morning gathering.

      (A) anticipation   (B) content   (C) revenge   (D) exception

(   ) 4. In the U.S., people over 21 are _____ to drink wine.

      (A) innovative   (B) harsh   (C) excessive   (D) eligible

(   ) 5. _____ the heavy snow, all flights over the Norway are cancelled.

      (A) In an effort to   (B) Up to   (C) As a result of   (D) In advance of

UNIT 12

The 99% Fight Back: the "Occupy" Movement

November, 2011

What began as a loosely organized protest against corporate greed in September has grown into a nationwide movement against economic inequality in the United States. Although the [1]Occupy Wall Street (OWS) movement originated in [2]New York City's financial district, similar "occupy" demonstrations have spread to cities across the country. The protestors have focused their anger on the people they call "the 1 percent," which refers to the corporate executives and financiers who control the majority of the nation's wealth, while they call themselves "the 99%," which refers to the majority of Americans who have borne the brunt of the current [3]economic downturn.

The Occupy Wall Street protestors began their demonstration on September 17 by setting up camp in [4]Zuccotti Park, which is near Wall Street in New York City. Over the following weeks, more and more people frustrated with an economy that features high unemployment together with rising corporate profits joined the movement as similar demonstrations began in other cities. The protests have received cautious support from some [5]Democrats, whereas [6]Republicans have mostly criticized the demonstrators. Organizers are beginning to struggle with the movement's growing size as the need for structured leadership arises and people begin to send monetary contributions.

One of the movement's most ambitious endeavors occurred in [7]Oakland, California on November 2. Demonstrators organized a massive street march that received support from local teachers and dock workers, which helped cause a virtual work stoppage at the country's fifth busiest port. Thus far the protests have been generally peaceful, although a former [8]Marine was injured by a police projectile in Oakland previously, causing more military veterans to join the movement. Local governments have begun to complain that the occupation is disrupting local services and traffic as they grow in size, but some of the movement's leaders fear that they will begin to lose support as colder weather sets in for the winter.

Choose the best answers.

(　　) 1. The passage is mainly about _____ .

    (A) the reason for the current economic downturn

    (B) what the protestors of the OWS movement were against for

    (C) what dock workers in Oakland really needed for their daily life

    (D) how Democrats supported the OWS movement

(　　) 2. What does the phrase "bear the brunt of" mean in the first paragraph?

    (A) To stop something from burning.

    (B) To help pump up something.

    (C) To keep an eye on something important.

    (D) To suffer the worst part of something unpleasant.

(　　) 3. According to the article, "the 1 percent" are _____ .

    (A) corporate executives　　　　(B) the majority of Americans

    (C) Republicans　　　　　　　　(D) most of the OWS protestors

(　　) 4. Which of the following about the OWS movement is correct?

    (A) The OWS movement started as a well-organized protest.

    (B) Less and less people joined the protest because of the loosely organization.

    (C) An unexpected demonstration in Oakland drew supports from local teachers.

    (D) The protests led to a series of violent attacks.

(　　) 5. The OWS movement's leaders worried about _____ .

    (A) a massive street march could bring about the economic downturn

    (B) protestors would lose support as the weather got cold in the winter

    (C) dock workers and local teachers began to complain about the occupation

    (D) the occupations might disrupt local services and traffic for a long time

>> Vocabulary

1. **occupy** [ˋɑkjə͵paɪ] *vt.* 佔領，佔據
   - Rebels have occupied the capital for two months.
   occupation [͵ɑkjəˋpeʃən] *n.* [U] 佔領
   - The movie *Seediq Bale* tells the story of the Wushe Incident during the Japanese occupation.

2. **corporate** [ˋkɔrpə͵ret] *adj.* 公司的，企業的
   - The logo of a bitten-off apple is an impressive corporate identity of this multinational corporation.

3. **greed** [ˋgrid] *n.* [U] 貪婪，貪心
   - Driven by greed for money, the police officer took bribes.

4. **nationwide** [͵neʃənˋwaɪd] *adj.* 全國性的，遍及全國的
   - According to a nationwide survey, over 50 percent of people are against the public policy.

5. **inequality** [͵ɪnɪˋkwalətɪ] *n.* [U] 不平等
   - A well-organized welfare system may help reduce social inequality.

6. **originate** [əˋrɪdʒə͵net] *vi.* 發源，起源
   - AIDS is believed to have originated from Africa.

7. **district** [ˋdɪstrɪkt] *n.* [C] 區域，地區
   - The couple bought a house in a coastal suburban district.

8. **executive** [ɪgˋzɛkjʊtɪv] *n.* [C] 主管領導
   - Mr. Chen is the top executive of this well-known car company.

9. **financier** [faɪnənˋsɪr] *n.* [C] 金融家
   - Fat-cat financiers were to blame for the Global Financial Crisis.

10. **unemployment** [͵ʌnɪmˋplɔɪmənt] *n.* [U] 失業
    - The government should take appropriate measures to help reduce unemployment.

11. **cautious** [ˋkɔʃəs] *adj.* 謹慎的
    - Sam is cautious about investing in the property market.

12. **whereas** [hwɛrˋæz] *conj.* 然而，儘管
    - Some approved the proposal, whereas others were against it.

13. **organizer** [ˋɔrgənˏnaɪzɚ] *n.* [C] (活動) 主辦者
   - The event organizer expects about twenty thousand people to attend the running festival this Sunday morning.
14. **monetary** [ˋmʌnəˏtɛrɪ] *adj.* 金錢的
   - Frank sent his wife a gift of high monetary value for her birthday.
15. **contribution** [ˏkɑntrəˋbjuʃən] *n.* [C] 捐款
   - We decided to make a contribution of NT5,000 to charity.
16. **ambitious** [æmˋbɪʃəs] *adj.* 野心勃勃的
   - Obviously, Amy Chua, the author of the book *Battle Hymn of the Tiger Mother*, is highly ambitious for her children.
17. **endeavor** [ɪnˋdɛvɚ] *n.* [C] (*fml.*) 努力，嘗試
   - The police made every endeavor to find the missing boy.
18. **massive** [ˋmæsɪv] *adj.* 大規模的，嚴重的
   - The protest movement led to massive changes in fiscal policy.
19. **virtual** [ˋvɝtʃʊəl] *adj.* 實際上的，實質上的
   - After a heated argument, my roommate and I became virtual strangers.
20. **veteran** [ˋvɛtərən] *n.* [C] 老兵，退伍軍人
   - My grandfather is a veteran of the Second World War.

≫ Idioms & Phrases

1. **refer to**　涉及…，與…有關
   - The word "premiere," meaning "first" in French, now refers to the first public performance of a movie.
2. **bear the brunt of sth.**　首當其衝，承受某事的主要壓力
   - Social welfare programs are believed to bear the brunt of cuts in government spending.
3. **thus far**　到目前為止，至今 (= so far)
   - Mrs. Miller's diamond ring has thus far been nowhere to be seen.
4. **set in**　(壞天氣、壞事等) 開始、到來
   - According to the weather forecast, the heavy rain is going to set in this evening.

≫補充

1. **Occupy Wall Street (OWS)**　佔領華爾街

   佔領華爾街的示威活動於 2011 年 9 月 17 日展開，以紐約市金融區華爾街附近的祖科蒂公園為大本營。參與佔領華爾街活動的人來自社會各階層，有教授、學生、白領族、工人、甚至是流浪漢，活動的口號是：「貪婪的百分之一對抗被苛待的百分之九十九 (the greedy 1% versus the hard-done-by 99%)，抗議經濟資源被社會極少數的富人把持，大多數的人卻受到不公平的待遇，藉以表達他們對金融體系的不滿，攀升的失業率、長期的貧困、貧富差距的懸殊，讓他們無法再忍受下去。

2. **New York City**　紐約市

   由荷蘭人於 1624 年建立，作為商業的交易站，當時被稱為新阿姆斯特丹。紐約自 1785 年到 1790 年為美國首都，在 1790 年後成為美國最大的都市之一。紐約由布朗區、布魯克林區、曼哈頓、皇后區、史坦島等五區組成。現為美國人口最多、最大的城市，是全球商業經貿的重心。觀光業是紐約相當重要的經濟來源，每年大約有四千多萬名觀光客造訪，著名地標有時代廣場、中央公園、自由女神像、帝國大廈等。

3. **economic downturn**　經濟衰退

   經濟學專有名詞，指經濟週期或景氣循環中，經濟出現負成長的階段。定義為在一年之中，一國的國內生產總值 (GDP) 連續兩季 (以上) 持續減少。

4. **Zuccotti Park**　祖科蒂公園

   坐落於紐約市曼哈頓下城區中的一個公園，2006 年整修後以該公園捐助者之一 John Zucccotti 為名，又稱作自由廣場公園。

5. **Democrat**　民主黨 (人)

   美國兩大政黨之一，最早是從 1792 年傑佛遜總統所創建的民主共和黨而來，為自由主義的政黨。代表顏色為藍色，象徵動物為驢子。出身該黨的代表性政治人物有小羅斯福、甘迺迪、柯林頓和歐巴馬等。

6. **Republican**　共和黨 (人)

   美國兩大政黨之一，由創建於 1854 年的北方各黨派人士所組成的聯盟而來，為保守主義的政黨。代表顏色為紅色，象徵動物為大象。出身該黨的代表性政治人物有林肯、老羅斯福、雷根、老布希和小布希等。

7. **Oakland**　奧克蘭

   為於美國西岸加州舊金山灣的主要港口城市，阿拉米達郡首府。

8. **Marine** 海軍陸戰隊

　　一般隸屬於海軍 (或獨立的軍種)，負責地面作戰、兩棲作戰及保護船艦登陸等特殊任務。

Fill in each blank with the correct word or phrase to complete the sentence. Make changes if necessary.

refer to	cautious	endeavor	contribution
greed	set in	ambitious	occupy

1. Luke is _____ about making any promise. He is a man of his word.
2. Those workers have _____ the factory. They refused to leave the place unless their boss agreed to offer a higher pay.
3. Driven by _____ for money, the actress tried everything to marry into the wealthy family.
4. Alex made every _____ to go to his ideal college.
5. The snow has _____ for a whole week. Therefore, the town was buried under five feet of snow.

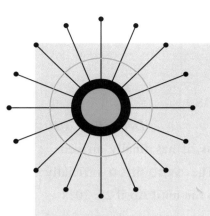

Local News

本土議題

Taipei Flora Expo Blooms

December, 2010

After years of preparation and publicity campaigns, it has finally arrived— [1]2010 Taipei International Flora Exposition has begun. The exposition officially opened to the public on November 6, and it is scheduled to run until April 25, 2011.

This is the first time that Taiwan has been chosen to host an [2]International Association of Horticultural Producers (AIPH) event, and Taipei has __1__ pulled out all the stops for this exposition. The event has been four years in the making, and it is reported that __2__ 13.8 billion New Taiwan dollars (456.95 million U.S. dollars) have been spent to bring it to life. __3__ a theme of "Rivers, Flowers, New Horizons," the expo covers 91.8 [3]hectares and includes four parks and 14 exhibition halls. Altogether, 32 million plants will be on display. Expo officials have stated that they expect that over 8 million visitors will attend this event, with more than 400,000 foreign tourists __4__ to visit the expo.

The Taipei Flora Expo has not been entirely free from controversy, __5__ . Some say that the government has spent too much money on the event; __6__ question the wisdom of holding this flower show during Taipei's rainy Fall and Winter seasons. Actually, the rain has already created problems during the opening ceremony's fireworks and has caused visitor attendance __7__ lower than expected during the expo's first weeks.

Despite these difficulties, the expo has received __8__ reviews from most of those who have attended it. Dr. Doeke Faber, president of the AIPH, stated, "In my opinion, the Taipei International Flora is the best one I have seen in 50 years." Other visitors have echoed this sentiment, with many saying that they appreciated having the chance to learn more about new types of eco-friendly technology, especially in the [4]Pavilion of Dreams and the [5]Pavilion of New Fashion (Far Eastern Group EcoARK) __9__ was made from 1.5 million recycled [6]PET bottles.

Without a doubt, the Taipei Flora Expo is one of the biggest and most important events that Taiwan has held in recent years. With so much to see and do at this exposition, it is definitely one event ___10___ can be visited and enjoyed multiple times over the next few months.

Choose the correct answers.

(	) 1. (A) mostly	(B) certainly	(C) relatively	(D) shortly
(	) 2. (A) as much so	(B) as much to	(C) too much to	(D) as much as
(	) 3. (A) By	(B) At	(C) With	(D) From
(	) 4. (A) to plan	(B) plan	(C) who planning	(D) planning
(	) 5. (A) thus	(B) yet	(C) however	(D) too
(	) 6. (A) others	(B) other	(C) ones	(D) the other
(	) 7. (A) to be	(B) be	(C) to being	(D) been
(	) 8. (A) careful	(B) positive	(C) common	(D) negative
(	) 9. (A) that	(B) , who	(C) which	(D) , which
(	) 10. (A) why	(B) that	(C) what	(D) it

>> Vocabulary

1. **bloom** [blum] *vi.* 開花
   • In Taiwan, most tung oil trees will start to bloom from late April.

2. **preparation** [ˌprɛpəˈreʃən] *n.* [U] 準備
   • The gymnast practices hard every day, in preparation for the Olympic Games.

3. **publicity** [pʌbˈlɪsətɪ] *n.* [U] 宣傳工作
   • The singer's sex scandal with her agent acted as a publicity stunt.

4. **exposition** [ˌɛkspəˈzɪʃən] *n.* [C] 展覽會
   • Book Exposition of America is the biggest of its kind in the U.S.

5. **schedule** [ˈskɛdʒʊl] *vt.* 預計
   • I am scheduled to meet with Dr. Philip at 5 o'clock.

6. **theme** [θim] *n.* [C] 主題，題目
   • Most of Pablo Neruda's poems are produced on the theme of love.

7. **horizons** [hə`raɪznz] *n. pl.* 視野，眼界
   - Working holiday may help broaden your horizons.

8. **exhibition** [ˌɛksə`bɪʃən] *n.* [C] 展覽
   - Claude Monet's paintings are now on exhibition at the art museum.

9. **ceremony** [`sɛrəˌmonɪ] *n.* [C] 儀式，典禮
   - I was too busy to attend my son's graduation ceremony.

10. **firework** [`faɪrˌwɝk] *n.* [C] 煙火
    - We set off fireworks to celebrate the New Year.

11. **attendance** [ə`tɛndəns] *n.* [U] 出席人數
    - The attendance at this public speech is higher than our expectation.

12. **echo** [`ɛko] *vt.* 附和
    - The literary critic didn't think highly of the novel, and the press echoed his criticism.

13. **sentiment** [`sɛntəmənt] *n.* [C] 意見，觀點
    - Many teachers and parents expressed similar sentiments about the education reform policy.

14. **appreciate** [ə`priʃɪˌet] *vt.* 感激
    - Thank you for your timely help. I really appreciate it.

15. **technology** [tɛk`nɑlədʒɪ] *n.* [U] 科技
    - The progress in computer technology has brought us much convenience.

16. **recycle** [ri`saɪkl̩] *vt.* 回收利用
    - Plastic containers can be recycled and made into clothing.

17. **multiple** [`mʌltəpl̩] *adj.* 數量多的
    - The driver suffered multiple injuries after the car accident.

≫ Idioms & Phrases

1. **pull out all the stops** 盡全力，全力以赴
   - The insurance salesman pulled out all the stops to win the contract.

2. **in the making** 歷時，在生產過程中
   - After countless fierce battles, the country finally won the war ten years in the making.

3. **bring...to life** 使…生動、有趣
   - The use of bright colors brings the animals in the painting to life.
4. **on display** 展示，展出
   - A collection of Chinese paintings are on display at the National Palace Museum.
5. **without a doubt** 無疑地
   - Without a doubt, Ken failed the test, since he hasn't studied for it.

≫補充

1. **Taipei Flora Expo (2010 Taipei International Flora Exposition)**
   2010 臺北國際花卉博覽會
   簡稱臺北花博、臺北國際花博，於 2010 年 11 月 6 日至 2011 年 4 月 25 日在臺北市舉行，是臺灣第一個正式獲得國際園藝家協會 (AIPH) 及國際展覽局 (BIE) 認證可主辦的國際園藝博覽會。

2. **International Association of Horticultural Producers (AIPH)**
   國際園藝家協會
   是由各國園藝家在瑞士於 1948 年所組成的協會，目前有 25 個會員國，共 33 個會員參與。AIPH 的會員每年於春季及秋季各集會一次，彼此交換栽培資訊與經驗，大會並將會議上的資訊整理成冊，出版統計年報。

3. **hectare** 公頃
   土地的丈量單位，一公頃等於一萬平方公尺。

4. **Pavilion of Dream** 夢想館
   夢想館位於臺北市的新生公園內，特色是結合了臺灣最新研發的尖端科技及藝術家的創意，應用在展館內。該館是臺北花博的展館中，唯一展現臺灣尖端科技的數位互動展館。

5. **Pavilion of New Fashion** 流行館
   由遠東集團所贊助興建、營運及佈展的流行館——遠東環生方舟。結構體以臺灣常見的竹子為主體，搭配建築回收的鋼架來強化建物的結構，同時讓這棟建築的碳排放量達到最低，而原本應使用磚塊水泥的建材，是以超過 152 萬支回收寶特瓶經處理後製成的寶特磚代替。質輕又堅固的寶特磚，使得流行館通過了地震及颱風的測試，是全球第一棟由寶特瓶所建造的綠建築。

6. **PET bottle** 寶特瓶
   PET 是聚對苯二甲酸乙二酯的簡稱，為製造寶特瓶的原料。

Pop Quiz

Fill in each blank with the correct word or phrase to complete the sentence. Make changes if necessary.

sentiment	in the making	appreciate	ceremony
recycle	horizons	on display	multiple

1. Pablo Picasso's paintings are _____ at the National Museum of History.
2. I wore a new dress to attend my high school classmate's wedding _____ .
3. My mother took all waste paper and newspapers to be _____ .
4. I really _____ having such a good friend, who always stands by me.
5. May decided to go on a volunteer vacation in Africa to broaden her _____ .

More Chinese Tourists, More Problems?

May, 2009

It was just less than a year ago when Taiwan opened its doors to tourists from the [1]People's Republic of China. On July 4, 2008, the first tour groups from China began to arrive, and the number of Chinese visitors to Taiwan has continued to increase, __1__ after daily [2]charter flights between Taiwan and China commenced on December 15. In fact, by __2__ April of 2009, more than 4,000 Chinese tourists were visiting Taiwan each day. This prompted Taiwan's [3]National Immigration Agency to raise the __3__ quota of Chinese tourists allowed into Taiwan to 7,200.

Yet, even though more and more Chinese tourists are visiting Taiwan, it seems, unfortunately, that incidents involving these tourists have been on the rise recently, too. On April 24, a tour bus carrying tourists from [4]Guangdong was crushed by a construction crane that fell down 37 floors as these tourists were on their way to visit Taipei 101. Three __4__ were killed and three others were injured in the incident. Then, on April 30, two Chinese tourists traveling with a tour group from [5]Fuzhou were __5__ injured by falling stones when they were walking in [6]Taroko National Park. One tourist was __6__ unconscious by falling stones, while the other suffered cuts and bone fractures. Both required surgery. And then, on May 1, a tourist from Guangdong fell 12 floors to his death from the balcony of his hotel room. This accident __7__ in [7]Puli Township, in [8]Nantou County. The sixty-seven-year-old victim had been part of a group of __8__ Chinese tourists on a five-day tour of Taiwan.

Even though three such serious incidents have occurred in such a short span of time, Chinese tour groups continue to visit Taiwan, and the number of Chinese tourists visiting Taiwan appears likely to continue to rise. Government officials have stated that they hope that one day 10,000 Chinese tourists will visit Taiwan every day, since this would __9__ Taiwan's tourism industry. However, the safety of all tourists who choose to visit Taiwan should be a top __10__ as well.

Exercise

Fill in each blank with the correct word or phrase.

(A) knocked	(B) seriously	(C) especially	(D) passengers	(E) took place
(F) early	(G) goal	(H) daily	(I) boost	(J) elderly

1. _____   2. _____   3. _____   4. _____   5. _____

6. _____   7. _____   8. _____   9. _____   10. _____

» Vocabulary

1. **commence** [kə`mɛns] *vi.* 開始，著手
   - The construction of the new factory will commence at 10 a.m. this Friday.
2. **prompt** [prɑmpt] *vt.* 促使
   - The threat of damaging her health prompted Tess to lose weight.
3. **quota** [`kwotə] *n.* [C] 定額，配額
   - The government has imposed quotas on the import of sports cars.
4. **unfortunately** [ʌn`fɔrtʃənɪtlɪ] *adv.* 不幸地
   - Unfortunately, I overslept and missed the school bus.
5. **incident** [`ɪnsədənt] *n.* [C] 事件
   - The witness tried hard to recall the shooting incident.
6. **involve** [ɪn`vɑlv] *vt.* 牽涉，牽連
   - There was a drug scandal involving the famous singer.
7. **construction** [kən`strʌkʃən] *n.* [U] 建造
   - The couple now live in rented housing since their house is still under construction.
8. **unconscious** [ʌn`kɑnʃəs] *adj.* 無知覺的，昏迷的
   - It is reported that a gangster was attacked and beaten unconscious on the street.
9. **fracture** [`fræktʃɚ] *n.* [C] 骨折
   - Teresa suffered a fracture of the arm, and the doctor told her that it needed six months to recover.

10. surgery [`sɝdʒərɪ] *n*. [U] 外科手術
   · The basketball player required surgery on his left knee.
11. balcony [`bælkənɪ] *n*. [C] 陽臺
   · Amber sat out on the balcony of the apartment to calm herself down.
12. span [spæn] *n*. [C] 一段時間
   · During the short span of our three-week stay in Paris, we have visited more than 20 museums.

≫Idioms & Phrases

1. on one's way to... 在前往⋯的途中
   · Mr. Lu had a flat tire on his way to the train station.

≫補 充

1. People's Republic of China 中華人民共和國
   通稱中國，首都北京。位於亞洲東部、太平洋西岸，領土面積約 960 萬平方公里，與 14 個國家接壤。人口約佔全球的五分之一，是世界上人口最多的國家。自改革開放後，中國經濟持續成長，是世界上經濟發展最快的國家之一。
2. charter flight 包機
3. National Immigration Agency 內政部入出國及移民署
   簡稱移民署，為中華民國負責管理入出國境與移民的最高機關，隸屬於內政部。主要工作有強化境外管理、國境線查驗功能，並對移入人口停留、居留、定居等不同階段之積極管理。
4. Guangdong 廣東省
   簡稱粵，是中國南部沿海的一個省份，省會廣州。廣東省位於南嶺以南，與香港、澳門、廣西、湖南、江西和福建接壤，與海南島隔海相望。廣東有「漁米之鄉」之稱，經濟相當發達。
5. Fuzhou 福州市
   為中國福建省的省會，位於福建省閩江下游出海口的福州平原上，是全省人口最多的城市。居民以福州族群為主，母語為福州話。

6. **Taroko National Park　太魯閣國家公園**

　為臺灣最早設立的國家公園之一，位於臺灣東部，跨花蓮縣、臺中市、南投縣三個行政區，有中橫公路通過園內。峽谷和斷崖為太魯閣國家公園的特色，「魯閣幽峽」名列臺灣八景之一。此外，園內的高山地帶保留了許多冰河時期的生物，如山椒魚等。

7. **Puli Township　埔里鎮**

　取自原住民社名埔裏社，位於臺灣南投縣北部，為臺灣本島地理中心。

8. **Nantou County　南投縣**

　位於臺灣中部，是臺灣唯一的內陸縣。境內有泰雅族、布農族、鄒族及邵族等原住民族群。南投被譽為臺灣的「大地之母」，臺灣最高峰玉山及最長河流濁水溪的源頭皆位於此。

Choose the best answer to each of the following sentences.

(　　) 1. My mother told me that I fell down the stairs when I was three, but I couldn't recall the _____ at all.

　　(A) ceremony　　(B) fracture　　(C) protest　　(D) incident

(　　) 2. _____, Mark was stuck in a traffic jam for two hours. He failed to make it to the meeting.

　　(A) Stereotypically　(B) Promptly　　(C) Unfortunately　(D) Likely

(　　) 3. The teacher's words of encouragement _____ Jerry to study hard.

　　(A) involved　　(B) symbolized　　(C) appreciated　　(D) prompted

(　　) 4. Suffering from heart disease, the little girl required heart _____.

　　(A) surgery　　(B) construction　　(C) industry　　(D) injury

(　　) 5. We found the homeless man lying _____ on the floor. He seemed to pass out.

　　(A) massive　　(B) unconscious　　(C) unfortunate　　(D) innovative

UNIT 15

To Build or Not to Build?

January, 2010

It has been one of the most controversial proposals in Taiwan in recent years. It has even played an important role in a recent election. And now it appears uncertainly that this project will ever begin. It, of course, is the [1]Suao-Hualien freeway project, more popularly known as the "Suhua freeway."

Opinions about this proposed new road clearly divide people into two groups. Some are strong supporters of the Suhua freeway project, including many politicians and most residents in eastern Taiwan. They argue that a new route between Suao township and Hualien city is desperately needed. It can be used not only to replace the original crooked and fragile road but also to boost the region's economy. Since this area consists mostly of farming communities, it has remained relatively underdeveloped, especially in comparison to other parts of the island. Furthermore, the new freeway would definitely help save a lot of time spent on traveling between Suao and Hualien—from almost three hours to only an hour or so.

However, many environmental activists have pointed that the construction of a new highway might cause extensive environmental damage to eastern Taiwan, which is famous for its naturally extraordinary scenic beauty. It would destroy this area's important habitat for many special plants and animals as well. Many experts also say this new road, which would include more than 40 kilometers of tunnels and 37 kilometers of bridges, might be even more dangerous, since its construction and the route itself would be so close to earthquake [2]fault lines. And, the most crucial question is: Do we really need the highly expensive and time-consuming construction of a new freeway to promise the future prosperity of eastern Taiwan?

Although the [3]Ministry of Transportation and Communications has reviewed the project and decided to take another proposal for improving the existing Suhua highway recently, the fate of the Suhua freeway remains up in the air because it is not the final call. It will be up to the people and politicians of Taiwan to come up with a solution that will best benefit eastern Taiwan, while still preserving the area's unique beauty and environment.

Exercise

Choose the best answers.

(   ) 1. What is the main idea of this passage?

    (A) The cost of the construction of the Suhua freeway project is too high.

    (B) There is a great deal of opposition to the Suhua freeway project.

    (C) How to boost eastern Taiwan's economic development.

    (D) There is great controversy over the Suhua freeway project.

(   ) 2. According to the passage, who do NOT support the Suhua freeway project?

    (A) People who live in Hualien.

    (B) Most of the residents in eastern Taiwan.

    (C) Environmental activists.

    (D) Many politicians in Taiwan.

(   ) 3. Which of the following is NOT a reason why people support the Suhua freeway project?

    (A) There's no direct route between Suao and Hualien now.

    (B) The Suhua freeway can help boost eastern Taiwan's economy.

    (C) The Suhua freeway can save a lot of travel time.

    (D) Those who live in the eastern part of Taiwan need a safer road.

(   ) 4. Which of the following statements is true about the Suhua freeway?

    (A) It includes less than 20 kilometers of tunnels.

    (B) It can help save a lot travel time from Hualien to Taitung.

    (C) It would be dangerous because it is close to earthquake fault lines.

    (D) It also aims to preserve habitats for many special plants and animals.

(   ) 5. Is the Suhua freeway going to be constructed?

    (A) It has not been decided yet.

    (B) No, because the residents are against the project.

    (C) Yes, it is under construction now.

    (D) It is not mentioned in the passage.

>> Vocabulary

1. **proposal** [prə`pozl̩] *n.* [C] 提議，建議
   - The government has approved proposals for economic reforms.

2. **route** [rut] *n.* [C] 路，路線
   - What's the shortest route from here to the train station? I am in a hurry.

3. **desperately** [`dɛspərɪtlɪ] *adv.* 極度，非常
   - The starving child looked around desperately for something to eat.

4. **crooked** [`krʊkɪd] *adj.* 彎曲的，不直的
   - A car accident happened on the crooked road last night.

5. **fragile** [`frædʒəl] *adj.* 脆弱的
   - The crystal vase is fragile. You have to handle it with care.

6. **mostly** [`mostlɪ] *adv.* 主要，大部分地
   - May goes to visit her grandparents mostly on Sundays.

7. **community** [kə`mjunətɪ] *n.* [C] 界，領域
   - Professor Lin has spent her whole life in the academic community.

8. **underdeveloped** [ˌʌndɚdɪ`vɛləpt] *adj.* 低度開發的
   - Many African countries, such as Chad and Liberia, are considered underdeveloped countries.

9. **furthermore** [`fɚðɚˌmor] *adv.* 此外
   - The house is too small; furthermore, it is far from the town.

10. **activist** [`æktɪvɪst] *n.* [C] 積極份子
    - The group of gay activists hope that the government would pass a bill to legalize same-sex marriage.

11. **extensive** [ɪk`stɛnsɪv] *adj.* 廣大的，大量的
    - Floods have caused extensive damage to the country's low-lying areas.

12. **scenic** [`sinɪk] *adj.* 風景優美的
    - Grand Canyon National Park is famous for its scenic beauty.

13. **habitat** [`hæbɪtæt] *n.* [C] 棲息地
    - The wetland provides an important habitat for birds.

14. crucial [`kruʃəl] *adj.* 關鍵性的，重要的
   • The support from Becky's parents is crucial to her success.
15. highly [`haɪlɪ] *adv.* 非常，很
   • Robert Frost's poems are highly praised.
16. time-consuming [`taɪm kən`sumɪŋ] *adj.* 費時的
   • Washing an airplane is very time-consuming, and it also costs lots of money.
17. prosperity [prɑs`pɛrətɪ] *n.* [U] 繁榮，成功
   • Tourism has brought economic prosperity to the old town.
18. preserve [prɪ`zɝv] *vt.* 保存
   • These environmental activists tried hard to preserve the ancient woodland.

≫ Idioms & Phrases

1. up in the air　尚未決定的
   • The project of building a cable car has been debated for years, but it is still up in the air.

≫ 補 充

1. **Suao Hualien (Suhua) freeway**　蘇花高速公路
   蘇花高速公路起於宜蘭縣蘇澳鎮，迄至花蓮縣吉安鄉，總長約 86 公里，橋樑總長約 37 公里，隧道總長約 40 公里，橋樑及隧道佔全線 90%，預估工期約需 7 到 8 年。因環評沒通過，已確定不興建。改進行蘇花公路改善計畫，簡稱「蘇花改」，路段從台九線蘇澳到崇德段，預計在 106 年完工通車。

2. **fault**　斷層
   斷層是指岩石破裂後，兩側岩石發生顯著的相對位移。斷層大小不等，大的斷層可貫穿整個岩石圈，水平則可綿延數千公里。由於地殼會在斷層處作垂直或水平移動，因此在斷層處經常會發生地震。

3. **Ministry of Transportation and Communications**　交通部
   交通部是管理全國交通事務之最高行政機關，負責通信 (郵政及電信)、運輸、氣象、觀光等四大領域，負責釐定交通政策、法令規章，並督導相關業務之執行。

Pop Quiz

Choose the best answer to each of the following sentences.

(　　) 1. Human cloning is a _____ controversial issue. Many people have strong opinions about it.

　　(A) promptly　　(B) highly　　(C) relatively　　(D) mostly

(　　) 2. Economic development may cause the destruction of wildlife _____, which makes many animals lose their natural home.

　　(A) themes　　(B) habitats　　(C) generations　　(D) communities

(　　) 3. The labor union put forward a _____ to reduce working hours from 48 to 40 per week.

　　(A) route　　(B) voucher　　(C) trap　　(D) proposal

(　　) 4. Rachel refused to answer my calls. _____, she has not even contacted me.

　　(A) Furthermore　　(B) Immediately　　(C) Unfortunately　　(D) Mostly

(　　) 5. A balanced diet plays a _____ part in maintaining health.

　　(A) crooked　　(B) fragile　　(C) crucial　　(D) time-consuming

Note

- --
- --
- --
- --
- --
- --
- --
- --
- --
- --
- --
- --
- --
- --
- --
- --
- --
- --
- --

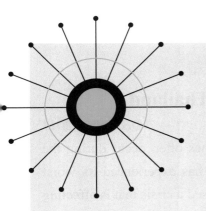

Natural
Disaster

天災

UNIT 16

Worst Flooding in 50 Years in ¹Thailand

December, 2011

Floods are nothing new to Thailand. In fact, minor ones often occur during the country's ²monsoon season. This year, however, Thailand has experienced its worst flooding in fifty years, ___1___ months of heavy rain have caused a crisis that is affecting not only Thailand, but also the rest of the world.

The trouble began as early as March of this year when certain areas of northern Thailand received an astonishing 344 percent more rain than usual. ___2___ rain continued throughout the rest of the summer, filling dams and causing water to gather in northern and central Thailand. In the past, this water would have slowly drained south to ³the Gulf of Thailand, ___3___ minimum damage. This year, ___4___ , the sheer amount of rain that Thailand received caused massive flooding that started in the north and continued down to the south.

Starting in late July, a massive amount of water began to make its way toward ⁴Bangkok, Thailand's capital. These floodwaters submerged thousands of acres of farmland. ___5___ early October, the historic city of ⁵Ayutthaya was flooded, and evacuations had begun in parts of central Thailand. Further south, the nine million residents of Bangkok began to brace for the coming floodwaters.

As the water moved south, it also flooded hundreds of factories in central Thailand. In recent years, Thailand has become a global center for the ___6___ of car and computer components. The 2011 flooding disrupted manufacturing activity in these plants. Experts are now predicting an increase in prices of external hard drives ___7___ this natural disaster.

So far, a few sections of Bangkok have ___8___ unaffected by the flooding, thanks to extensive drainage systems and other preparations. Relief agencies warned, however, that the threat of disease from the unsanitary conditions caused by the flooding still remains. For its part, the Thai government has already promised a large cleanup and aid program for the areas ___9___ by this year's floods.

To date, the floods of 2011 have already caused more than 800 deaths and US$5.9 billion in damage in Thailand. This flooding has also wreaked havoc on global supply chains for cars and computers.   10 , the 2011 floods in Thailand will be remembered for many years to come.

Exercise

Choose the correct answers.

(   ) 1. (A) or   (B) as   (C) but   (D) if

(   ) 2. (A) Breaking-record   (B) Break-record

          (C) Record-breaking   (D) Record-broken

(   ) 3. (A) to cause   (B) and causing   (C) causing   (D) caused

(   ) 4. (A) instead   (B) yet   (C) too   (D) however

(   ) 5. (A) By   (B) At   (C) On   (D) For

(   ) 6. (A) production   (B) entertainment   (C) opposition   (D) controversy

(   ) 7. (A) in order to   (B) because of   (C) because   (D) as a result

(   ) 8. (A) sounded   (B) kept   (C) looked   (D) remained

(   ) 9. (A) to be affected   (B) affecting   (C) which affected (D) affected

(   ) 10. (A) Fortunately   (B) Promptly   (C) Clearly   (D) Relatively

>> Vocabulary

1. astonishing [əˋstɑnɪʃɪŋ] *adj.* 驚人的
   - I found it quite astonishing that my classmate had undergone plastic surgery.

2. drain [dren] *vi.* (液體) 流出
   - The large amount of rainwater brought by the typhoon finally drained into the river.

   drainage [ˋdrenɪdʒ] *n.* [U] 排水，放水
   - The poor drainage system is unable to prevent the fishing village from being flooded during the typhoon season.

3. minimum [ˋmɪnəməm] *adj.* 最小的，最低的
   - In order to make the loss to the minimum degree, Mark reported his lost credit cards as soon as he found that his wallet had been stolen.

4. sheer [ʃɪr] *adj.* 全然的，純粹的
   - All the tourists are impressed by the sheer beauty of the Grand Canyon.

5. capital [`kæpətl] *n.* [C] 首都
   - Taipei is the capital of Taiwan.

6. submerge [səb`mɝdʒ] *vt.* 淹沒，浸沒
   - After the heavy rain, the low-lying area was totally submerged by water.

7. acre [`ekɚ] *n.* [C] 英畝
   - Mr. Chen, who possesses a 1000-acre ranch, is a landlord.

8. farmland [`fɑrm,lænd] *n.* [U] 農地，農田
   - The farmer works hard on the farmland from sunrise to sunset.

9. evacuation [ɪ,vækjʊ`eʃən] *n.* [C] 撤離，疏散
   - The commander ordered the evacuation of the troops from the island.

10. brace [bres] *vt.* 做準備
    - I am bracing myself for the upcoming exams.

11. component [kəm`ponənt] *n.* [C] (機器、設備等) 零件
    - The fax machine can't work because some of its vital components are broken.

12. disrupt [dɪs`rʌpt] *vt.* 使中斷，使混亂
    - The peace talk was disrupted for a while because of the protest demonstration.

13. expert [`ɛkspɝt] *n.* [C] 專家
    - Professor Martin is an expert in the ancient civilization of Greece.

14. external [ɪk`stɝnəl] *adj.* 外部的，外接的
    - Without a built-in DVD player on her laptop, Sue used an external one to play the disc.

15. unsanitary [ʌn`sænə,tɛrɪ] *adj.* 不衛生的，不潔的
    - It's unsanitary to eat with your bare hands, not to mention that you don't even wash them before eating.

16. wreck [rik] *vt.* 造成嚴重破壞
    - The long-lasting snow storm wreaked havoc on the small northern town.

17. havoc [`hævək] *n.* [U] 災害，禍患
    - The severe earthquake caused havoc throughout the country.

1. **thanks to**　幸虧，由於
   - Thanks to the brave firefighter, the baby boy survived the fire.
2. **to come**　未來的
   - Matt promised his wife that he wouldn't play cards again in the several days to come.

≫ 補 充

1. **Thailand**　泰國

   東南亞國家之一，古稱暹羅，首都曼谷。東臨寮國和柬埔寨，南接泰國灣和馬來西亞，西面則是緬甸和安達曼海。約有六千多萬人口，泰族佔總人口的 40%，主要宗教為佛教。泰國在十一月至二月為乾季，三到五月為熱季，七至九月受季風影響，為雨季。

2. **monsoon**　季風

   又稱季候風，指的是因海陸比熱不同，導致大氣環流與降水所產生的季節性變化，季風區通常會有明顯的雨季與旱季之別，兩季盛行的風向角度會達到 120 度以上。季風主要發生在南亞、東亞、西非幾內亞以及澳洲北部沿海地帶。

   monsoon season　雨季

   指的是降水量因季節變換而產生差異的地區，降水相對較多的月份稱為雨季，其特點是幾乎每天都會下雨，有時甚至會連下數日不斷。在不同的氣候類型中，雨季月份也不盡相同，例如，東亞季風區的雨季主要為夏季 (7 到 9 月)，南亞季風區在 6 至 11 月，而地中海型氣候的雨季則是在冬季。

3. **Gulf of Thailand**　泰國灣

   又稱暹羅灣，是泰國南部的海灣，東臨柬埔寨、越南，西邊則是泰國和馬來西亞。泰國灣長 720 多公里，寬在 480 至 560 公里之間，總水域面積約 32 萬平方公里，平均水深僅 45 公尺。

4. **Bangkok**　曼谷

   泰國首都，是泰國的政治、經濟、文化、科技、教育等中心。曼谷位於昭批耶河東岸，鄰近泰國灣。由於佔地廣大且水上交通便利，因此有「東方威尼斯」的美稱，但也由於地勢較低 (平均海拔僅 2 公尺左右)，在雨季時經常面臨洪水的威脅。

5. **Ayutthaya** 大城府

又稱阿育他亞府，位於泰國中部、曼谷北方約 76 公里處，為歷史悠久的古都，府內有諸多名勝古蹟。主要地形為廣闊的平原，由於三條河在此處匯流，因此水產豐富，農業相當發達，為泰國最大的產米區。

Pop Quiz

Choose the best answer to each of the following sentences.

( ) 1. Continuous strikes would wreak _____ on the country's economy.

     (A) drainage   (B) monetary   (C) havoc   (D) publicity

( ) 2. Even a big eater is surprised at the _____ size of the hamburger, which is 15-inch high.

     (A) unsanitary   (B) external   (C) minimum   (D) sheer

( ) 3. As a(n) _____ on global warming, Professor Paul claimed that the Arctic could be ice-free in summer within twenty years.

     (A) laborer   (B) expert   (C) organizer   (D) miner

( ) 4. Traffic will be _____ tomorrow because of the road closure. I suggest that you change your route.

     (A) submerged   (B) braced   (C) recycled   (D) disrupted

( ) 5. _____ your help, I passed all my exams.

     (A) Thanks to   (B) Up to   (C) Referring to   (D) In response to

UNIT 17

Earthquake and [1]Tsunami Devastate Japan

April 1, 2011

On Friday, March 11, a massive earthquake hit Japan at 2:46 p.m. local time. The [2]epicenter of the earthquake was   1   about 130 kilometers east of [3]Sendai, and some reports said that the quake measured 9.0 on the [4]Richter scale,   2   it the most powerful earthquake in Japan's history.

Although the earthquake caused considerable damage, it was the tsunami that followed that   3   devastated many parts of Japan. Almost immediately after the earthquake, government officials in Japan began to issue tsunami warnings. Then, only one hour or so after the earthquake, a tsunami was seen flooding Sendai Airport, with news footage showing waves sweeping away airplanes and other vehicles as walls of water moved   4 . Sadly, the tsunami was reported to have swept away several towns along the coast of Japan. Homes and buildings were washed away, and some towns were reduced to nothing more than piles of rubble.

To make matters worse, several of Japan's nuclear power plants were also affected by the natural disaster. Though these nuclear power stations automatically shut down after the earthquake,   5   from the tsunami overwhelmed the [5]Fukushima I and II stations and damaged the emergency generators there. This   6   a power failure to the cooling system, which led to explosions and radiation leaks. More than 200,000 people nearby were evacuated as workers scrambled to deal with these potential nuclear [6]meltdowns.

Dubbed the "[7]East Japan Great Earthquake" by some, this natural disaster was well reported on the Internet, with   7   uploading video footage of the earthquake and the tsunami almost in real time. Perhaps because of this, donations and offers of   8   from around the world began pouring in almost immediately following this disaster. Many countries have also been   9   to pitch in with help, including Taiwan, which was sending a donation of NT$100 million as well as rescue teams to Japan.

In the days following these disasters, the Japanese prime minister [8]Naoto Kan commented that "in the 65 years after the end of World War II, this is the __10__ and the most difficult crisis for Japan." Without a doubt, the Japanese are having a difficult time rebuilding their lives. However, the aid and prayers from all over the world will certainly be of great help during the period.

Exercise

Fill in each blank with the correct word.

(A) actually	(B) located	(C) waves	(D) caused	(E) making
(F) locals	(G) quick	(H) toughest	(I) assistance	(J) inland

1. _____   2. _____   3. _____   4. _____   5. _____

6. _____   7. _____   8. _____   9. _____   10. _____

Vocabulary

1. **devastate** [ˋdɛvəsˏtet] *vt.* 徹底破壞，摧毀
   - Floods devastated the whole village. Most houses were swept away, and hundreds of lives were lost.
2. **considerable** [kənˋsɪdərəbl̩] *adj.* 相當多的，相當大的
   - Sam experienced considerable pressure to meet a tight deadline.
3. **issue** [ˋɪʃʊ] *vt.* 宣布，公布
   - The government official issued a statement, denying having a green card.
4. **rubble** [ˋrʌbl̩] *n.* [U] 瓦礫堆
   - The explosion destroyed the building and reduced it to rubble.
5. **plant** [plænt] *n.* [C] 工廠
   - Frank worked at a huge chemical plant.
6. **disaster** [dɪˋzæstɚ] *n.* [C] 災難，災害
   - The 921 earthquake in 1999 is one of the most serious disasters that have happened in Taiwan.
7. **automatically** [ˏɔtəˋmætɪkl̩ɪ] *adv.* 自動地
   - The main door will open automatically when you stand in front of it.

8. overwhelm [ˌovɚˋhwɛlm] *vt.* (水) 淹沒
   • The pouring rain these days caused flooding, which overwhelmed the town.

9. explosion [ɪkˋsploʒən] *n.* [C] 爆炸
   • The gas explosion caused a big fire, and dozens of people were injured.

10. radiation [ˌredɪˋeʃən] *n.* [U] 輻射
    • Hair loss is one of the symptoms of radiation sickness.

11. leak [lik] *n.* [C] (液體、氣體等) 漏出
    • The radiation leaks at the Chernobyl Nuclear Power Plant caused great damage to the surrounding areas.

12. evacuate [ɪˋvækjʊˌet] *vt.* 撤離，疏散
    • The police evacuated the whole city to escape the bombing.

13. scramble [ˋskræmbl̩] *vt.* 艱難地 (或倉促地) 完成
    • The forces were scrambling to control the uncontrollable situation.

14. potential [pəˋtɛnʃəl] *adj.* 潛在的，可能的
    • Parents should never leave their children under the age of six alone to avoid the potential dangers.

15. upload [ʌpˋlod] *vt.* 上載
    • It may take an hour for a file this size to upload.

16. donation [doˋneʃən] *n.* [C] 捐贈物，捐款
    • Flood victims needed donations of food and basic necessities.

17. prayer [prɛr] *n.* [C] 祈禱
    • Amy said a prayer for her sick classmate, hoping God will bless her.

≫ Idioms & Phrases

1. to make matters worse   更糟的是
   • A forest fire is raging the protected area. To make matters worse, the dry weather theses days makes it more difficult to put out the fire.

2. pitch in   投入，參與
   • If we all pitch in, the project will be finished in no time.

≫補充

1. **tsunami** 海嘯

   此字源自日語「津波」，意思為「港邊的波浪」。海嘯是一種具有強大破壞力的海浪。當地震發生在海底時，因震波的動力而引起海水劇烈的起伏，形成強大的波浪、向前推進，稱之為海嘯。人類對地震、海嘯等災變，只能透過觀察和預測來做預防以降低損失，但無法阻止它們的發生。

2. **epicenter** 震央

   當地震發生時，地震震源向上垂直投影到地面的位置，也就是地面離震源最近的地方，稱之為震央。

3. **Sendai** 仙台

   是日本宮城縣縣廳的所在地，亦是日本東北地方最大的城市。伊達政宗自 1600 年開始在仙台築城，之後不斷進行開發，使該地自那時就相當繁榮。

4. **Richter scale** 芮氏地震規模

   此為表示地震規模大小的標度。芮氏地震規模最早是在 1935 年由兩位來自美國加州理工學院的地震學家芮克特和古騰堡共同制定的。芮氏地震規模的主要缺點在於它與震源的物理特性沒有直接的聯繫，並且在規模 8.3～8.5 左右會產生飽和效應，使得一些強度明顯不同的地震在用傳統方法計算後，得到的芮氏地震規模數值卻一樣。

5. **Fukushima** 福島

   是日本東北地方的一個城市，福島縣縣廳的所在地。

6. **meltdown** 爐心熔毀

   又稱為核熔燬或熔毀，是核反應爐因無法及時冷卻而熔化所造成的損毀。爐心熔毀後會造成具有放射性的物質外洩，對人類及其他生物的健康有莫大的影響。

7. **East Japan Great Earthquake** 東日本大地震

   是指在 2011 年 3 月 11 日發生在日本東北地方的近海地震，接踵而來的大海嘯，重創了日本岩手縣、宮城縣、福島縣以及茨城縣這些位於太平洋沿岸的城鎮，預計死亡人數達一萬五千多人，行蹤不明者有兩千多人。同時，受到大海嘯侵襲的福島第一、第二核能發電廠，由於氫氣爆炸、燃料棒外露，引發嚴重核災，造成史無前例的災難，其影響範圍包括東北、北海道、關東等地。

8. **Naoto Kan** 菅直人 (1946～)

   是日本政治家，有「草根大臣」、「市民政治家」、「藍領政治家」等稱譽。

Pop Quiz

Choose the best answer to each of the following sentences.

(　　) 1. Jean's parents have a(n) _____ influence on her. She obeys her parents in all things.

    (A) automatic　　(B) unconscious　　(C) eligible　　(D) considerable

(　　) 2. The doctor _____ a warning that obesity might cause many health problems.

    (A) evacuated　　(B) wrecked　　(C) devastated　　(D) issued

(　　) 3. The new product is examined carefully to avoid any _____ problems.

    (A) permissive　　(B) public　　(C) potential　　(D) prestigious

(　　) 4. The Hurricane Katrina was one of the worst natural _____ to hit the U.S.

    (A) disasters　　(B) explosions　　(C) donations　　(D) prayers

(　　) 5. Tom overslept and missed the school bus. _____, he forgot to bring his homework.

    (A) Without a doubt　　　　　　(B) To make matters worse

    (C) On the way　　　　　　　　(D) Up in the air

UNIT 18

Grounded by the Ash

May, 2010

When it first erupted on March 20, 2010, the [1]Eyjafjallajokull volcano in southern [2]Iceland caused only a few local problems. However, a second eruption on April 14 suddenly sent a massive cloud of ash into the sky. Within two days, the ash cloud had reached more than eight kilometers in height and had drifted into the skies of northern Europe, shutting down air traffic and stranding passengers in airports around the globe since April 15.

Officials decided to cancel flights as the ash drifted toward Europe because it contained small particles of [3]silicate that could severely damage jet engines. During two separate incidents in the 1980s, passenger jets unknowingly flew through clouds of volcanic ash, causing the engines to shut down. Crews were able to restart the engines in both cases, but only after the airplanes had descended several thousand meters.

Airports as far away as Rome were forced to close as the ash drifted south and east. Passengers struggled to find alternate means of transportation to return from vacations and business trips. Hundreds of athletes planning to travel from Europe to the United States to compete in the [4]Boston Marathon on April 19 missed the race after months of training. Overall, an estimated 1.2 million people were affected each day while flights were grounded.

Airlines began to complain that governments were being too cautious about the ash after several days of cancellations. When flights finally resumed after six days, airlines had lost close to $2 billion from the disruption. Some airlines demanded that governments compensate them for the lost money, but officials insisted that it was better to err on the side of caution. The global impact of the volcano highlighted the need for governments and businesses to develop contingency plans to deal with problems caused by natural disasters.

Choose the best answers.

(　　) 1.　This article is mainly about _____.

(A) how people prevented the unexpected eruption of volcano

(B) how the volcanic ash affected the mass transportation from place to place

(C) what the governments should do in advance to prevent natural disasters

(D) why some athletes couldn't compete in the Boston Marathon

(　　) 2.　According to the article, we may refer that flights resumed on _____ , 2010.

(A) April 21　　　(B) May 1　　　(C) April 14　　　(D) April 20

(　　) 3.　What does the phrase "err on the side of" in the fourth paragraph mean?

(A) Do nothing at all though it is really needed.

(B) Do something what it is really needed.

(C) Do something more than it is really needed.

(D) Do something less than it is really needed.

(　　) 4.　Which of the following descriptions is NOT true?

(A) Major airports in Western Europe were forced close due to the volcanic ash.

(B) It was estimated that airlines had lost nearly $20 billion dollars at this time.

(C) Some airlines planned to ask for the financial aid from the governments.

(D) Many marathon runners missed the race because of the natural disaster.

(　　) 5.　According to the passage, which is true about the two separate incidents in 1980s?

(A) Two airplanes flew through the volcano and unfortunately crashed.

(B) An airplane safely passed over the sky above the Eyjafjallajokull volcano.

(C) A flight to Iceland was forced to cancel because of the volcanic ash.

(D) The clouds of volcanic ash caused the two jets' engines to shut down.

1. **ground** [graʊnd] *vt.* 使停飛
   - Because of the fierce winter storm, all airplanes have been grounded for two days.

2. **eruption** [ɪˋrʌpʃən] *n.* [C] 噴發，爆發
   - Frequent volcanic eruptions are believed to be one of reasons that indirectly lead to the extinction of dinosaurs 65 million years ago.

3. **drift** [drɪft] *vi.* 飄
   - Lying on the meadow, we can see the clouds slowly drifting across the sky.

4. **strand** [strænd] *vt.* 受困，使滯留
   - The heavy fog left two thousand tourists stranded at the airport.

5. **particle** [ˋpɑrtɪkl̩] *n.* [C] 微粒，顆粒
   - Caused by the inhalation of dust particles, the miner suffered from black lung disease.

6. **descend** [dɪˋsɛnd] *vi.* 下降
   - Passengers fastened their seatbelts when the plane began to descend.

7. **alternate** [ˋɔltɚnɪt] *adj.* 替代的，交替的
   - Due to the traffic jam on the highway, Leo had no choice but to take an alternate way.

8. **means** [minz] *n.* [C] (*pl.*～) 方法，手段
   - Zoe had no means of turning down Fred's invitation to dinner.

9. **transportation** [͵trænspɚˋteʃən] *n.* [U] 交通運輸 (系統)
   - For most students, bus is their main means of transportation.

10. **cancellation** [͵kænsl̩ˋeʃən] *n.* [C] 取消
    - The snow storm led to the cancellation of most flights.

11. **resume** [rɪˋzum] *vt.* 重新開始、繼續
    - After taking six-month parental leave, Mandy resumed her job as a nurse.

12. **disruption** [dɪsˋrʌpʃən] *n.* [C] 混亂
    - The terrorist attack caused severe social disruption.

13. **compensate** [ˋkɑmpən͵set] *vt.* 賠償
    - The government promised to compensate the earthquake victims for the damage to their houses.

14. **caution** [ˋkɔʃən] *n.* [U] 小心，謹慎

   • These political activists need to be treated with some caution.

15. **highlight** [ˋhaɪ͵laɪt] *vt.* 強調，突顯

   • The news report highlighted the gap between rich and poor in Greece.

16. **contingency** [kənˋtɪndʒənsɪ] *n.* [C] 偶然事件

   • We have made some contingency plans, in case it rains.

≫Idioms & Phrases

1. **shut down**　關閉

   • Many banks were forced to shut down because of the economic recession.

2. **err on the side of...**　過於⋯

   • The financial expert thought that it was better for investors to err on the side of caution when time was hard.

≫補　充

1. **Eyjafjallajokull**　艾雅法拉冰蓋

   冰島文中為「島嶼山上的冰河」之意。艾雅法拉冰蓋是位於冰島南部一座約為 100 平方公里大的冰河，底下覆蓋了一座約 1666 公尺的火山。艾雅法拉冰蓋冰河火山曾於 920 年、1612 年、1821 年—1823 年和 2010 年爆發。2010 年 4 月 14 日噴發時，大量的火山灰散布在歐洲上空，使得歐洲多數機場關閉，航空班次大亂。

2. **Iceland**　冰島

   位於北大西洋中，介於格陵蘭島與英國間的島國。由於接近北極圈，全國約 11% 土地為冰河覆蓋。冰島四周環海，為寒流及暖流交會之處，全年溫差不大，平均溫度為 2 至 6 度。首都雷克雅維克，人口約三十多萬人。

3. **silicate**　矽酸鹽

   為矽氧化合物 (Si_xO_y)，由矽氧所組成的岩石有花崗岩、石英等。地球地殼大多由矽酸鹽構成。

4. **Boston Marathon**　波士頓馬拉松

   創立於 1897 年，在美國麻薩諸塞州的波士頓每年四月的第三個星期一舉行的國際馬拉松比賽。是目前歷史最悠久及最著名的馬拉松賽事，每年平均有兩萬多人參與此盛事。

Pop Quiz

Fill in each blank with the correct word or phrase to complete the sentence. Make changes if necessary.

resume	alternate	means	err on the side
shut down	compensate	contingency	highlight

1. A special bonus can be used as a _____ of rewarding employees for their efforts.

2. The chemical factory was accused of discharging waste material into the river. Thus, it was forced to _____ .

3. The study _____ the problem of the one-child policy, which led to discrimination against female newborns.

4. The restaurant promised to _____ customers for their losses. Each customer could get money-off coupons.

5. Tim will _____ working as soon as he feels better.

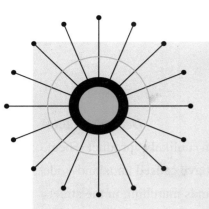

Health

健　康

UNIT 19

Where's the Beef?

December, 2009

A new controversy has erupted in Taiwan over an unlikely product—beef. Specifically, imported beef products from the United States have caused an island-wide stir, with politicians objecting to these imports, and thousands marching in the streets of Taipei on November 14. These politicians and protesters ___1___ their opposition to the government's plans to resume the import of different types of U.S. beef products.

In 2003, the Taiwanese government banned all imports of U.S. beef. This step was ___2___ after reports stated that [1]bovine spongiform encephalopathy (BSE), more commonly known as "mad cow disease," had been found in American cattle. At the time, the ban was seen as a sensible move, ___3___ according to some scientists, eating the brains and [2]spinal cords of animals ___4___ BSE can cause a serious, sometimes fatal, disease in human beings.

The ban was once partly lifted in 2005, but it was soon brought ___5___ after a second case of BSE was discovered in America. In 2006, Taiwan's [3]Department of Health (DOH) decided to permit [4]boneless beef from cattle of a certain age to be imported. Over the three years that followed, Taiwan faced ___6___ pressure from the U.S. to allow more imports of U.S. beef. Finally, in October 2009, Taiwan's ban on U.S. [5]bone-in beef, [6]ground beef, and cow organs from cattle younger than 30 months was lifted.

___7___ this step was welcomed by American beef exporters and U.S. government officials, it was not so popular in Taiwan. Politicians from both major political parties expressed their concern about this move, and many Taiwanese citizens expressed their ___8___ of health risks and the possible spread of mad cow disease to Taiwan. Some also accused Taiwan's current government of bowing to pressure from the U.S. and disregarding public health safety in Taiwan. Many ___9___ the government to renegotiate this agreement.

For its part, DOH officials have insisted that strict inspection measures are in place to ensure the public's safety. For the time being, however, the debate in Taiwan over whether to import—or even eat—American beef will __10__ continue.

Exercise

Choose the correct answers.

(   ) 1. (A) have been voicing   (B) had voiced

             (C) voice   (D) will voice

(   ) 2. (A) run   (B) found   (C) kept   (D) taken

(   ) 3. (A) since   (B) or   (C) and   (D) but

(   ) 4. (A) at   (B) of   (C) with   (D) by

(   ) 5. (A) down   (B) up   (C) back   (D) out

(   ) 6. (A) improving   (B) increasing   (C) decreasing   (D) developing

(   ) 7. (A) Yet   (B) If   (C) In spite of   (D) Although

(   ) 8. (A) riots   (B) fears   (C) means   (D) horizons

(   ) 9. (A) cared for   (B) took to   (C) called for   (D) set in

(   ) 10. (A) likely   (B) relatively   (C) simply   (D) mostly

≫ Vocabulary

1. **stir** [stɝ] *n.* [C] 激動，憤怒
   - The president's insulting remarks caused quite a stir among citizens.
2. **object** [əbˋdʒɛkt] *vi.* 反對
   - Kate's father dislikes her boyfriend. Thus, he strongly objects to their marriage.
3. **ban** [bæn] *vt.* 禁止
   - In Taiwan, smoking is banned in public places.
   ban [bæn] *n.* [C] 禁令
   - The government has imposed a ban on child labor.
4. **sensible** [ˋsɛnsəbḷ] *adj.* 明智的，合理的
   - I think the sensible thing to do is to stay calm when one is in danger.
5. **fatal** [ˋfetḷ] *adj.* 致命的
   - Alcoholism is a potentially fatal disease, which will cause severe damage to a drinker's body and affect his or her psychological behavior.

6. **permit** [pɚ`mɪt] *vt.* 允許，准許
   - People who wear slippers are not permitted to visit the museum.

7. **exporter** [ɪk`spɔrtɚ] *n.* [C] 出口商，出口國
   - Thailand has become the world's biggest rice exporter.

8. **concern** [kən`sɝn] *n.* [U] 擔心
   - Many parents voiced their concern over the policy on higher education.

9. **accuse** [ə`kjuz] *vt.* 控訴
   - That woman was accused of theft. She stole thousands of dollars from tourists.

10. **disregard** [ˌdɪsrɪ`gɑrd] *vt.* 不顧，漠視
    - Tina disregarded her parents' advice and decided to quit her job.

11. **renegotiate** [ˌrinɪ`goʃɪˌet] *vi.* 重新協商
    - The government insisted that these houses should be torn down and refused to renegotiate with the landlords.

12. **insist** [ɪn`sɪst] *vi.* 堅持，執意
    - The host insisted that all guests should eat and drink to their heart's content

13. **inspection** [ɪn`spɛkʃən] *n.* [U] 檢查，審查
    - Regular inspection must be carried out before driving cars.

14. **ensure** [ɪn`ʃʊr] *vt.* 確保
    - To ensure your safety, please fasten your seat belt during the flight.

≫ Idioms & Phrases

1. **for the time being**　目前，暫時
   - Teresa hasn't found a full-time job and worked part-time in a restaurant for the time being.

≫ 補 充

1. **bovine spongiform encephalopathy (BSE)**　牛腦海綿狀病變
   俗稱狂牛症，是由蛋白質感染因子所造成的疾病。牛隻一旦發病，會先出現驚恐及易被激怒的狂牛行為，慢慢地變得行動困難、虛弱，然後便會在幾個星期內死亡。牛死後經解剖發現到大腦有萎縮的現象，及大量的神經細胞死亡。此種病源的蛋白因子具抗熱性、又耐化學處理，不易用蛋白酵素分解。

如果食用病牛的身體組織或器官，也會讓人類產生類似的致命症狀。狂牛症最初是於 1996 年在英國被確認，後來在世界各地都有病例，以歐洲地區最多。因為狂牛症病原在人體的潛伏期極長，可能有許多人受到感染但未發病，所以對人類所造成的生命威脅還無法確定。

2. **spinal cord** 脊髓
   脊椎骨內的物質，有許多神經連結腦部和身體各部位。

3. **Department of Health (DOH)** 衛生署
   衛生署是我國最高衛生行政機關，隸屬於行政院。管轄醫事、藥政、食品衛生、護理及健康照護，以及諸多與衛生醫療保健相關的處室組織。

4. **boneless beef** 不帶骨牛肉

5. **bone-in beef** 帶骨牛肉

6. **ground beef** 牛絞肉

Pop Quiz

Choose the best answer to each of the following sentences.

(   ) 1. There is growing _____ over the widening gap between rich and poor, which might lead to social instability.

(A) radiation (B) monetary (C) concern (D) inspection

(   ) 2. Max was not _____ to go out with his friends because he was grounded for a week.

(A) permitted (B) disturbed (C) symbolized (D) disregarded

(   ) 3. It is _____ to bring a shopping list when you go shopping. It can help you save money.

(A) innovative (B) fatal (C) massive (D) sensible

(   ) 4. Ken _____ his classmate of cheating on exams.

(A) renegotiated (B) preserved (C) accused (D) ensured

(   ) 5. The company has imposed a(n) _____ on dress code. Each employee has to wear uniform.

(A) stir (B) ban (C) acre (D) exporter

Food Scare Grows in Taiwan

July, 2011

It all began quietly in March of 2011. Unknown to most people at that time, Taiwan's [1]Food and Drug Administration (FDA) found traces of a toxic chemical, [2]Di(2-ethylhexyl) phthalate, better ___1___ as DEHP, in sixteen sport and soft drinks. Often used to make [3]PVC pipes, this [4]plasticizer has been found to cause cancer and other ___2___ problems in humans who have consumed it.

Over the weeks that followed, the FDA ___3___ several tests to determine if other food and drink products had been tainted with DEHP. Then, on May 23, the FDA announced to the ___4___ that certain items had been contaminated with this plasticizer. In the days that followed, products were removed from store shelves, and the government began to require manufacturers of five major categories of food and drink—sports drinks, juices, tea drinks, fruit jams and syrups, and some tablets and powders—to prove that their products were free of harmful chemicals.

Investigators believe that one company is primarily responsible for this crisis. Yu Shen Chemical Company (昱伸香料公司), Taiwan's biggest supplier of [5]emulsifiers, has been selling this plasticizer as a food [6]additive for possibly the past fifteen years. Emulsifiers are often used as a [7]clouding agent in some types of food and drinks. ___5___, Yu Shen Chemical Company used DEHP as a substitute for [8]palm oil, the traditional and more expensive ingredient in emulsifiers. ___6___, another company, Pin Han Perfumery Company (賓漢香料公司), was also found to have used DEHP as a clouding agent.

How serious this food scare will affect Taiwan in the long run remains to be seen. For now, many people are scared and ___7___ about exactly which food and drinks are safe to consume. For their part, manufacturers and companies have rushed to assure people that their products are ___8___ and free of DEHP. [9]Shih Yen-shiang, Taiwan's Minister of Economic Affairs, has estimated that this DEHP scandal will end up costing the food sector in Taiwan more than NT$10 billion, since retailers are forecasting a 10 to 20 percent drop in revenue as a result of the crisis.

As the scale of the problems caused by the DEHP scandal continues to grow, it may take some time before the public's confidence in Taiwan's food and drink products returns. Yet, some hope that this food scare will lead to ____9____ regulation of food and drink items. It may also lead to greater public awareness about the ____10____ of food safety.

Exercise

Fill in each blank with the correct word or phrase.

(A) confused	(B) known	(C) stricter	(D) health	(E) Moreover
(F) safe	(G) importance	(H) public	(I) Unfortunately	(J) carried out

1. _____ 2. _____ 3. _____ 4. _____ 5. _____

6. _____ 7. _____ 8. _____ 9. _____ 10. _____

≫ Vocabulary

1. administration [ədˌmɪnəˋstreʃən] *n*. [C] 行政機構
   - Environmental Protection Administration is in charge of protecting the environment by enforcing regulations based on laws.

2. toxic [ˋtɑksɪk] *adj.* 有毒的
   - Nuclear waste is highly toxic; it will remain dangerous for hundreds of thousands of years.

3. consume [kənˋsum] *vt.* 吃，喝
   - Mary always consumes large amounts of coffee every morning.

4. taint [tent] *vt.* 污染
   - The river has been tainted with toxic waste.

5. contaminate [kənˋtæməˌnet] *vt.* 污染
   - The drinking water in this area has been contaminated with industrial waste dumped by chemical factories.

6. manufacturer [ˌmænjuˋfæktʃərɚ] *n.* [C] 製造商
   - Toyota is the largest car manufacturer in the world.

7. category [`kætə,gorɪ] *n.* [C] 種類，類別
   - The test results can be divided into three main categories.

8. syrup [`sɪrəp] *n.* [U] 糖漿
   - The girl poured some maple syrup over the pancakes.

9. tablet [`tæblət] *n.* [C] 藥片，藥丸
   - Mrs. Paul swallowed some sleeping tablets to help her get some sleep.

10. investigator [ɪn`vɛstə,getɚ] *n.* [C] 調查者
    - The investigators of this murder case finally tracked the murderer down in Hualien.

11. substitute [`sʌbstə,tjut] *n.* [C] 代替物
    - Beans are a healthy substitute for meat.

12. ingredient [ɪn`gridɪənt] *n.* [C] 成分，材料
    - We bought all the ingredients for making cookies—flour, butter, eggs, and sugar.

13. minister [`mɪnɪstɚ] *n.* [C] 部長
    - The Minister of Transport promised to solve the problem of traffic congestion in the big city.

14. estimate [`ɛstə,met] *vt.* 估計，估算
    - The teacher estimated that about eighty percent of his students passed the test.

15. scandal [`skændl̩] *n.* [C] 醜聞
    - The sex scandal about the president and his secretary has ruined his reputation.

16. sector [`sɛktɚ] *n.* [C] (國家經濟) 部門，領域
    - Joining the WTO had a major impact on the business sector of Taiwan.

17. forecast [`for,kæst] *vt.* 預測，預報
    - Rain is forecast for tomorrow.

18. revenue [`rɛvə,nju] *n.* [U] 收益，收入
    - The company's new product was a great success. Thus, its annual revenues rose by 60%

19. scale [skel] *n.* [U] 規模，範圍
    - We were shocked by the sheer scale of the damage while finding that the roof was tore off by the storm.

20. regulation [`rɛgjə,leʃən] *n.* [C] 規定，法規
    - Not only drivers but also pedestrians should follow traffic regulations.

1. in the long run　最終，終於
   - The old man suffered from liver cancer and passed away in the long run.
2. be free of　沒有…，不含…
   - The maple syrup is free of artificial colors and flavorings.
3. end up　最後就…
   - Lucas was a compulsive gambler. He ended up losing all his money.

≫補 充

1. **FDA**　食品藥物管理局
   隸屬於行政院衛生署，執行業務主要為強化食品、藥物、新興生技產品、化妝品之管理及風險評估，落實源頭管理，健全輸入食品管理體系，發展核心檢驗科技，提升管理、檢驗與研究水準，以能達到食品藥物管理一元化的目標。

2. **Di (2-ethylhexyl) phthalate (= DEHP)**　鄰苯二甲酸二 (2- 乙基己基) 酯
   為鄰苯二甲酸與 2- 乙基己醇生成的酯類化合物。DEHP 是一種常用的塑化劑，可以增加塑膠的延展性與彈性，是使用最廣的塑化劑。DEHP 是一種環境荷爾蒙，已被證實會干擾人體體內荷爾蒙的訊息傳遞，以及影響男性生殖系統的發育。若孕婦體內的 DEHP 過高，會導致甲狀腺素分泌過低，影響胎兒中樞神經和成長。環保署將 DEHP 列管為第四類毒性化學物質，國際癌症研究所將 DEHP 歸類為 2B 級致癌物，和 DDT、鉛同級。

3. **PVC**　聚氯乙烯
   全名為 Polyvinyl Chloride，簡稱 PVC。由於其防火耐熱的特性，聚氯乙烯被廣泛用於各式各樣產品，如電線外皮、鞋、手提袋、食物保鮮膜等。在高溫的燃燒過程中會釋放出氯化氫、氯氣和其他有毒氣體。PVC 加工產品的主要問題在於製造過程當中，一定要加入添加劑或塑化劑，但這些化學物質大多有害，可能會滲出或氣化，甚至有致癌的風險。

4. **plasticizer**　塑化劑
   或稱增塑劑、可塑劑，是一種增加材料的柔軟性或是材料液化的添加劑，其添加對象包含了塑膠、混凝土、水泥、石膏等。

5. **emulsifier**　乳化劑
   是常見的食品添加物，其分子通常具有親水基和親油基，易在水和油介面形成吸附層，進而改變乳化體中各物相之間的表面活性，形成均勻的乳化體，故能改變食物的口感及外觀。

常見的乳化劑有甘油脂肪酸酯、聚甘油脂肪酸酯、蔗糖脂肪酸酯以及大豆磷脂等。

6. **food additive** 食品添加劑

食品添加劑是指為改善食品品質和色、香、味而加入食品中的物質。一般來說，食品添加劑可分為天然和化學合成兩大類，天然食品添加劑是指利用動植物或微生物的代謝產物等為原料，經提煉所獲得的天然物質；化學合成的食品添加劑是指用化學方式，使元素或化合物通過氧化、還原、縮合、聚合等合成反應而得到的物質。

7. **clouding agent** 起雲劑

為食品添加劑的一種。為了幫助食品的乳化，經常使用於運動飲料、非天然果汁及果凍、果醬等食品中，讓飲料避免混合物沉澱或油水分離，並可增加飲料中的白霧感及濃稠感。

8. **palm oil** 棕櫚油

棕櫚油被廣泛用於烹飪和食品製造業，被當作食用油和人造奶油來使用。棕櫚油屬性溫和，是製造食品的好材料。從棕櫚油的組合成分看來，其高固體性質甘油含量能讓食品避免氫化而保持平穩，並有效抗氧化，因此棕櫚油深受食品製造業的喜愛。

9. **Shih Yen-Shiang** 施顏祥 (1950～)

國立臺灣大學化學系學士、美國麻省理工學院博士，1986 年起加入經濟部，歷任中小企業處處長、臺灣菸酒公司局長、工業局局長、經濟部長等職。

Pop Quiz

Choose the best answer to each of the following sentences.

(　　) 1. The mayor has recently been involved in corruption _____ , which ruined his reputation.

　　(A) shifts　　(B) substitutes　　(C) sectors　　(D) scandals

(　　) 2. _____ chemicals were discharged into the ocean, damaging the fragile ecology of the coral reefs.

　　(A) Innovative　　(B) Crooked　　(C) Toxic　　(D) Permissive

(　　) 3. The canned food is _____ . People who eat it will vomit and have the runs.

　　(A) estimated　　(B) consumed　　(C) contaminated　　(D) forecast

(　　) 4. Liz took some _____ to help ease the headache.

　　(A) tablets　　(B) ingredients　　(C) manufacturers　　(D) regulations

(　　) 5. Tim likes to eat fast food and _____ putting on much weight.

　　(A) sets in　　(B) ends up　　(C) calls for　　(D) is free of

UNIT 21

Bug Crisis

October, 2010

People throughout the United States are watching out for bugs. [1]Bedbugs and [2]stink bugs are invading houses and damaging crops all over the country. Although they virtually disappeared from the United States after World War II, bedbugs began to make a comeback in the 1990s. Natives of Asia, stink bugs first appeared in the United States around 1998. Both bugs reproduce rapidly, and their large numbers are making people worry about how to get rid of them.

Bedbugs are small and can enter buildings through gaps in windows and doors. Once inside, they find their way to dark places such as suitcases and dresser drawers. They especially tend to hide in mattresses, from which they emerge at night to bite the unsuspecting people sleeping on them. Once bedbugs have infected a mattress, the only way to get rid of them is to throw away the mattress.

Although stink bugs are bigger and more imposing than bedbugs, they do not bite people. Stink bugs get their name from the foul odor that they emit when people crush them. They feed on fruits and vegetables, which makes them troublesome to farmers. The bugs make their way inside houses when people open doors, and they swarm over everything.

In Asia, stink bugs are kept under control by [3]wasps that eat their eggs. Without a natural enemy in the United States for either stink bugs or bedbugs, getting rid of them is proving to be extremely difficult. Experts suggest that people seal their houses as much as possible, but the bugs can often get in when people are not noticing. Research into eliminating stink bugs includes traps that attract their young, whereas measures against bedbugs include using [4]sniffer dogs to find their hiding places.

Choose the best answers.

( ) 1. What is the article mainly about?

   (A) How bedbugs and stink bugs made a comeback in the United States.

   (B) How people prevent the stinky bugs from emitting stinky odor.

   (C) How people choose a clean and comfortable mattress safe from bedbugs.

   (D) How people in the United States train sniffer dogs to look for stink bugs.

( ) 2. Which of the following descriptions about bedbugs is correct?

   (A) Bedbugs are bigger than stink bugs.

   (B) Bedbugs feed on fruits and vegetables on the farms.

   (C) Bedbugs could be found by using sniffer dogs.

   (D) Bedbugs like to hide in the dark places.

( ) 3. The phrase "make their way" in the third paragraph means "_____."

   (A) be far away in distance   (B) go to a place

   (C) change their decision   (D) be in a good place

( ) 4. Which of the following is the enemy of stink bugs?

   (A) Bedbugs.   (B) Foul odor.   (C) Wasps.   (D) Traps.

( ) 5. According to the passage, which of the following is NOT true?

   (A) Stink bugs first appeared in the United States around 1998.

   (B) The only way to get rid of bedbugs is to throw away infected mattresses.

   (C) Experts suggest people eliminate stink bugs by setting up traps.

   (D) Bedbugs reproduce slowly because they emerge at night.

» Vocabulary

1. **virtually** [ˋvɝtʃʊəlɪ] *adv.* 幾乎，差不多

   • Virtually everyone wants to hit the jackpot.

2. **reproduce** [ˏriprəˋdjus] *vi.* 繁殖，生殖

   • Salmon would return from the sea to the river to reproduce.

3. **rapidly** [ˋræpɪdlɪ] *adv.* 快速地，迅速地

   • The tropical island has been changing rapidly because its tourism industry is growing more than ever.

4. dresser [`drɛsɚ] *n.* [C] 衣櫥
   - A dresser or a chest of drawers in a bedroom is used for storing clothes.
5. mattress [`mætrəs] *n.* [C] 床墊
   - In order to get a good night's sleep, Kate decided to buy a memory foam mattress.
6. imposing [ɪm`pozɪŋ] *adj.* 壯觀的，令人印象深刻的
   - The Tokyo Skytree is the tallest and most imposing building in Japan.
7. foul [faʊl] *adj.* 惡臭的，難聞的
   - Though garlic is believed to be good for people, it makes them have foul breath.
8. odor [`odɚ] *n.* [U] 氣味、臭味
   - My foreign friend cannot stand the unpleasant odor of stinky tofu.
9. emit [ɪ`mɪt] *vt.* 散發 (光、熱、聲音、氣味等)
   - Eason emits a low sound to attract my attention.
10. crush [krʌʃ] *vt.* 壓壞，壓碎
    - Judy crushed the walnuts with a nutcracker.
11. troublesome [`trʌbl̩səm] *adj.* 令人煩惱的，討厭的
    - Teresa is a troublesome child because of her bad temper.
12. swarm [swɔrm] *vi.* 成群地來回移動
    - Fans swarmed into the airport as the popular singer showed up over there.
13. eliminate [ɪ`lɪmə,net] *vt.* 消滅
    - If you want to lose weight, you had better eliminate sweet food from your diet.
14. measure [`mɛʒɚ] *n.* [C] 措施
    - The Mexican government took tough measures to combat drugs trafficking.

>> Idioms & Phrases

1. watch out for　密切注意
   - The police were informed to watch out for the terrorist attack during the European summit.
2. make a comeback　復出，重返
   - The rock band plans to make a comeback with a new album this year.

3. **feed on**　以⋯為食
   - Pandas feed on bamboo.
4. **make one's way**　前往，去
   - Those tourists made their way to the museum after they got off their buses.

≫補充

1. **bedbug**　床蝨
   屬於臭蟲科。床蝨主要以吸血維生，以口器刺穿人類或哺乳類動物的肌膚來吸血，會在皮膚上留下兩個洞。人若被床蝨叮咬後，會引起皮膚發癢、過敏、傷口紅腫。床蝨體型極小，扁平呈橢圓形、無翅膀。成蟲的胸部腹面有一對臭腺，會分泌帶有特殊臭味的物質，因此有臭蟲之名。成蟲把卵產在牆壁、床板等縫隙中，並把這些地方當作棲息地。雖然多數人稱此為臭蟲，但本文中所提到的 stink bugs 所指的是不同種類的昆蟲。

2. **stink bug**　臭蟲
   屬於椿象總科，或稱椿象，因背部呈現盾牌形，也稱作 shield bug。在第一、二對腳上有臭腺，會分泌帶有臭味的液體，作為受到攻擊或侵擾的防禦武器。雌蟲會以植物的莖葉作為產卵的地方，主要以吸食植物汁液為生，對農夫而言是種害蟲。

3. **wasp**　黃蜂
   又稱胡蜂、螞蜂、寄生蜂。雌蜂身上有一螫針，在遇到攻擊或干擾時，會群起攻擊對方，使人中毒甚至於死亡。黃蜂會對一些害蟲加以捕食或寄生，因此可被利用在農業的病蟲害防治上。

4. **sniffer dog**　嗅探犬
   是指受過特別訓練來執行偵測爆裂物、毒品、找尋蜂巢或是執行救災等任務的犬隻。美國近來為了日益猖獗的床蝨問題，因此也訓練能找出床蝨的嗅探犬。

Pop Quiz

Choose the best answer to each of the following sentences.

(   ) 1. Rising unemployment has become a(n) _____ problem. Some studies show
that there is a link between unemployment and crime rates
(A) imposing   (B) permissive   (C) troublesome   (D) rapid

(   ) 2. The police warned that tourists should _____ for pickpockets.
(A) watch out   (B) make their way
(C) make a comeback   (D) feed on

(   ) 3. In Taiwan, the birth rate has declined _____. Many married couples don't
want to have children.
(A) stereotypically   (B) rapidly   (C) unfortunately   (D) virtually

(   ) 4. The Environmental Protection Administration took appropriate _____ to help
lessen the effects of air pollution.
(A) mattresses   (B) themes   (C) dressers   (D) measures

(   ) 5. The police surrounded the train station to _____ the possibility of a bomb
attack.
(A) crush   (B) qualify   (C) eliminate   (D) tolerate

Note

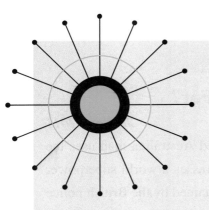

Technology

科 技

UNIT 22

Has [1]WikiLeaks Gone Too Far?

January, 2011

It sounds like something out of a movie. A silver-haired Australian man uses the Internet to **reveal** top-secret information that __1__ embarrasses a world superpower __1__ **alters** the course of world affairs. Then, the man is detained by the British police to face charges in Sweden concerning sex-related crimes, but is later released on bail. __2__ , a series of cyber attacks are carried out by "[2]hacktivists" to punish certain companies, in order to show support for this website. Yet, this is one story that comes straight out of today's headlines, and not out of a Hollywood **thriller**. For the past few months, WikiLeaks and its **secretive spokesperson** [3]Julian Assange __3__ the hottest topic in international news.

WikiLeaks was __4__ in 2006. Its goal was to bring attention to documents from news leaks and **anonymous submissions**, many of which might **normally** have gone unnoticed. Over the years that followed, WikiLeaks became better known around the world, and Assange came to be seen __5__ its spokesperson. In April of 2010, WikiLeaks posted a video that was said to show Iraqi civilians and journalists being killed by American **forces** in 2007. Later, in July of 2010, WikiLeaks released more than 76,900 documents about the United States war effort in Afghanistan.

WikiLeaks was quickly **denounced** by members of the U.S. military, who claimed that these actions put American soldiers at great __6__ in Afghanistan and Iraq. However, others supported WikiLeaks, including many **journalists** and news organizations, who stated that this website was just exercising its right __7__ free speech.

Then, in the most **explosive** incident yet, WikiLeaks began to __8__ U.S. State Department **diplomatic** cables available to the world. Some of these secret **communications** embarrassed American government **officials**. __9__ , some people said that these classified documents just revealed that government officials were doing their jobs.

Has WikiLeaks gone too far? Is it dedicated to revealing the truth or creating chaos? One thing is   10   : sometimes real life can be more interesting—and more bizarre—than anything on a movie screen.

Exercise

Choose the correct answers.

(   ) 1. (A) too...to   (B) not only...but also
            (C) not...but   (D) so...that

(   ) 2. (A) Suddenly   (B) Meanwhile   (C) Firstly   (D) Finally

(   ) 3. (A) have been   (B) were   (C) are   (D) will be

(   ) 4. (A) boosted   (B) consumed   (C) emitted   (D) launched

(   ) 5. (A) at   (B) by   (C) as   (D) of

(   ) 6. (A) craze   (B) theme   (C) risk   (D) issue

(   ) 7. (A) on   (B) of   (C) for   (D) to

(   ) 8. (A) let   (B) name   (C) lay   (D) make

(   ) 9. (A) However   (B) Besides   (C) Thus   (D) For example

(   ) 10. (A) excessive   (B) certain   (C) radical   (D) massive

≫ Vocabulary

1. reveal [rɪ`vil] *vt.* 透露，洩漏
   - The auctioneer refused to reveal the name of the private buyer for the famous painting.
2. alter [`ɔltɚ] *vt.* (使) 改變
   - The experience of working holiday in Australia has radically altered Ben's life.
3. thriller [`θrɪlɚ] *n.* [C] 驚悚小說、電影
   - The writer's new novel is a thriller. It's a story about a serial killer.
4. secretive [sɪ`kritɪv] *adj.* (想法、行動等) 隱藏的
   - The actress is secretive about her private life.
5. spokesperson [`spoks͵pɝsn̩] *n.* [C] 發言人
   - The spokesperson for the car company said it would take full responsibility for the accident.

6. **anonymous** [ə`nɑnəməs] *adj.* 匿名的
- The gangster made an anonymous phone call to the witness, warning her not to tell the truth in court.

7. **submission** [səb`mɪʃən] *n.* [C] 呈交，提交
- The deadline for the submission of applications is May 3rd.

8. **normally** [`nɔrmlɪ] *adj.* 通常
- Normally, it takes Mrs. White an hour to prepare meals for her family.

9. **force** [fors] *n.* [C] 軍隊，部隊
- The big city was destroyed by military forces in the war.

10. **denounce** [dɪ`naʊns] *vt.* 譴責，指責
- The man was denounced as a betrayer because he worked for the enemy.

11. **journalist** [`dʒɝnlɪst] *n.* [C] 新聞記者
- After graduation, Fanny works as a financial journalist.

12. **explosive** [ɪk`splosɪv] *adj.* 爆炸性的
- The abolition of the death penalty is an explosive issue.

13. **diplomatic** [ˌdɪplə`mætɪk] *adj.* 外交的
- The country broke off diplomatic relations with its neighboring country last month.

14. **communication** [kəˌmjunə`keʃən] *n.* [C] 信息，通信
- There must be something wrong! I haven't received any communications from my brother since last Sunday.

15. **official** [ə`fɪʃəl] *n.* [C] 官員
- Mr. Chen has been a government official for more than thirty years.

16. **dedicated** [`dɛdəˌketɪd] *adj.* 專心致志的
- Dr. Sloan is dedicated to her scientific experiment.

17. **chaos** [`keɑs] *n.* [U] 混亂
- The living room was in chaos after the birthday party and we had to clear it up.

18. **bizarre** [bɪ`zar] *adj.* 奇異的，古怪的
- It was bizarre to see Rebecca wear a fur coat on such a hot day.

>>Idioms & Phrases

1. **go too far**   做得過份
   - Sue went too far. She stood me up again!

>>補 充

1. **WikiLeaks**   維基解密
   維基解密是一個國際性的非營利媒體組織，專門揭露匿名來源及網路洩露的各國機密文件。網站主導者為朱利安‧阿桑奇。維基解密因為洩露了美國軍事及外交機密，近來引起美國政府與世界各國的高度關注。

2. **hacktivist**   思想駭客
   指會入侵網站並竄改資料的人，通常是要宣揚自己特定的宗教立場、政治理念或對其他特定事件的想法。

3. **Julian Assange**   朱利安‧阿桑奇
   維基解密網站主導者。據說是維基解密的創辦人，但他迴避這個身分並稱自己為維基解密的發言人與首席編輯。

Pop Quiz

Fill in each blank with the correct word to complete the sentence. Make changes if necessary.

forces	alter	dedicated	normally
bizarre	communication	reveal	chaos

1. Smartphones have dramatically _____ modern people's lives. Many people are becoming increasingly dependent on their smartphones.
2. The nationwide strike has thrown the country into _____.
3. _____, the temperature in Pingtung is higher than that in Taipei in the winter.
4. Frank _____ that he had a crush on Amber.
5. Mr. Lin is _____ to his work. For him, work is high on his list of priorities.

UNIT 23

[1]iPhone Madness Again

August, 2010

After months of anticipation, Apple released its newest version of the iPhone, the iPhone 4, in five countries on June 24, 2010. Although its debut was marked by a supply shortage and antenna problems, the iPhone 4 lived up to its hype with new __1__ such as video calling and high-definition video. Apple announced that it would start selling the iPhone 4 in 17 more countries on July 30.

When the first version was released in January 2007, the iPhone became one of the most popular [2]smartphones in the world because of its __2__ [3]touch screen, flexible internet connectivity, and sleek design. __3__, the iPhone could play videos and music, just like Apple's popular line of [4]iPods.

Apple began accepting [5]pre-orders for the iPhone 4 on June 15, but high __4__ forced the company to halt pre-orders within hours. Even after the phone arrived in stores on June 24, demand remained so __5__ that the iPhone 4 was still unavailable on a walk-in basis in many stores more than a month later.

The biggest __6__ surrounding the iPhone 4 involved problems with its antenna. Soon after its release, users discovered that they __7__ reception while making calls if they held the phone in a manner that covered up an important part of the antenna, which is located around the edge of the phone. In a news conference on July 16, Apple cofounder [6]Steve Jobs announced that the company would __8__ free "[7]bumper" cases, which help ease the reception problems, for all customers who purchase the device before September 30. Jobs also noted that other smartphones experience similar problems, and dismissed the notion that Apple had made a __9__ designed product.

In addition to the antenna problems, production issues have plagued the white version of the iPhone 4. Apple announced that it would not be available until later in 2010, and for now customers can only purchase the black version. __10__ the controversy surrounding its release, Apple's iPhone 4 remains very popular, with 1.7 million units sold the first weekend that it was released.

Exercise

Fill in each blank with the correct word.

(A) high	(B) provide	(C) controversy	(D) features	(E) innovative
(F) lost	(G) Moreover	(H) poorly	(I) demand	(J) Despite

1. _____   2. _____   3. _____   4. _____   5. _____

6. _____   7. _____   8. _____   9. _____   10. _____

» Vocabulary

1. **release** [rɪ`lis] *vt.* 發行，上架
   - The computer company will release its new product next week.

2. **debut** [de`bju] *n.* [C] 首次亮相
   - The band Mayday's debut album was released in 1997.

3. **shortage** [`ʃɔrtɪdʒ] *n.* [C] 缺乏，不足
   - The country faced a critical food shortage after a long drought.

4. **antenna** [æn`tɛnə] *n.* [C] 天線 (*pl.* antennas/antennae)
   - In the past, people put the outdoor antennas on the rooftop to receive TV signals.

5. **hype** [haɪp] *n.* [U] 促銷廣告
   - Don't believe all the hype. The movie is kind of a disappointment.

6. **flexible** [`flɛksəbl̩] *adj.* 靈活的，可變通的
   - To meet all customers' needs, the travel agency offers flexible packages all the year.

7. **halt** [hɔlt] *vt.* 停止
   - The government implemented economic reforms in an effort to halt recession.

8. **unavailable** [ˌʌnə`veləbl̩] *adj.* 無法得到，難以獲得
   - The high-priced car is unavailable to ordinary people.

9. **reception** [rɪ`sɛpʃən] *n.* [U] (無線電、電視的) 接收效果
   - Recently, many cell phone users complain about the poor reception in this area.

10. **conference** [`kɑnfərəns] *n.* [C] 會議，研討會
    - Dr. Robert will attend an international conference on global warming.

11. experience [ɪk`spɪrɪəns] *vt.* 經歷，遭遇
   - Mrs. Wang experienced problems with her teenage son, who was unwilling to interact with anyone.
12. dismiss [dɪs`mɪs] *vt.* 不予理會
   - It's better to dismiss all the gossip you hear. Otherwise, you may bother yourself about the opinion of others.
13. notion [`noʃən] *n.* [C] 想法
   - I reject the notion that money is everything.
14. plague [pleg] *vt.* 困擾，折磨
   - Most of the Internet users are plagued by spam mails every day.

≫ Idioms & Phrases

1. live up to   符合 (期待)
   - The scenery of Taroko National Park lives up to its reputation.
2. on a...basis   基於…方式、原則
   - Customers are seated on a first-come, first-served basis in this restaurant.

≫ 補 充

1. iPhone   蘋果智慧型手機
   2007 年由蘋果公司所設計的多功能智慧型手機系列，除了一般手機的功能外，還有整合照相手機、PDA、媒體播放器及無線通訊的功能。另外也有支援收發電子郵件、網路瀏覽、即時網路通訊等服務，利用多點觸控螢幕來操控。曾被《時代雜誌》選為「2007 最佳發明」之一。

2. smartphone   智慧型手機
   有別於一般基本手機功能的高階功能手機， 在手機內安裝與電腦相容的作業系統 (如 Windows Mobile、iOS、Linux、Android 等)，提供多媒體播放、上網瀏覽、收發郵件、即時通訊、登入線上社群等多功能服務。

3. touch screen   觸控式螢幕，觸控面板
   透過機器上電子螢幕的圖像操作介面，用手或是觸控筆來進行資訊的查詢或是輸入。普遍運用在提款機、電子遊樂器、智慧型手機及平板電腦等。

4. iPod   蘋果數位多媒體播放器

2001 年由蘋果公司設計的攜帶型數位多媒體播放器。以設計簡單、便於使用的介面為特色，透過 iTunes 軟體進行音樂的傳輸及管理，同時也提供 iTunes Store 的線上付費音樂服務。

5. **pre-order** 預購

指商品尚未發售前，開放預先購買的行銷策略。利用預先購買，保證在正式販賣時可直接取貨，或是給消費者相關贈品、折扣等優惠，使新產品能受到消費者注意的行銷手法。

6. **Steve Jobs** 史提夫・賈伯斯 (1955–2011)

是美國蘋果公司的創辦人之一，曾任董事長及執行長職位，亦是皮克斯動畫的創辦人及執行長。賈伯斯被認為是電腦業界的標誌性人物，人們把他視為是麥金塔電腦、iPod、iPhone、iPad 等知名數位產品的締造者。曾七次登上《時代雜誌》的封面，被認為是全球最為成功的發明家及商人之一。

7. **bumper** 保護套

此字原為「汽車頭尾的保險桿」之意。在此指 iPhone 4 天線問題事件中，蘋果公司贈送的可以包覆在機體四角的橡膠保護套。

Pop Quiz

Choose the best answer to each of the following sentences.

(　) 1. The actress challenged the _____ that aging is inevitable. She tried everything possible to avoid looking old.

　(A) antenna　　(B) sector　　(C) notion　　(D) proposal

(　) 2. The government decided to _____ work on the nuclear plant, for safety's sake.

　(A) dismiss　　(B) voice　　(C) halt　　(D) plague

(　) 3. There was a severe water _____ . Thus, the local government imposed water restrictions.

　(A) conference　　(B) shortage　　(C) route　　(D) debut

(　) 4. Catherine was born with a silver spoon in her mouth; she never _____ financial difficulties during her lifetime.

　(A) releases　　(B) disrupts　　(C) eliminates　　(D) experiences

(　) 5. The musician thought his performance didn't _____ his expectations. He wanted to improve his skills at playing the piano

　(A) live up to　　(B) lead to　　(C) come to　　(D) take to

UNIT 24

Rise of the Thinking Machines

March, 2011

In the battle of man **versus** machine, humans might have something to learn from their **creations**. An [1]artificial intelligence (AI) computer system named [2]Watson beat two of the best **contestants** ever to play [3]*Jeopardy!*, the popular television quiz show in the United States. In a two-day **tournament** against [4]Ken Jennings, who held a record of winning 74 games **in a row**, and [5]Brad Rutter, who is the show's all-time money winner, Watson defeated its human **competitors handily**. The victory gave [6]IBM, the computer's creator, a $1 million prize and left humans to wonder about the meaning of Watson.

Watson is actually a collection of many IBM [7]servers connected together to increase the system's **overall** power. This "thinking machine" uses its special software that allows it not only to understand human speech but also to respond to questions in a [8]synthesized voice. When asked a question, Watson quickly searches through its vast **array** of stored knowledge, such as **encyclopedias**, dictionaries, literary works, and the full text of Wikipedia. It can **process** a million books per second and responds based on three most probable answers that it can find in the [9]database.

During the *Jeopardy!* game, a video screen **represented** Watson as an [10]avatar alongside the human competitors. Unlike humans, Watson cannot leave its room at IBM and cannot work without electricity. However, the computer has an **enormous** advantage in the speed with which it presses the [11]buzzer that contestants use to respond to questions. The **participant** (the person or machine) that buzzes in first is allowed to answer the question, and Watson can buzz in much quicker than humans.

Once defeat was certain, Ken Jennings wrote a **humorous** message on his video screen: "I, for one, welcome our new computer overlords." However, most **analysts** agreed that Watson's victory was good for humans. Watson's success **demonstrates** that AI system can be built to **analyze** complex problems and suggest solutions based on **intricate** patterns, which is a skill that people can use to solve challenges in various fields such as security, health care, and finance.

Exercise

Choose the correct answers.

(   ) 1. The article is mainly about _____ .

(A) how IBM developed a new AI system to respond to its users' questions

(B) how the TV quiz show *Jeopardy!* became popular in the United States

(C) how the thinking machine beat human contestants and won the quiz game

(D) how the thinking machine can buzz in much quicker than humans

(   ) 2. According to the article, _____ won the two-day tournament.

(A) Ken Jennings   (B) Brad Rutter

(C) the engineer of Watson   (D) the AI system Watson

(   ) 3. The phrase "in a row" in the first paragraph means " _____ ."

(A) at a slow pace   (B) one after another

(C) a continuous supply   (D) in a difficult situation

(   ) 4. Which of the following statements about Watson is NOT correct?

(A) It can leave IBM freely and go anywhere to work with people.

(B) It is an AI computer system that can think and speak.

(C) It can understand what people say and respond to their questions.

(D) It can help people quickly search for the information.

(   ) 5. Which of the following statements is correct?

(A) Brad Rutter can press the buzzer quicker than Watson.

(B) Watson held the record of being the all-time money winner of *Jeopardy!*.

(C) Most experts thought that Watson's victory was good for humans.

(D) Watson tried so hard to defeat its human competitors.

》Vocabulary

1. **versus** [ˋvɝsəs] *prep.* 對抗
   - It is Roger Federer versus Rafael Nadal in the Wimbledon semifinal.
2. **creation** [krɪˋeʃən] *n.* [C] 創造品
   - An ipod is considered one of the greatest technological creations in the 21st century.

3. **contestant** [kən`tɛstənt] *n.* [C] 參賽者
   - The contestant who ate the most hamburgers in eight minutes could receive a reward of $10,000.
4. **tournament** [`tɜ·nəmənt] *n.* [C] 錦標賽
   - Though the golfer lost one game of the tournament last week, he is still ranked number one in the Men's World Golf Rankings.
5. **competitor** [kəm`pɛtətɚ] *n.* [C] 參賽者
   - Over 25,000 competitors ran the Boston Marathon this year.
6. **handily** [`hændɪlɪ] *adv.* 輕鬆地，容易地
   - The top tennis player handily beat his opponent in the first round.
7. **overall** [ˌovɚ`ɔl] *adj.* 總體的，全面的
   - The couple held a luxurious wedding ceremony. Its overall cost was $100,000.
8. **array** [ə`re] *n.* [C] 大堆，大批
   - There is a wide array of books for you to choose from.
9. **encyclopedia** [ɪnˌsaɪklə`pidɪə] *n.* [C] 百科全書
   - Jerry, who knows a lot of information about many different subjects, is called as a walking encyclopedia.
10. **process** [`prɑsɛs] *vt.* (用電腦) 處理
    - With the latest CPU technology, this new type of tablet computer can process detailed research data.
11. **represent** [ˌrɛprɪ`zɛnt] *vt.* 代表
    - The chief officer was chosen to represent the country at the international conference.
12. **enormous** [ɪ`nɔrməs] *adj.* 巨大的，極大的
    - Mr. Chen has invested an enormous amount of money in the bond market.
13. **participant** [pɑr`tɪsəpənt] *n.* [C] 參加者，參與者
    - The TV talent show attracted over 10,000 participants in the first audition.
14. **analyst** [`ænəlɪst] *n.* [C] 分析師
    - The political analyst predicted that the mayor would be re-elected for a second term.

analyze [`ænə,laɪz] *vt.* 分析
- The scientist is busy analyzing data in order to get the experimental results.

15. humorous [`hjumərəs] *adj.* 幽默的，有幽默感的
- The movie is a humorous account of Mr. Bean's trip to France.

16. demonstrate [`dɛmən,stret] *vt.* 證明，證實
- The study demonstrated that over 60% schoolchildren have ever been bullied.

17. intricate [`ɪntrəkɪt] *adj.* 錯綜複雜的
- The Persian carpet is a mass of color and has intricate patterns.

≫Idioms & Phrases

1. in a row　連續地
- Mr. Huang has worked overtime two weeks in a row.

≫補 充

1. **artificial intelligence (AI)**　人工智慧
由約翰・麥卡錫於 1956 年創造出來的語彙，其原定義為：the science and engineering of making intelligent machines，也就是由人創作出來的電腦系統所表現出來的智能，同時也指的是專門研究、設計電腦系統來模擬人類智能行為的一個研究領域，現在可以應用在指紋識別、人臉識別及專家系統 (如 OS 系統中的人工智慧軟體 Siri) 等。

2. **Watson**　華森
以 IBM 公司創始人湯瑪斯・華森命名的程式，能夠以自然語言來回答問題。為測試其能力，在 2011 年 2 月挑戰美國電視益智問答節目《危險邊緣》的比賽，結果打敗該節目擁有最多勝利紀錄的肯・杰寧斯及最高獎金得主布萊德・洛特。

3. **Jeopardy!**　《危險邊緣》
1964 年開播至今的美國電視益智問答節目，比賽的題目涵蓋了歷史、文學、藝術、流行文化、科學、運動、地理、文字遊戲等多方面。節目以特別的答題模式來進行，參賽者依據以答案形式提供的線索，用問題的方式來回答，每次由三位參賽者來進行三輪的比賽。

4. **Ken Jennings**　肯・杰寧斯 (1974–)
為美國電視益智問答節目《危險邊緣》中連勝紀錄保持人。

5. **Brad Rutter**　布萊德・洛特 (1978–)
為美國電視益智問答節目《危險邊緣》中最高獎金得主。

6. IBM (International Business Machines Corporation)
國際商業機器股份有限公司

由湯瑪斯・華森於 1911 年成立的跨國知名科技資訊服務公司，總部位於美國紐約，在全球 160 多個國家設有分公司。以製造銷售電腦硬體、軟體，並提供企業資訊設備建構、諮詢的服務，同時也在材料、化學等不同科學領域上進行創新研發。

7. server　(電腦) 伺服器

為使用者提供執行和管理服務的電腦軟體系統，依據功能來區分有：檔案伺服器、資料庫伺服器、郵件伺服器、網頁伺服器及列印伺服器等。

8. synthesized voice　合成語音

是指將輸入的文字或儲存於電腦中的文件模擬人聲發出語音的技術，可以應用在智能玩具、電子辭典、電子導航等。

9. database　資料庫

為電腦化的資料儲存系統，使用者可以進行新增、存取及刪除資料的動作。

10. avatar　(網路聊天用的) 化身

11. buzzer　蜂鳴器

蜂鳴器是一種一體化結構的電子儀器，廣泛用於電腦、影印機、報警器、電子玩具、定時器等電子產品中做為發聲器件。

Pop Quiz

Choose the best answer to each of the following sentences.

(　　) 1. Steve always tells _____ jokes and makes people laugh.
　　　　(A) cautious　　　(B) humorous　　　(C) superior　　　(D) intricate

(　　) 2. The math genius _____ solved the complex math problem in a second.
　　　　(A) handily　　　(B) enormously　　　(C) unfortunately　　(D) stereotypically

(　　) 3. The stock market _____ estimated that the financial sector would make a comeback.
　　　　(A) analyst　　　(B) competitor　　　(C) organizer　　　(D) participant

(　　) 4. The research _____ the connection between smoking and lung cancer.
　　　　(A) represented　　(B) appreciated　　(C) demonstrated　　(D) eliminated

(　　) 5. Amy's boyfriend gave her an _____ bunch of roses on Valentine's day.
　　　　(A) overall　　　(B) alternate　　　(C) extensive　　　(D) enormous

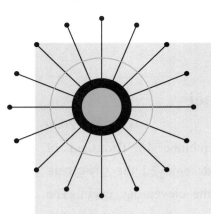

Sports
運　動

UNIT 25

2009 [1]Deaflympics in Taipei

October, 2009

The 2009 Summer Deaflympics came to a close on September 15. Thousands of deaf athletes ___1___ their coaches and families and friends enjoyed the **gracious hospitality** of their Taiwanese hosts over the ___2___ of the eleven-day event. The games **were** also **blessed with** nice weather, which came as a pleasant surprise after earlier reports had **indicated** that rain might **dampen** the occasion.

This year's Deaflympics **kicked off with** a **spectacular** opening ceremony at [2]Taipei Municipal Stadium on September 5. Fireworks filled the night sky, and [3]A-mei flew through the air on special cables ___3___ she sang the Deaflympic theme song "Dreams You Can Hear." A special candlelight **vigil** was also held to mourn for the victims of the Typhoon Morakot disaster. Then, the **towering** Deaflympic flame was lit, and the games were ready to begin.

Twenty sports were featured in this year's event, including badminton, soccer, tennis, and swimming, and the competitions were held at **venues** all around Taipei. Taiwan did very well in these games, ___4___ 11 gold **medals**, 11 silver medals, and 11 **bronze** medals. This placed Taiwan fifth overall in the medal standings and gave Taiwan its best-ever finish in the Deaflympics.

Throughout the event, the streets of Taipei, ___5___ around Taipei Municipal Stadium, were filled with foreign athletes and visitors. Many of the ___6___ could also be seen running in local parks and training at athletic centers around Taipei. The athletes ___7___ part in the games praised organizers for making everything run so smoothly. In particular, the thousands of volunteers, many of whom ___8___ basic [4]sign language and were always ready to help out with a smile, were frequently **commended**.

The 2009 Summer Deaflympics came to an end with a ___9___ Taiwanese party. More than 350 round tables were ___10___, and athletes and guests were served a wide variety of Taiwanese **specialties**, including [5]steamed dumplings, [6]tempura, [7]beef noodle soup, [8]shaved ice with mango, and [9]bubble tea. The Deaflympic **torch** and flag were then **passed on to** [10]Athens, where will host the next event in 2013.

Exercise

Choose the correct answers.

(   ) 1. (A) in addition   (B) rather than   (C) up to   (D) along with

(   ) 2. (A) course   (B) waste   (C) logic   (D) mix

(   ) 3. (A) but   (B) as   (C) because   (D) or

(   ) 4. (A) of   (B) at   (C) with   (D) by

(   ) 5. (A) virtually   (B) unfortunately   (C) especially   (D) relatively

(   ) 6. (A) organizers   (B) participants   (C) ministers   (D) activists

(   ) 7. (A) who taking   (B) taken   (C) to take   (D) taking

(   ) 8. (A) had learned   (B) will learn   (C) are learning   (D) learn

(   ) 9. (A) traditional   (B) multiple   (C) sensible   (D) tragic

(   ) 10. (A) pumped up   (B) come to   (C) set up   (D) led to

≫ Vocabulary

1. **gracious** [`greʃəs] *adj.* 親切的，和善的
   - Andy was so gracious that he even invited us to his villa this summer.

2. **hospitality** [ˌhɑspɪ`tælətɪ] *n.* [U] 殷勤招待
   - Thanks for your kind hospitality during our stay at your place.

3. **indicate** [`ɪndə͵ket] *vt.* 指出
   - The research indicated that smartphones have a major impact on modern people's lives.

4. **dampen** [`dæmpən] *vt.* 使掃興
   - The humiliating defeat never dampened Steve's enthusiasm for decision.

5. **spectacular** [spɛk`tækjələ] *adj.* 壯麗的，壯觀的
   - The Grand Canyon National Park has spectacular scenery.

6. **vigil** [`vɪdʒəl] *n.* [C] 守夜祈禱
   - Mrs. Warren kept a constant vigil at her husband's bedside.

7. **towering** [`taʊrɪŋ] *adj.* 高聳的，高大的
   - We all admired the majesty of the towering cliffs.

8. venue [`vɛnju] *n.* [C] 集合地，發生地
   - The jazz pianist will perform at four different concert venues.
9. medal [`mɛdl̩] *n.* [C] 獎章
   - The top-flight gymnast won two gold medals in the Olympics.
10. bronze [brɑnz] *adj.* 青銅的
    - There is a bronze statue of the former president in the park.
11. commend [kə`mɛnd] *vt.* 讚揚，稱讚
    - The French restaurant is highly commended for its excellent cuisine.
12. specialty [`spɛʃəltɪ] *n.* [C] 特產
    - Classic chocolate cake is the specialty of this bakery.
13. torch [tɔrtʃ] *n.* [C] 火炬，火把
    - The Olympic torch will be transported from Greece to the host country.

≫ Idioms & Phrases

1. be blessed with sth.　有幸享有
   - The comedian is blessed with a good sense of humor.
2. kick off (with sth.)　(以…) 開始
   - The show kicked off with a song and dance number.
3. pass sth. on to sb.　將某物傳遞給某人
   - Sam passed the information on to his co-workers.

≫ 補 充

1. **Deaflympics**　聽障奧林匹克運動會
   簡稱聽障奧運或聽奧，原名「世界聾人運動會」，每四年舉辦一次，分為夏季與冬季兩種賽事。2001 年起獲得國際奧委會同意，得以冠上 "lympics" 字尾而形成現今的名稱，但不算是奧運比賽，類似的例子有肢體殘障者所參加的殘障奧運和智能障礙者所參加的特殊奧運。2009 年在臺北舉辦的夏季聽障奧運為第 21 屆。聽障奧運的參賽者必須有一定程度的聽覺障礙，比賽進行時會以揮旗或閃燈等方式來代替哨音。

2. **Taipei Municipal Stadium**　臺北市立體育場
   或稱臺北田徑場，為一座綜合性體育場，臺北市為了主辦聽障奧運而加以重新改建，可容納約兩萬人，聽障奧運的開幕式、閉幕式、田徑賽及足球決賽都在此場館舉行。

3. **A-mei** 張惠妹 (1972–)

臺灣女歌手，卑南族人。1996 年推出首張專輯後立刻獲得成功，受歡迎程度持續不墜，在華語歌壇擁有很高的地位，是首位登上《時代雜誌》亞洲版封面、且入選亞洲二十大風雲人物的歌手。她為 2009 年聽障奧運主唱主題曲「聽得見的夢想」。

4. **sign language** 手語

手語是一種不使用語音，而是用手勢、身體動作、臉部表情來表達意思的溝通方式。

5. **steamed dumpling** 蒸餃

6. **tempura** 甜不辣

7. **beef noodle soup** 牛肉麵

8. **shaved ice with mango** 芒果剉冰

9. **bubble tea** 珍珠奶茶

於 1980 年代發明於臺灣的茶類飲料，是將粉圓加入奶茶中而成，由於口感特殊，所以廣受歡迎，也成為臺灣最具代表性的飲料之一。

10. **Athens** 雅典

希臘首都，同時也是最大的城市，位於巴爾幹半島南端，三面環山，一面傍海，人口約有三百多萬。雅典為古希臘城邦文化的中心，是西方文明的起源地，有許多歷史古蹟。

Pop Quiz

Fill in each blank with the correct word or phrase to complete the sentence. Make changes if necessary.

venue	be blessed with	commend	medal
kick off	spectacular	hospitality	indicate

1. The couple _____ a baby girl. They have always longed for a child.
2. Thanks for your _____ during our trip to London.
3. We stopped halfway to admire the _____ mountain scenery.
4. With his outstanding performance, the athlete won a gold _____.
5. The study _____ that there is a link between unemployment and depression.

UNIT 26

[1]World Cup 2010 in [2]South Africa

August, 2010

The 2010 World Cup will be remembered as a tournament of firsts. It was the first time that an African nation had held the World Cup soccer ___1___ . It was also the first time for Spain to win this much coveted title.

South Africa was the [3]host country for this year's World Cup. The nation went all out for the World Cup, building several magnificent stadiums around the country, including [4]Soccer City in [5]Soweto. ___2___ , some visitors and even some players complained about the freezing weather in South Africa during the tournament. Other visitors had problems with the ___3___ transportation there.

On the pitch, however, the 2010 World Cup was definitely full of plenty of ___4___ soccer action. The final game between Holland and Spain was certainly no ___5___ . This championship had fans on the edge of their seats for the entire match. The game even went into [6]extra time, until Spain's [7]Andres Iniesta scored a goal to give Spain a 1–0 victory and the World Cup trophy. The win gave Spain its first World Cup title, ___6___ Holland suffered its third defeat in a World Cup championship game.

Another first for this World Cup was the [8]vuvuzela. This traditional South African "stadium horn" became a fixture at World Cup matches. Some people loved these ___7___ horns, while others hated them. For people watching the matches on television, these horns often ___8___ like a swarm of angry bees.

Finally, one more first for the 2010 World Cup was the appearance of [9]Paul, the psychic octopus. This two-year-old octopus was able to successfully predict eight of the winners in this year's competition. Paul predicted that Spain would beat Holland in the ___9___ and that Germany would beat Uruguay in the third-place match. Paul even received death threats from some angry German fans after successfully predicting their team's defeat, with some threatening to turn Paul into sushi.

___10___ , the 2010 World Cup will be one that fans around the world will remember for a long time. It was the first World Cup to be held in Africa, and it had vuvuzelas, a psychic octopus, and Spain's first-time champion.

Exercise

Fill in each blank with the correct word or phrase.

(A) Unfortunately	(B) exception	(C) while	(D) sounded	(E) competition
(F) Without a doubt	(G) loud	(H) exciting	(I) final	(J) public

1. _____ 2. _____ 3. _____ 4. _____ 5. _____

6. _____ 7. _____ 8. _____ 9. _____ 10. _____

» Vocabulary

1. **covet** [`kʌvɪt] *vt.* 覬覦，渴望
   - The actress has long coveted the chance to play in a Hollywood movie.
2. **magnificent** [mæg`nɪfəsənt] *adj.* 壯麗的，宏偉的
   - The sunrise over Mt. Ali is magnificent. You should go there to see the breathtaking view.
3. **complain** [kəm`plen] *vi.* 抱怨
   - Nick complained to the teacher about his classmate's bad behavior.
4. **freezing** [`frizɪŋ] *adj.* 極冷的
   - It is freezing outside; it makes me shiver with cold.
5. **plenty** [`plɛntɪ] *pron.* 大量，許多
   - You have plenty of time to get the job done.
6. **championship** [`tʃæmpɪən͵ʃɪp] *n.* [C] 錦標賽
   - Los Angeles Lakers had ever won sixteen NBA championships.
7. **score** [skor] *vt.* (比賽中) 得分
   - Frank scored a goal two seconds before the time ran out and won the championship for his team.
8. **trophy** [`trofɪ] *n.* [C] 獎盃
   - A trophy will be given to the winner of the competition.
9. **suffer** [`sʌfɚ] *vt.* 遭受，承受
   - The bank suffered much loss of business due to the economic recession.

10. **horn** [hɔrn] *n.* [C] 號角
   - The exciting game started with a single blow of the horn.
11. **fixture** [ˈfɪkstʃɚ] *n.* [C] 固定裝置、配件
   - The old light fixtures in the office will be replaced by LED lighting soon.
12. **swarm** [swɔrm] *n.* [C] (昆蟲的) 群，蜂群
   - Do you see a swarm of bees around the tree? There must be a beehive in the branches.
13. **psychic** [ˈsaɪkɪk] *adj.* 通靈的
   - Helen claims that she has psychic power which enables her to know what other people are thinking.
14. **predict** [prɪˈdɪkt] *vt.* 預測
   - Newspapers predicted that the celebrity would divorce her husband.
15. **threat** [θrɛt] *n.* [C] 威脅，恐嚇
   - Drunk driving is a threat to public safety.

   threaten [ˈθrɛtn̩] *vt.* 威脅，恐嚇
   - The owner of the company has been threatened to pay millions for his son's life.

≫ Idioms & Phrases

1. **go all out** 用盡全力
   - These dancers went all out for victory. They practiced the dance until it was perfect.
2. **on the edge of one's seat** 非常興奮，極為激動
   - The action movie was so exciting that it kept me on the edge of my seat the whole time in the theater.

≫ 補 充

1. **World Cup** 世界盃足球賽
   是一個國家級男子足球隊之間的國際比賽，由國際足球總會 (FIFA) 每四年舉辦一次，是世界足壇規模最大、水準最高的賽事。世界盃的首屆比賽是在 1930 年舉辦，冠軍為烏拉圭隊。比賽分成會外賽和會內賽兩部份，會外賽決定哪 32 支球隊能打入決賽圈，然後在主辦國進行為期一個月的會內賽來爭奪世界盃冠軍。

2. **South Africa**　南非

全名為南非共和國，位於非洲大陸最南端，領土的東、西、南三面分別瀕臨印度洋、大西洋和南冰洋，海岸線綿延三千公里。南非擁有三個首都：行政首都為普利托里亞，司法首都為布隆泉，立法首都為開普敦。南非是非洲經濟最發達的國家，發展程度好的區域包括開普敦、約翰尼斯堡等，但其他地區的發展程度卻非常有限，造成南非國內嚴重的貧富差距問題。

3. **host country**　(比賽、會議等) 主辦國

4. **Soccer City**　足球城體育場

1989 年落成，位於南非約翰尼斯堡，為 2010 年南非世界盃決賽舉行場地。

5. **Soweto**　索維托

為約翰尼斯堡西南方都會區的一部分，足球城體育場所在地。

6. **extra time**　延長賽

7. **Andres Iniesta**　安德烈斯·伊涅斯塔

西班牙巴塞隆納人，2002 年 10 月首次在歐洲冠軍聯賽中代表巴塞隆納隊出戰比利時的布魯日。2010 年的南非世界盃決賽中，他在延長賽時踢進決定性的一球，使得終場西班牙以 1:0 擊敗荷蘭，奪得首次世界盃冠軍。

8. **vuvuzela**　巫巫茲拉

一種長約一公尺的號角。在南非的世足賽中，球迷常使用這種號角為球隊加油打氣。巫巫茲拉的響度可以達到近 130 分貝，對未經防護的人耳會造成永久損傷。

9. **Paul**　神算章魚保羅

是德國奧伯豪森一間水族館內的章魚。在 2010 年的世界盃足球賽中，章魚保羅準確預測出多場比賽的結果，在球賽期間蔚為熱門話題。

Pop Quiz

Choose the best answer to each of the following sentences.

(　　) 1. The businessman _____ huge losses because he had made a wrong investment.

      (A) released　　(B) suffered　　(C) scored　　(D) threatened

(　　) 2. Faucets, sinks, and toilets are all common bathroom _____.

      (A) threats　　(B) horns　　(C) fixtures　　(D) trophies

(　　) 3. The expert _____ that coal would run out in less than 50 years.

      (A) predicted　　(B) emitted　　(C) coveted　　(D) demanded

(　　) 4. The witch is _____ and can know what will happen in the future.

      (A) fatal　　(B) psychic　　(C) magnificent　　(D) freezing

(　　) 5. The horror movie was truly terrifying. It had the audience _____.

      (A) on display　　 (B) make their way

      (C) in a row　　 (D) on the edge of their seats

UNIT 27

Super Sunday

March, 2009

The [1]Pittsburgh Steelers scored a [2]touchdown with 35 seconds left to defeat the [3]Arizona Cardinals 27–23 in [4]Super Bowl XLIII on February 1, 2009. [5]Wide receiver [6]Santonio Holmes caught the winning pass from [7]quarterback [8]Ben Roethlisberger to cap an eight-play, 78 yard drive. The Steelers won their sixth Super Bowl, and Holmes earned the most valuable player award for his performance.

The first Super Bowl was played on January 15, 1967, and the game originally featured the champion of the [9]National Football League (NFL) versus the champion of the [10]American Football League (AFL). When the two leagues merged in 1970, the game became the new NFL's championship game. Over time, the Super Bowl has become the most-viewed television event in the United States. Approximately 98.7 million people watched this year's game, a new record.

Most people in the United States consider Super Bowl Sunday to be something of a national holiday. Besides the game itself, much of the hype revolves around the Super Bowl's television ads. Companies such as Apple and Coca Cola spend millions of dollars for 30-second commercials that are analyzed as much as the game. In addition, the half-time show regularly attracts big stars like [11]Paul McCartney, [12]the Rolling Stones, and [13]Bruce Springsteen.

Americans love football because it is a fast, physical game. Throughout the season, fans passionately root for their team to reach the Super Bowl. Before games, people arrive at the stadium early for [14]tailgate parties where they eat and celebrate interesting traditions. For example, fans of the [15]Green Bay Packers wear foam hats that are shaped like a piece of cheese and call themselves "cheeseheads." Many fans are so devoted to football that they feel sad once the Super Bowl is over, but all they can do is count the days until the new season begins.

Exercise

Choose the best answers.

(   ) 1. The passage is mainly about _____.

    (A) the outstanding performance of Ben Roethlisberger in the game

    (B) how the Pittsburgh Steelers won the Super Bowl

    (C) Super Bowl, the most popular sports event in the United States

    (D) the halftime show of the Rolling Stones

(   ) 2. Who won the most valuable player award in Super Bowl XLIII?

    (A) Paul McCartney.   (B) Bruce Springsteen.

    (C) Ben Roethlisberger.   (D) Santonio Holmes.

(   ) 3. The phrase "root for" in the last paragraph means to "_____" someone in a game.

    (A) support   (B) force   (C) introduce   (D) threat

(   ) 4. Which of the following statements about the Super Bowl is true?

    (A) The Super Bowl is originally the NFL championship game.

    (B) The Pittsburgh Steelers had won the Super Bowl five times before 2009.

    (C) The Super Bowl's commercials are not as popular as the game itself.

    (D) Over 100 millions of football fans watched the Super Bowl XLIII.

(   ) 5. According to the passage, which of the following is NOT true?

    (A) Fans of the Green Bay Packers usually wear "cheeseheads" in a game.

    (B) The NFL and the AFL merged after the first Super Bowl.

    (C) Many big stars would join the halftime show.

    (D) The Arizona Cardinals was defeated in the Super Bowl XLIII.

≫ Vocabulary

1. **cap** [kæp] *vt.* 超越，勝過

   • In *One Thousand and One Nights*, Scheherazade capped a new story with another to save her own life.

2. **valuable** [ˋvæljəb!] *adj.* 很有用的，很重要的

   • Those working holidays in New Zealand gave Crook valuable experience.

3. champion [`tʃæmpɪən] *n*. [C] 冠軍，優勝者
   - The heavyweight boxer beat all opponents and became the world champion.
4. merge [mɝdʒ] *vi*. 合併
   - It is reported that the two car companies plan to merge next year.
5. approximately [ə`prɑksəmɪtlɪ] *adv*. 大約，大概
   - It takes Matthew approximately two hours to commute from Taoyuan to Taipei.
6. half-time [`hæf͵taɪm] *n*. [U] (足球、籃球比賽) 中場休息
   - New York Knicks was still leading San Antonio Spurs by 49–46 just two minutes before half-time.
7. regularly [`rɛgjələlɪ] *adv*. 頻繁地，經常地
   - Mrs. Rogers goes to the nearby supermarket regularly.
8. physical [`fɪzɪkl] *adj*. 粗野的，激烈的
   - American football is a physical game, in which players use some forms of physical contact to reach the goal.
9. passionately [`pæʃənɪtlɪ] *adv*. 熱情地，狂熱地
   - Fans gathered outside the stadium and passionately shouted out their idol's name.
10. stadium [`stedɪəm] *n*. [C] 體育館
    - The government decided to build a new stadium with a capacity of 50,000.
11. foam [fom] *n*. [C] 泡綿
    - The new sofa bed Leo bought last week consists of a single comfortable foam mattress.

≫ Idioms & Phrases

1. revolve around 以…為中心
   - Mrs. Brown's everyday life revolves around her children.
2. root for 為…加油
   - We root for our national baseball team to succeed in the World Baseball Classic.

1. **Pittsburgh Steelers** 匹茲堡鋼人隊

   為美國國家美式足球聯盟 (NFL) 旗下之美國美式足球聯會 (AFC) 北區的球隊，創立於 1933 年，以賓西法尼亞州的匹茲堡為根據地，是目前獲得最多超級盃冠軍的隊伍。

2. **touchdown** (橄欖球、美式足球) 達陣得分

   美式足球常見的得分方式。進攻球員將球帶入對方達陣區或在達陣區中成功接住傳來的球，即為成功達陣。達陣成功可以為該隊贏得 6 分，同時獲得一次 1 分加踢或 2 分轉換進攻的機會。

3. **Arizona Cardinals** 亞利桑那紅雀隊

   為美國國家美式足球聯盟 (NFL) 旗下之國家美式足球聯會 (NFC) 西區的球隊，創立於 1898 年，以亞利桑那州的格蘭戴爾為根據地，是目前歷史最悠久的美式足球隊伍。

4. **Super Bowl** 超級盃

   超級盃是美國國家美式足球聯盟的年度冠軍賽，每年會在一月最後一個或二月第一個星期天舉行，故該天又稱為「超級盃星期天」。超級盃多年來都是全美收視率最高的電視節目，並逐漸成為一個非官方的全國性節日，在超級盃開場前和中場休息的時候，會有很多流行歌手進行表演。

5. **wide receiver** (美式足球球員) 外接手，接球手

   為美式足球球員位置之一，任務為負責接住來自四分衛的傳球，又稱為 wideouts 或 receiver，為比賽中行動最快速敏捷、也是最受注目的球員之一。

6. **Santonio Holmes** 聖東尼奧‧荷姆斯

   美國佛羅里達州人，2006 年加入匹茲堡鋼人隊成為背號 10 號接球手。因在第 43 屆超級盃中優異的表現，獲選為最有價值球員。

7. **quarterback** (美式足球球員) 四分衛

   為美式足球球員位置之一，任務為負責發動進攻、掌控場上進攻。開球後通常將球傳給其他球員進攻，也會自己帶球向前推進。

8. **Ben Roethlisberger** 班‧羅斯里伯格

   美國俄亥俄州人，匹茲堡鋼人隊主力四分衛，2004 年獲選為「NFL 年度最佳進攻新秀」，至今率隊獲得兩座超級盃冠軍。

9. **National Football League (NFL)** 國家美式足球聯盟

   為美國職業美式足球組織，成立於 1920 年。該聯盟現有 32 支代表區域或城市的隊伍，分

成美國美式足球聯會 (AFC) 及國家美式足球聯會 (NFC)，再依所屬地分為東西南北四區。球季於每年九月至十二月間進行約 17 週的例行賽，每隊需進行 16 場比賽。各聯會戰績最佳的 6 隊會進入季後賽爭取晉級，最後再由兩個聯會冠軍隊伍進行年度的超級盃大賽。

10. **American Football League (AFL)** 美國美式足球聯盟

為美國職業美式足球組織，成立於 1959 年，1969 年球季結束後跟國家美式足球聯盟 (NFL) 合併，該聯盟原本的 10 支隊伍後來便成為美國足球聯會 (AFC) 的骨幹球隊。

11. **Paul McCartney** 保羅‧麥卡尼 (1942–)

前英國樂團披頭四主要創作人之一，創作如 *Hey Jude*、*Yesterday*、*Let It Be* 等多首膾炙人口的歌曲。為目前金氏世界紀錄流行音樂最暢銷音樂人，據統計有 60 張金唱片，唱片總銷量更超越兩億張。近年致力於保護動物、音樂教育及第三世界救助等慈善活動。

12. **The Rolling Stones** 滾石樂團

1962 年成軍的知名英國搖滾團體，以改編藍調、節奏藍調、鄉村、搖滾等音樂風格成名，後來不斷加入不同音樂曲風。此外，主唱米克‧傑格及吉他手凱斯‧理查斯的詞曲創作也讓「滾石」至今仍為廣受歡迎的搖滾天王團體。

13. **Bruce Springsteen** 布魯斯‧史普林斯汀 (1949–)

美國知名鄉村搖滾創作歌手，善於透過歌曲來表達中下階層群眾的心聲，有「工人皇帝」的稱號，曾獲得 20 座葛萊美獎、2 座金球獎及 1 座奧斯卡獎，全球唱片銷售多達一億兩千多萬張。

14. **tailgate party** 後車廂派對

美國運動比賽或是有些演唱會開始前，球迷或歌迷聚集在球場停車場中聚餐的場合。通常參與的人會將汽車的車尾門打開，然後一起烤肉野餐，享受漢堡、熱狗、燒烤食物及啤酒，同時還會有些餘興節目或遊戲。有些無法進場的群眾會攜帶電視音響設備，在球場前收看球賽，與場內同步感受現場的氣氛。

15. **Green Bay Packers** 綠灣包裝工隊

為美國國家美式足球聯盟 (NFL) 旗下之國家美式足球聯會 (NFC) 北區的球隊，創立於 1919 年，以威斯康辛州的綠灣為根據地，該隊曾贏得四次超級盃冠軍。綠灣包裝工隊更是該州居民身份認同的重要一部分，因為威州酪農業發達，是美國乳酪的主要生產中心，所以許多球迷會帶著起司形狀的帽子來替球隊加油。

Pop Quiz

Fill in each blank with the correct word or phrase to complete the sentence. Make changes if necessary.

valuable	regularly	merge	revolve around
root for	champion	approximately	stadium

1. The department store announced that it was going to _____ with the supermarket in order to gain more market share.
2. Mr. Wang's life _____ work; he works his butt off for the company.
3. Exercising _____ can help you stay fit and healthy.
4. The baseball game will be held at the new _____ tomorrow afternoon.
5. The research is a _____ source of information on school bullying.

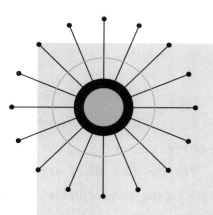

Arts & Entertainment

文化娛樂

UNIT 28

The King of Pop

August, 2009

[1]Michael Jackson, known around the world as the King of Pop, died at the age of 50 on June 25 in Los Angeles, California. With hits ___1___ *Thriller*, *Bad*, *Black or White*, and *Heal the World*, Jackson earned millions of fans around the world with his catchy songs and incredible dance moves. Although his reputation ___2___ a setback in 2005 when he was accused of molesting a young boy, a jury later acquitted Jackson of the charges, and he had announced a series of comeback concerts in London just months before he died.

Born on August 29, 1958, Michael Jackson rose to fame at the age of 11 ___3___ the lead singer of the Jackson 5, a singing group consisting of him and four of his brothers. By the late 1970s, Michael became a successful solo artist, and his fame reached a new level with the ___4___ of the album *Thriller* in 1982. *Thriller* ___5___ included the hits *Beat It* and *Billie Jean*, won a record eight [2]Grammy Awards and became the ___6___ album of all time.

___7___ Michael Jackson released several other popular records, his private life began to overshadow his singing career. From the early 1980s, Jackson's ___8___ noticeably changed. His skin became lighter and lighter, and his face showed evidence of several [3]plastic surgeries. Jackson eventually had three children, but questions remain ___9___ whether or not he was their biological father.

More than 17,000 people attended a memorial service for Jackson on July 7. The service celebrated Jackson's contributions to the world, and it included tributes from entertainers such as [4]Mariah Carey, [5]Lionel Richie, and [6]Stevie Wonder. Jackson's 11-year-old daughter, Paris, made a touching tribute to her father at the end of the ceremony, ___10___ back tears to declare that he was "the best father you could ever imagine."

Choose the correct answers.

( ) 1. (A) rather than (B) lead to (C) instead of (D) such as

( ) 2. (A) suffered (B) occupied (C) issued (D) halted

( ) 3. (A) as (B) of (C) by (D) from

( ) 4. (A) sector (B) measure (C) release (D) debut

( ) 5. (A) which (B) , which (C) , who (D) that

( ) 6. (A) sold-best (B) selling-best (C) best-selling (D) best-sell

( ) 7. (A) Before (B) Because (C) And (D) Although

( ) 8. (A) appearance (B) scandal (C) threat (D) tablet

( ) 9. (A) as if (B) as to (C) but for (D) up to

( ) 10. (A) to hold (B) and holding (C) holding (D) held

» Vocabulary

1. **catchy** [`kætʃɪ] *adj.* 易記的
   - To drive consumers to purchase products, most TV advertisements are designed with catchy slogans and sentimental stories.

2. **incredible** [ɪn`krɛdəbl] *adj.* 難以置信的
   - La Sagrada Familia, Antoni Gaudi's unfinished masterpiece, is really an incredible church, which attracts millions of tourists around the world every year.

3. **reputation** [ˌrɛpjə`teʃən] *n.* [C] 名譽，名聲
   - The five-star hotel gained a good reputation for its service.

4. **setback** [`sɛt͵bæk] *n.* [C] 挫折
   - The candidate suffered a major setback when he was accused of offering bribes.

5. **molest** [mə`lɛst] *vt.* 猥褻，騷擾
   - The lovely girl was molested by a gang of teenagers while strolling in the park.

6. **acquit** [ə`kwɪt] *vt.* 宣判…無罪
   - After months of investigation and trial, the jury acquitted the man of murder.

7. **solo** [`solo] *adj.* 單獨的，獨自的
   - No one offered help. Ted got the job done with his solo effort.

8. **overshadow** [ˌovɚˋʃædo] *vt.* 使…蒙上陰影
   - The baseball gambling scandals overshadowed Taiwan's professional baseball games.
9. **career** [kəˋrɪr] *n.* [C] 生涯，職業
   - The actor started his acting career at the age of sixteen.
10. **noticeably** [ˋnotɪsəblɪ] *adv.* 顯著地，明顯地
    - Mr. Wang was noticeably affected by the long-term unemployment. He felt very depressed about the future.
11. **eventually** [ɪˋvɛntʃʊlɪ] *adv.* 最後，最終
    - After days of work, Gina eventually finished the report.
12. **biological** [ˌbaɪəˋlɑdʒɪkl̩] *adj.* 生物的
    - The girl had a totally different life after losing her biological parents in a huge apartment blaze last year.
13. **memorial** [məˋmorɪəl] *adj.* 紀念的
    - To commemorate Master Sheng-yen, Dharma Drum Mountain organized a simple Buddhist memorial service.
14. **tribute** [ˋtrɪbjut] *n.* [C][U] (表示敬意) 致敬，致哀
    - Tributes have been pouring in from all over the country for the famous singer who passed away last night.
    - The memorial concert is a special occasion that excellent musicians gather to pay tribute to the world-famous classical music conductor Herbert von Karajan.
15. **touching** [ˋtʌtʃɪŋ] *adj.* 感人的，動人的
    - The balcony scene in *Romeo and Julie* is so touching that many lovers shed tears.

≫ Idioms & Phrases

1. **rise to fame**　一舉成名
   - Susan Boyle rose to fame in the TV show *Britain's Got Talent*.
2. **hold back**　控制、抑制 (情緒等)
   - In the negotiation process, Max managed to hold back his anger and listen to how the representative of the car company responded.

≫補 充

1. **Michael Jackson** 麥克・傑克森 (1958–2009)

   美國知名流行歌手,曾被譽為「流行音樂之王」。11 歲時,以 Jackson 5 團體出道,13 歲發行首張個人專輯,專輯《顫慄》(*Thriller*) 為至今史上銷量最高的唱片,高達一億多張。單曲 *Thriller* 的音樂錄影帶被認為是影響二十世紀流行音樂文化的重要作品。生平共獲得 15 座葛萊美獎、2 次進入搖滾名人堂,與貓王、披頭四並列為流行音樂偉大歌手。原訂於 2009 年 7 月 13 日開始復出演唱會巡迴之旅,但不幸於同年 6 月 25 日猝死於家中。

2. **Grammy Award** 葛萊美獎

   與告示牌音樂獎、全美音樂獎、搖滾名人堂等同列為美國四大音樂獎盛事。葛萊美獎由美國錄音學院負責頒發,共有 78 個獎項,涵蓋 30 多種音樂類型。葛萊美獎於 1959 年 5 月 4 日首度頒發,獎座造型是一個小型鍍金留聲機。

3. **plastic surgery** 整形手術

   是指透過外科手術來改善外貌,藉以讓人增加自信。整容通常指臉部整形,包括割雙眼皮、墊下巴、隆鼻等。

4. **Mariah Carey** 瑪莉亞・凱莉 (1970–)

   美國知名流行歌手、詞曲創作人、音樂製作人。1990 年發行首張專輯獲得空前成功,在美國就賣出了九百萬張,並連續 11 週位居告示牌排行榜銷售冠軍。曾獲頒 5 座葛萊美獎、11 座全美音樂獎等大小音樂獎項,唱片銷量達兩億多張。

5. **Lionel Richie** 萊諾・李奇 (1949–)

   美國知名搖滾流行歌手、詞曲創作人、音樂製作人,曾獲 5 座葛萊美獎,唱片銷量超過一億張。演唱過無數知名經典金曲,如 1984 年洛杉磯奧運會主題曲 *All Night Long*、1985 年與麥克・傑克森共同創作的 *We Are the World* 等。

6. **Stevie Wonder** 史提夫・汪達 (1950–)

   美國知名黑人盲人歌手,擅長多種樂器、音樂創作及製作。1961 年以年僅 11 歲的音樂神童姿態被唱片公司發掘,1962 年發行首張唱片,1970 及 1980 年代創作大量歌曲,被譽為美國流行音樂最有影響力的音樂人,至今有 9 首年度冠軍單曲,曾獲 22 座葛萊美獎及 1 座奧斯卡最佳電影歌曲獎。

Pop Quiz

Fill in each blank with the correct word to complete the sentence. Make changes if necessary.

overshadow	acquit	touching	reputation
career	solo	catchy	noticeably

1. After a thorough investigation, the court found the woman innocent and _____ her of the murder.
2. Mrs. Tommy couldn't go through the pain of divorce and has become _____ more depressed.
3. Amy started her teaching _____ after graduation from college.
4. The wise old man has a _____ for offering useful advice.
5. The story was so _____ that a lot of people were moved to tears.

UNIT 29

Addicted to [1]Social Games

December, 2009

Many people use [2]Facebook to stay in touch with their friends and families. Now, a lot of those Facebook users find themselves doing more than just sharing pictures and posting [3]status updates. Games such as [4]*Mafia Wars* and [5]*FarmVille* have brought people together in ___1___ worlds, where they carry out Mafia jobs or tend farms. Not only do these games engross the players' endless time in front of the computer, they also make millions of dollars for the ___2___ of the games.

Most Facebook games follow a standard pattern. In *Mafia Wars*, gamers become the boss of a virtual mafia family and make virtual money to purchase weapons and properties. To gain [6]experience points (XP) and reach the next level, the players could ___3___ master jobs or fight with other Mafia families. Moreover, they obtain a [7]Daily Chance lottery ticket to gain some random items from the collection or bigger prizes. Meanwhile, *FarmVille* lets players set up a virtual farm, where they grow crops and raise livestock to earn more virtual coins. Farmer players gain XPs to reach the ___4___ level and expand farms by having more neighbors, coins, and cash. All of these games incessantly promote themselves to players by asking them to notify friends of their recent achievements and offering daily virtual gifts to invite more ___5___ players from your list of friends to join the games. In the end, many players are unconscious of becoming ___6___ addicted to the online social games.

If players use up all of their virtual money, these games offer the ___7___ of using real money to buy more. In *Mafia Wars*, $5 buys 21 [8]Godfather Reward Points, which might seem like a good deal for the player, but it really ___8___ being a genuine goldmine for [9]Zynga, the maker of *Mafia Wars*. In 2009, Zynga will ___9___ close to $250 million, mostly through the small purchases that players make using games like *Mafia Wars* and *FarmVille*.

Facebook games like these succeed because they are easy to play; they also make it easy for players to become addicted to virtual success. Although no one really loses these games, the only ___10___ are the people making real money.

Exercise

Fill in each blank with the correct word or phrase.

(A) ends up	(B) fully	(C) creators	(D) either	(E) choice
(F) winners	(G) earn	(H) upper	(I) potential	(J) virtual

1. _____ 2. _____ 3. _____ 4. _____ 5. _____

6. _____ 7. _____ 8. _____ 9. _____ 10. _____

Vocabulary

1. **addicted** [ə`dıktıd] *adj.* 沉迷的
   - The teenage boy is addicted to surfing the Internet; he spends almost 12 hours on it a day.

2. **post** [post] *vt.* (在網路上) 張貼訊息
   - Plurk users can freely post text messages, share photos, and quickly respond to comments.

3. **tend** [tɛnd] *vt.* 照顧，照料
   - Mrs. Larry tends her pet dog well and takes it for a walk every day.

4. **engross** [ın`gros] *vt.* 佔去 (某人的) 時間、注意力，使全神貫注
   - Mark was so engrossed in the game that he totally forgot to eat his lunch.

5. **pattern** [`pætən] *n.* [C] 模式，方式
   - Edgar Allen Poe's short stories are believed to set the pattern for modern detective fiction.

6. **purchase** [`pɜtʃəs] *vt.* 購買
   - To avoid waiting in line in front of the ticket window of the movie theater, moviegoers now usually purchase movie tickets online a week in advance.

   purchase [`pɜtʃəs] *n.* [C] 購買
   - If you want to have a full refund on electronics in the store, don't forget your receipt within a week from the time of purchase.

7. **property** [`prɑpətı] *n.* [C] 房地產
   - The rich man owns several residential properties in Paris and London.

8. random [`rændəm] *adj.* 隨機的
   - All the packages look the same, so the chance to get the big prize is random.
9. collection [kə`lɛkʃən] *n.* [C] 收集品
   - The private museum displayed a collection of antique furniture.
10. livestock [`laɪv͵stɑk] *n. pl.* 家畜
    - Mr. McDonald raises livestock such as cows, pigs, and sheep on his farm.
11. incessantly [ɪn`sɛsn̩tlɪ] *adv.* 不斷地，不停地
    - The couple quarreled incessantly, and thus they ended in divorce.
12. notify [`notə͵faɪ] *vt.* 通知，告知
    - Tim notified his team members that the original proposal was changed.
13. deal [dil] *n.* [C] 交易
    - During the anniversary sale, you can get some good deals on make-up.
14. genuine [`dʒɛnjʊɪn] *adj.* 真正的
    - These art experts in the museum recognized that the painting was genuine.
15. goldmine [`goldmaɪn] *n.* [C] 賺錢的生意
    - After the success of Facebook and Twitter, people find the social networking service a real goldmine on the Internet.

≫ Idioms & Phrases

1. stay in touch (with sb.)　(與某人) 保持聯絡
   - Though John and Ben haven't seen each other for five years, they still stay in touch via Facebook every now and then.
2. use sth. up　把…用盡
   - Alex decided to use up all the foreign currencies before returning to Taiwan.

≫ 補 充

1. social games　社交遊戲
   又稱 social gaming。與電視遊樂器遊戲性質不同，社交遊戲通常指的是會與人產生互動的遊戲，如棋盤遊戲、即時線上格鬥遊戲、角色扮演遊戲等。

2. **Facebook　臉書**

當今最熱門的社群網站。由馬克‧祖克柏於 2004 年與幾位哈佛大學的同學一起創立的網站。當初原本只在哈佛大學學生間使用，作為同學及朋友間聯繫的工具。後來慢慢擴展到全世界，目前約有六億多人登記使用臉書。使用者可以在臉書上張貼分享自己的即時訊息、照片或影片給自己的朋友們，同時也可以進行即時通訊以及玩免費線上遊戲。

3. **status update　狀態更新**

為微型部落格或是社群網站的多媒體溝通模式。使用者利用部落格、社群網站平台或手機來傳遞簡短訊息或是搭配影音檔案，張貼在自己的個人空間內和朋友、家人分享。

4. **Mafia Wars　黑幫戰爭**

Zynga 網路遊戲公司設計的一款以黑手黨家族為背景的多人線上遊戲。該遊戲獲得 2009 年威比獎的「人民之聲」獎。

5. **FarmVille　農場鄉村**

Zynga 網路遊戲公司設計的一款「即時線上農場模擬遊戲」，在臉書上相當熱門。該遊戲讓玩家管理虛擬農場，並體驗耕種作物、飼養家畜等工作。

6. **experience point　經驗值**

縮寫為 Exp 或是 Xp。一種在多數角色扮演遊戲中用來量化玩家進行遊戲進度的單位值。通常遊戲玩家必須完成某些指定任務、突破關卡或是幫助隊友才能獲得對等的經驗值。

7. **Daily Chance lottery ticket　每日彩券**

《黑幫戰爭》遊戲每天提供玩家的一張虛擬樂透彩券。

8. **Godfather Reward Point　教父回饋點數**

《黑幫戰爭》遊戲中，玩家完成工作等級後所給予的回饋點數。玩家可以利用回饋點數來購買許多特殊稀有的虛擬寶物。

9. **Zynga　社群網路遊戲公司**

2007 年創立於美國加州舊金山的社群網路遊戲公司，主要提供遊戲玩家在 Facebook 、MySpace 及 iPhone 等平台使用該公司設計的免費遊戲。該公司設計多款熱門遊戲，如：《黑幫戰爭》、《農場鄉村》、《咖啡世界》、《魚塘鄉村》等。

Pop Quiz

Choose the best answer to each of the following sentences.

(　　) 1. Mandy likes to _____ things online because online shops never close.

    (A) notify   (B) tend   (C) analyze   (D) purchase

(　　) 2. A _____ of Claude Monet's paintings was exhibited in the art museum.

    (A) goldmine   (B) component   (C) collection   (D) tournament

(　　) 3. Lucas is _____ to computer games. He stays in his room with his computer the whole time.

    (A) gracious   (B) genuine   (C) addicted   (D) random

(　　) 4. The two car companies are discussing a business _____ .

    (A) deal   (B) swarm   (C) property   (D) pattern

(　　) 5. Mrs. Robert baked some cookies and _____ all the flour and eggs.

    (A) held back   (B) used up   (C) ended up   (D) stayed in

UNIT 30

The Spectacle of [1]Avatar: A Movie of the Future

January, 2010

Not only is *Avatar* the most expensive film ever made, it may also change the way that people watch movies. Directed by [2]James Cameron, who also created the hit movies [3]*The Terminator* and [4]*Titanic*, *Avatar* reportedly cost almost $300 million to make and was filmed by using 3-D technology. Viewers do more than simply watch *Avatar*: they experience it.

Avatar is set in the year 2154 on the distant moon of [5]Pandora, where humans are trying to take control of a substance that will save Earth from destruction. A team of scientists places [6]Jake Sully, a wounded ex-marine, inside a hybrid creation called an avatar, which looks and acts like the [7]Na'vi, the natives of Pandora. However, instead of going undercover and stealing the Na'vi's secrets, Sully falls in love with the Na'vi princess and joins them to fight off a human invasion and save Pandora from conquest.

Even though it is a science fiction, some people still go to see *Avatar* again and again because of its visual effects. In addition to the impressive 3-D technology, the virtual inhabitants of Pandora are also visually stunning. Created by using [8]stop-motion technology in which computers transform the movements of real people into the on-screen aliens, the 10-foot-tall Na'vi captivate the viewers with their blue skin and cat-like eyes, and look just as real as the human actors. Cameron even hired a linguist to create a unique Na'vi language to make the aliens seem even more authentic.

In its premiere at the box office, *Avatar* earned approximately $278 million, breaking the record for the most money earned by a movie over an opening weekend. With its epic story of love and adventure, as well as its breathtaking special effects, *Avatar* will likely continue to be a hit for many weeks to come.

 **Exercise**

Choose the best answers.

(　　) 1. This article is mainly about _____.

    (A) the geographical location of Pandora

    (B) what makes the movie *Avatar* such a huge success

    (C) how to create a unique Na'vi language

    (D) the movie director's interview and critics' comments

(　　) 2. The word "hybrid" in the 2nd paragraph refers to "_____."

    (A) different   (B) random   (C) mixed   (D) biological

(　　) 3. Which of the following statements about *Avatar* is NOT true?

    (A) A Na'vi is about 10-foot-tall with blue skin and cat-like eyes.

    (B) *Avatar* is reportedly the most expensive film ever made.

    (C) *Avatar* is a sci-fi movie with the 3-D technology and visual effects.

    (D) The Na'vi language is based on African languages.

(　　) 4. The character Jake Sully in *Avatar* is _____.

    (A) a scientist doing research on Pandora

    (B) an ex-marine from Earth

    (C) a Na'vi linguist living with the Na'vi

    (D) the Na'vi princess

(　　) 5. Which of the following statements about *Avatar* is true?

    (A) The 3-D and stop-motion technologies make *Avatar* the most popular movie ever made.

    (B) The 3-D technology of Avatar transforms the movements of cats into the on-screen aliens.

    (C) Cameron hired a Na'vi to teach all actors how to speak Na'vi language fluently.

    (D) The opening weekend of *Avatar* at the box office was not as good as *Titanic* did in 1997.

1. **spectacle** [ˋspɛktəkl̩] *n.* [C] 奇觀，壯觀
   - The Ming Hwa Yuan Taiwanese Opera Company's *"The Legend of the White Snake"* is well-known for its marvelous spectacle of multimedia and choreography.

2. **destruction** [dɪˋstrʌkʃən] *n.* [U] 毀滅，破壞
   - The long-term drought has caused widespread destruction to crops.

3. **marine** [məˋrin] *n.* [C] 海軍陸戰隊員
   - Marines are specialized soldiers trained for military operations at sea and on land.

4. **hybrid** [ˋhaɪbrɪd] *adj.* 混種的
   - A mule, the hybrid animal, is the offspring of a female horse and a male donkey.

5. **undercover** [͵ʌndɚˋkʌvɚ] *adv.* 暗中進行地
   - To crack down on organized crime, the police had assigned secret detectives to work undercover in the gang for years.

6. **invasion** [ɪnˋveʒən] *n.* [C] 侵略，侵犯
   - The French invasion of Russia of 1812 began with Napoleon's ambition and ended with his military misjudgment.

7. **conquest** [ˋkɑnkwɛst] *n.* [U] 征服，佔領
   - The soldiers paraded through the city to celebrate their successful conquest of it.

8. **inhabitant** [ɪnˋhæbətənt] *n.* [C] 居民
   - New York City, the most populous metropolitan area in the United States, is a big city with over 8 million inhabitants.

9. **stunning** [ˋstʌnɪŋ] *adj.* 驚人的
   - The view from the top of Taipei 101 is really stunning.

10. **on-screen** [ˋɑn͵skrin] *adj.* 螢幕上的
    - Robert and Kristen are not only an on-screen couple but they are also seeing each other off the screen.

11. **captivate** [ˋkæptə͵vet] *vt.* 吸引，使迷住
    - Cirque du Soleil's astonishing performances have captivated millions of people around the world.

12. **linguist** [ˈlɪŋgwɪst] *n.* [C] 語言學家
   - A linguist is a professional expert who studies languages.

13. **authentic** [ɔˈθɛntɪk] *adj.* 真實的
   - With the help of Shakespeare experts, the manuscript has proved to be his authentic handwriting.

14. **premiere** [prɪˈmɪr] *n.* [C] 首映
   - The director and the leading actor will attend the world premiere in Los Angeles this Friday evening.

15. **breathtaking** [ˈbrɛθˌtekɪŋ] *adj.* 驚人的，令人嘆為觀止的
   - It is an unforgettable experience to see the breathtaking sunset at Sun Moon Lake.

≫ Idioms & Phrases

1. **fight off**　擊退，阻止
   - The girl fought off the robber despite the fact that she was thin and small.

≫ 補 充

1. **Avatar**　《阿凡達》
   2009 年票房冠軍電影，詹姆士‧卡麥隆導演，利用 3D 合成攝影系統拍攝而成。背景設定在 2154 年的潘朵拉星球，人類為了挖掘該星球上珍貴礦物，利用基因技術將人類與納美人混種出「阿凡達」，並利用「阿凡達」與納美人接觸以達成最終目的。

2. **James Cameron**　詹姆士‧卡麥隆 (1954–)
   加拿大籍電影導演，曾導過多部熱門強片，如《魔鬼終結者》、《異形 2》、《鐵達尼號》及《阿凡達》等。

3. **The Terminator**　《魔鬼終結者》
   1984 年由阿諾‧史瓦辛格主演，詹姆士‧卡麥隆所執導的科幻電影。電影時間設定在 1984 年，來自 2029 年未來世界的機器人殺手穿越時空到現代，為的是暗殺人類救世主的母親。

4. **Titanic**　《鐵達尼號》
   1997 年美國災難愛情電影，由李奧納多‧狄卡皮歐和凱特‧溫斯蕾主演，詹姆士‧卡麥隆執導。電影描寫 1912 年超級郵輪「鐵達尼號」首航，在北大西洋誤撞冰山的船難事件中，一個窮光棍小子傑克與富家女蘿絲的生死之戀。鐵達尼號沈船的情境是以電腦特效製作，使其成為二十世紀製作成本最高的電影 (2 億美金)。

5. **Pandora**　潘朵拉星球

電影《阿凡達》中的虛構星球，與地球大小相似，屬於波呂斐摩斯星的 14 顆衛星之一。對人類而言，這個星球保有地球所失去的原始自然環境，但大氣中的氣體對人類有害，夜間森林的生物會自然發出螢光。

6. **Jake Sully**　傑克‧蘇利

電影《阿凡達》中的男主角，前海軍陸戰隊員，被派遣到潘朵拉星球參與「阿凡達計畫」，負責操控混種人。但因緣際會接觸納美人的生活，最終成為納美人的一分子，協助他們抵禦人類的入侵。

7. **Na'vi**　納美人

電影《阿凡達》中居住在潘朵拉星上的虛構外星人種。納美人平均約有三公尺高，擁有光滑的藍色皮膚、一對琥珀色雙眼以及長尾巴。他們被人類視為野蠻未開化的原住民，有些人類輕蔑地稱他們為「藍色猴子」。

8. **stop-motion**　停格動畫

為一種動畫拍攝手法，就是一次只拍一個畫面，每拍完一張就必須調整人偶、物品的動作後再繼續拍攝，因此過程相當繁瑣耗時。利用這種拍攝方式製作的黏土動畫有《聖誕夜驚魂》、《酷狗寶貝》和《笑笑羊》等。

Pop Quiz

Fill in each blank with the correct word to complete the sentence. Make changes if necessary.

hybrid	destruction	undercover	breathtaking
premiere	on-screen	conquest	captivate

1. The action movie will have its _____ at the Grauman's Chinese Theatre in August.

2. We were awed by the _____ scenery of the Niagara Falls.

3. Tom Hanks and Meg Ryan played an _____ couple in the film *You've Got Mail*.

4. The building of the tunnel led to the _____ of the forest since many trees were cut down.

5. These children were _____ by the interesting story.

Vocabulary Index
單字索引

Answer Key

01 Exercise

AABCD   DBDCA

Pop Quiz

1. launched   2. certainly   3. tension
4. risky   5. condemn/condemned

02 Exercise

HBIJE   CDAFG

Pop Quiz

1. D   2. C   3. D   4. B   5. A

03 Exercise

ABDCC

Pop Quiz

1. B   2. D   3. A   4. C   5. A

04 Exercise

DCBBA   CDDCB

Pop Quiz

1. spurred   2. fled   3. luxurious
4. voices   5. protest

05 Exercise

AEHBC   DFIGJ

Pop Quiz

1. B   2. C   3. C   4. A   5. D

06 Exercise

DBCDB

Pop Quiz

1. care for   2. established   3. step down
4. coincidence   5. elections

07 Exercise

BACCD   DBACD

Pop Quiz

1. ordeal   2. collapse   3. relatively
4. rescued   5. consequences

08 Exercise

EIDAC   BFJHG

Pop Quiz

1. C   2. A   3. C   4. D   5. D

09 Exercise

ADACB

Pop Quiz

1. B   2. D   3. D   4. C   5. B

10 Exercise

CCDBA   ADCBB

Pop Quiz

1. profit   2. symbolizes   3. fellow
4. compete   5. in advance

11 Exercise

IEBHD   AJCFG

Pop Quiz

1. B   2. A   3. D   4. D   5. C

12 Exercise

BDACB

Pop Quiz

1. cautious   2. occupied   3. greed
4. endeavor   5. set in

13 Exercise

BDCDC   AABDB

Pop Quiz

1. on display   2. ceremony   3. recycled
4. appreciate   5. horizons

14 Exercise

CFHDB   AEJIG

Pop Quiz

1. D   2. C   3. D   4. A   5. B

15 Exercise

DCACA

Pop Quiz

1. B   2. B   3. D   4. A   5. C

16 Exercise

BCCDA   ABDDC

Pop Quiz

1. C   2. D   3. B   4. D   5. A

17 Exercise

BEAJC   DFIGH

Pop Quiz

1. D   2. D   3. C   4. A   5. B

18 Exercise

BACBD

Pop Quiz

1. means   2. shut down   3. highlighted
4. compensate   5. resume

19 Exercise

ADACC   BDBCA

Pop Quiz

1. C   2. A   3. D   4. C   5. B

20 Exercise

BDJHI   EAFCG

Pop Quiz

1. D   2. C   3. C   4. A   5. B

21 Exercise

ADBCD

Pop Quiz

1. C   2. A   3. B   4. D   5. C

22 Exercise

BBADC   CDDAB

Pop Quiz

1. altered   2. chaos   3. Normally
4. revealed   5. dedicated

23 Exercise

DEGIA   CFBHJ

Pop Quiz

1. C   2. C   3. B   4. D   5. A

24 Exercise

CDBAC

Pop Quiz

1. B   2. A   3. A   4. C   5. D

25 Exercise

DABCC   BDAAC

Pop Quiz

1. are blessed with   2. hospitality
3. spectacular   4. medal   5. indicates

26 Exercise

EAJHB   CGDIF

Pop Quiz

1. B   2. C   3. A   4. B   5. D

27 Exercise

CDABB

Pop Quiz

1. merge   2. revolves around
3. regularly   4. stadium   5. valuable

28 Exercise

DAACB   CDABC

Pop Quiz

1. acquitted   2. noticeably   3. career
4. reputation   5. touching

29 Exercise

JCDHI   BEAGF

Pop Quiz

1. D   2. C   3. C   4. A   5. B

30 Exercise

BCDBA

Pop Quiz

1. premiere   2. breathtaking
3. on-screen   4. destruction
5. captivated

Intermediate Reading:
英文閱讀 *High Five*

掌握大考新趨勢，搶先練習新題型！

王隆興　編著

★全書分為 5 大主題：生態物種、人文歷史、科學科技、環境保育、醫學保健，共 50 篇由外籍作者精心編寫之文章。

★題目仿 111 學年度學測參考試卷命題方向設計，為未來大考提前作準備，搶先練習第二部分新題型——混合題。

★隨書附贈解析夾冊，方便練習後閱讀文章中譯及試題解析，並於解析補充每回文章精選的 15 個字彙。

透過閱讀，你我得以跨越時空，一窺那已無法觸及的世界

閱讀經典文學時光之旅：英國篇
宋美璍　編著

閱讀經典文學時光之旅：美國篇
陳彰範　編著

- 各書精選8篇經典英美文學作品，囊括各類議題，如性別平等、人權、海洋教育等。獨家收錄故事背景知識補充，帶領讀者深入領略經典文學之美。
- 附精闢賞析、文章中譯及電子朗讀音檔，自學也能輕鬆讀懂文學作品。
- 可搭配新課綱加深加廣選修課程「英文閱讀與寫作」及多元選修課程。

三民網路書店　會員

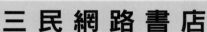

獨享好康大放送

通關密碼：A9599

書種最齊全
服務最迅速

憑通關密碼
登入就送100元e-coupon。
(使用方式請參閱三民網路書店之公告)

生日快樂
生日當月送購書禮金200元。
(使用方式請參閱三民網路書店之公告)

好康多多
購書享3%～6%紅利積點。
消費滿350元超商取書免運費。
電子報通知優惠及新書訊息。

超過百萬種繁、簡體書、原文書5折起　　三民網路書店 www.sanmin.com.tw

★ 108課綱、全民英檢中級必備

Intermediate Reading
新聞宅急通

C

翻譯與解析

三民英語編輯小組　彙編

三民書局

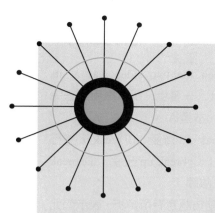

Translation &
Analysis

今年春天，南北韓緊張情勢升高，全球將關注焦點轉向朝鮮半島。北韓態度強硬，聲稱已測試另一枚核彈，雙方關係處於近年來最低迷，也可能是最危險的時刻。

第二次世界大戰結束前，韓國都還是個統一的國家。大戰結束後爆發激烈內戰，北方有中國的支持，而南方則有美國當靠山。雙方交戰至 1953 年才簽署暫時性和平協議。在接下來這些年，並未爆發進一步的大型戰爭，但雙方均互相嚴密監視。即使到了今天，南北韓都仍有軍隊駐守在分隔兩國的邊界上。

然而到了今年春天，北韓開始有了威脅雙方和平的行動。四月時，北韓發射一枚長程飛彈，全世界其他國家，包括聯合國在內，均譴責北韓的此一舉動。而北韓的回應竟是在 5 月 25 日宣稱已成功完成第二次核武測試。該國的第一次測試是於 2006 年進行。北韓還表示將不再遵守讓韓戰於 1953 年終止的暫時性和平協議。

為何北韓目前的行事如此危險且無法預測?有人認為是因為南韓近來在美國帶領下，加入阻止核武擴散的行動。長年以來，美國一直不斷試著要讓北韓終止其核武計畫。也有人認為這只是北韓神秘領導人金正日想引人注意罷了。專家也認為北韓亟需經濟援助，而最近的這些舉動可能是嘗試爭取協助的籌碼。

無論如何，北韓近來的行動確實對南北韓五十餘年來的相對和平造成威脅。

Exercise 解析

(A) 1. 時態早於下句 (the relationship between the two sides was at its lowest . . .) 發生，所以應用過去完成式，故選(A)。

(A) 2. (A) break out 爆發；(B) break in 強行進入；(C) break up 分手；(D) break down 故障。

(B) 3. 此句前後語意有所轉折，表示南北韓是由不同國家支持，所以應選有轉折語氣的連接詞，故選(B)。

(C) 4. 後接複數名詞，故選(C)。

(D) 5. 選項皆為複合形容詞。(A) 低風險的；(B) 長壽的；(C) 影響深遠的；(D) 遠程的。

(D) 6. 選項(A) 應改成 inclusive of；選項(B) 的時態與前後文不符；若用選項(C)，此句內容則須改成：The rest of the world, the United Nations included, ...。所以答案為選項(D)。

(B) 7. (A) 贈送；(B) 發生；(C) (偶然) 遇見；(D) 實現。

(D) 8. 後文說明原因，故選(D)。

(C) 9. 根據 for years，可以知道此句時態用完成式，美國一直都試著要讓北韓終止其核武計畫，故選(C)。

(A) 10. (A) 很，非常；(B) 幾乎；(C) 幾乎不；(D) 不久。

Pop Quiz 解答
1. launched　2. certainly　3. tension
4. risky　5. condemn / condemned

挪威諾貝爾委員會出人意表地宣布，將 2009 年諾貝爾和平獎頒給美國總統歐巴馬。由於歐巴馬上任還不到一年，因此這決定跌破許多人眼鏡。儘管委員會解釋，歐巴馬總統獲獎原因在於「不遺餘力加強國際外交和民族間的合作關係」，但評論家仍有怨言，認為委員會只是因為歐巴馬在國際間極受歡迎才頒獎給他。

瑞典的炸藥發明家諾貝爾於 1896 年去世，當時他在遺囑中聲明要將遺產用來創立獎項，以表揚物理、化學、醫學、文學及和平方面的成就。此獎於 1901 年首次頒發，被稱為桂冠得主的得獎人會獲得一張獎狀、一面獎牌以及約一百四十萬美元的獎金。因為每年和平獎總是最後頒發，所以許多人都將它視為其中最崇高的獎項。

諾貝爾獎多半表揚通過長時間考驗的成就，但許多和平獎得主都是因為近期表現而獲獎，而這也往往引發爭議，因為許多得主雖然製造和平卻也帶來戰爭。舉例來說，季辛吉因與越南和談而在 1973 年獲頒和平獎，但他之前其實參與過籌畫柬埔寨祕密轟炸行動，造成當時數千柬埔寨人民喪生。

就連歐巴馬總統的支持者也同意，現在就頒給他這麼崇高的獎項作為表揚似乎是太早了。許多人認為頒這獎給總統只是讓他徒增無謂的壓力。雖然有些人建議歐巴馬總統婉拒這份榮耀，但他仍決定要領取這個獎項，以「呼籲所有國家採取行動，以面對二十一世紀的種種挑戰。」

Exercise 解析

1. __H__ 此格應填動詞，從上下文意可以知道將諾貝爾和平獎頒給歐巴馬總統的決定使許多人驚訝，故選(H)。

2. __B__ 此格應填形容詞，根據文意選(B)。

3. __I__ 此格應填名詞，推論應該選跟物理、化學等有關的學術範疇，故選(I)。

4. __J__ 此格應填名詞，應為獲頒諾貝爾獎後會得到的東西，故選(J)。

5. __E__ 此格應填副詞，most 與兩個音節以上的形容詞連用，形成最高級，故選(E)。

6. __C__ 此格應填過去分詞 (片語)，根據文意選(C)。

7. __D__ 因為先行詞 (Henry Kissinger) 為一專有名詞，所以用非限定關係子句，對象為人，故關代用 who，故選(D)。

8. __A__ 此格應填副詞，加上後有 to 不定詞，推論答案為(A)，表示「太⋯以致於不能⋯」的句型。

9. __F__ 此格應填介系詞，put pressure on sb. (to do sth.) 表示「對某人施加壓力 (去做某事)」，答案為選項(F)。

10. __G__ 此格應填動詞，根據後面動詞為「should + V」，故選(G)，此為 S_1 + suggest + that S_2 (+ should) + be/V... 的句型。

Pop Quiz 解答				
1. D	2. C	3. D	4. B	5. A

獵殺世界頭號恐怖份子行動告終

奧薩瑪・賓拉登是全球通緝的頭號恐怖分子，他最出名的身分也許是蓋達組織的創始人，蓋達組織就是發動美國 911 攻擊事件的恐怖組織。賓拉登出生於沙烏地阿拉伯一個十分虔誠的穆斯林家庭，在大學時便開始對宗教產生極大的興趣。有人認為他在 1979 年輟學並前往阿富汗抵抗蘇聯部隊的侵略。在蘇聯被擊退後，他對伊斯蘭教的一個激進教派產生興趣，此教派聲稱美國政府迫害中東的伊斯蘭教徒。於是，賓拉登的蓋達組織在世界各地發動了一連串的恐怖攻擊，其中包括 1993 年紐約世貿中心爆炸案、1996 年 19 名駐沙烏地阿拉伯的美軍遇害案、1998 年美國駐肯亞及坦尚尼亞的大使館爆炸案、以及造成逾三千人死亡的 911 攻擊事件。

911 攻擊事件過後，當時的美國總統小布希發誓一定要逮到賓拉登，不論死活。2001 年 12 月，賓拉登差點在阿富汗的托拉波拉山區被抓到，但他仍逃脫成功並在接下來數年持續躲避追捕。

賓拉登持續在逃將近十年，多年來全世界都想知道他到底藏身何處。接著在 2011 年 5 月 2 日晚間，美國總統歐巴馬發表一則驚人的聲明：「今天，在我的指示下，美國在巴基斯坦阿伯塔巴德對一座建築群發動了鎖定對象的任務，一支美國小隊以無比的勇氣和能力執行該任務。沒有任何美國人受傷，他們悉心避免傷及平民。在一陣交火後，他們殺了奧薩瑪・賓拉登並取得他的屍體。」

美國部分地區為賓拉登的死訊歡欣鼓舞。但在世界上的其他地區，恐怖組織卻也誓言要替賓拉登之死進行復仇攻擊。也有許多人希望賓拉登的死能讓美國開始撤軍並終止在阿富汗的軍事行動。反戰組織的成員則表示，既然獵殺賓拉登的行動已經告終，或許和平終於能夠降臨該地區。

Exercise 解析

(A) 1. 第一段在介紹賓拉登的生長背景，以及蓋達組織在世界各地發動了一連串的恐怖攻擊，第二、三段是美國總統布希和歐巴馬誓言對抗賓拉登，並終於逮到他，第四段是賓拉登的死訊使美國人民欣喜若狂，期許中東國家可以感受和平氛圍。故知本文主旨在討論賓拉登之死的影響，故選(A)。

(B) 2. 答案線索在第一段，故選(B)。

(D) 3. 答案線索在第四段，蓋達組織是在 1993 年發動紐約世貿中心爆炸案，並非在他死後才策動，故(D)為非。

(C) 4. 沒有美國士兵遭到射殺，故(A)為非；賓拉登在襲擊行動中當場遭到擊斃，故(B)為非；軍方並未傷及無辜平民，故(D)為非。

(C) 5. 該組織並未要求美國從阿富汗撤軍，故(A)為非；在阿富汗抵抗蘇聯部隊是賓拉登在 1979 年所做的事，與該組織無關，故(B)為非；文中並未提及，故(D)為非。

Pop Quiz 解答

1. B	2. D	3. A	4. C	5. A

2011 年 1 月 14 日，突尼西亞總統扎因・阿比丁・班・阿里在統治 23 年後，因不滿政府高壓統治的抗議浪潮而逃離該國。人民從 2010 年 12 月開始走上街頭表達對其政權獨裁政策、貪腐以及該國經濟蕭條現況的不滿。突尼西亞臨時政府則要求以國際力量逮捕現在躲在沙烏地阿拉伯的班・阿里。

突尼西亞革命導源於名叫穆罕默德・布瓦吉吉的街頭小販，他為抗議不公而引火自焚。他的死之後成為其他人組織暴動的象徵，致使數十人死亡。然而政府無力遏止動盪的情勢。日益增加的抗議群眾對於統治者享受奢華生活，而一般老百姓卻找不到工作也無法負擔基本生活開銷的狀況感到十分憤怒。班・阿里答應舉行公開選舉的承諾也不足以平息動亂，他下臺之後，總理穆罕默德・甘努奇組成了臨時政府。

甘努奇上臺後首先的動作之一就是在 1 月 20 日釋放 1800 名政治犯，但示威行動因為前總統陣營的人馬仍把持要位而持續進行。臨時政府發布控告班・阿里貪污罪名的逮捕令，並呼籲國際扣留前總統的家人。一位突尼西亞記者為這個政治動盪取名「茉莉花革命」。由於有社群網站的幫忙，有些觀察者甚至將其稱為「推特革命」。其他北非及中東國家開始有類似的聲音，要求政治改革，這都應該歸功於突尼西亞人在這次革命中所做的努力。歐巴馬總統及其他歐盟國家領袖們聲援支持突尼西亞的示威人士，但他們否認有介入策劃這起革命。

Exercise 解析

(D) 1. (A) 除…之外 (還)；(B) 至於…；(C) 取代，代替；(D) 以及，和。

(C) 2. 先行詞 (班・阿里) 為唯一特定的人物，所以用用非限定的關係子句，先行詞前須加上逗點，且不可以用 that，故選(C)。

(B) 3. 此為分詞構句，原句為：...and they (those riots) caused dozens of deaths.。省略了連接詞和相同主詞，動詞為主動動作，所以改成現在分詞，故選(B)。

(B) 4. 上下文意語氣有所轉折，故選(B)。

(A) 5. 此為分詞片語，原句為：...an interim unity government which was led by Tunisia's prime minister...，省略了關係代名詞，並將被動語態改成過去分詞而成，故選(A)。

(C) 6. 此格填連接詞，根據語意，故選(C)。

(D) 7. (A) 恢復知覺；(B) (飛機) 起飛；(C) 克服；(D) 要求，請求。

(D) 8. 介系詞 with 在此表示「用，以」。

(C) 9. 此格應選可引導子句，兼具名詞和關係代名詞的功能的複合關係代名詞，故選(C)。

(B) 10. (A) 含有；(B) 否認；(C) 失敗，未能；(D) 用於 (產生…效果)。

Pop Quiz 解答

1. spurred	2. fled	3. luxurious
4. voices	5. protest	

一名男子在托登罕市被警方槍殺後，英國爆發了一連串的動亂。被槍殺的馬克・杜根現年 29 歲，8 月 4 日時死於一場可疑的警匪槍戰。兩天後，上百名示威者聚集在當地警局，替他們認為的「執法過當」討回一個公道。部分群眾向警車丟擲瓶罐並縱火燒掉其中一部車後，開始發生暴動。接下來的幾天，暴動向英國包括曼徹斯特、伯明罕、利物浦、倫敦等各大主要城市蔓延。等騷動開始平息下來時，全英國已有超過三千人遭到逮捕。

隨著燒毀、洗劫商店等事件發生，大暴動影響了英國人的日常活動。8 月 11 日，英國首相大衛・卡麥隆在國會報告時指出這場暴動是「純屬犯罪行為」。政府對動亂反應強勢，僅僅倫敦就部署了超過一萬名警力來恢復秩序。而政府最具爭議性的行動之一是下令嚴懲被指控參與暴力事件的民眾。法院速審速決並重判毫無前科的人，引來批評的聲浪，直指政府比較想要殺雞儆猴而非主持正義。

政治人物及其他官員努力想瞭解為何會發生如此大規模的動亂。為避免未來發生類似的動亂，首相卡麥隆下令檢討並研擬政府該如何修正政策。雖然政府強調此次暴動是國家道德危機造成的結果，但很多人認為，暴民之中很多是來自貧窮的郊區，他們對社會不平等的不滿才是造成此次動亂的主因。

Exercise 解析

1. __A__ 根據 hundreds of，此格應填複數名詞，故選(A)。

2. __E__ 此格應填動詞 (片語)，根據語意選(E)。view/regard/see/look (up)on/think of A as B 將 A 視為 B。

3. __H__ 此格應填動詞 (片語)，根據 violence，故選(H)。

4. __B__ 此格應填形容詞來修飾名詞，根據後面的 throughout the country，可以知道這場暴動是大規模的，故選(B)。

5. __C__ 此為分詞構句，原句為：..., and called them "criminality, pure and simple."，省略了連接詞，並將主動語態的動詞改為現在分詞，故答案為選項(C)。

6. __D__ 此格應填副詞來修飾動詞，根據語意選(D)。

7. __F__ 此格應填形容詞，根據後面的介系詞 in，故選(F)。

8. __I__ 此格應填可以連接兩個句子的複合關係代名詞，故選(I)。

9. __G__ 此格應填名詞，根據語意選(G)。

10. __J__ play a part in sth. 表示「在某事中發揮作用」。

Pop Quiz 解答

1. B	2. C	3. C	4. A	5. D

UNIT 06

終獲自由

民主運動領袖翁山蘇姬在被緬甸 (英文今稱 Myanmar，舊稱 Burma) 政府視為政治犯將近二十年後，終於在 2010 年 11 月 13 日獲釋。翁山蘇姬自她從政以來，有將近 15 年的時間遭到軟禁。在監禁期間，她曾獲允諾只要離開緬甸就能得到自由，但她拒絕了。這或許解釋了為何翁山蘇姬成為全球民運人士勇氣與希望的象徵。

翁山蘇姬是 1947 年時被暗殺的緬甸獨立英雄翁山將軍的第三個孩子，也是唯一的女兒。在留學旅居國外多年後，她為了照顧生病的母親於是在 1988 年返國。巧合的是，執政黨領袖吳奈溫將軍在當時下臺了。翁山蘇姬公開呼籲成立一個民主政府，並協助建立了全國民主聯盟 (NLD)。她接著迅速成為緬甸民主運動中的重要人物，並領導全國民主聯盟在 1990 年的大選贏得壓倒性的勝利。然而，從 1962 年開始統治緬甸的軍政府卻拒絕兌現大選結果，不但緊握權力不放，更將翁山蘇姬軟禁起來。即使在被軟禁家中的期間，翁山蘇姬仍然持續擔任全國民主聯盟領袖。回應她替緬甸爭取民主所付出的努力，翁山蘇姬在 1991 年獲頒諾貝爾和平獎。

2010 年 5 月，由於抵制反抗軍政府所安排的又一輪不公平選舉，全國民主聯盟因而被強制解散。雖然翁山蘇姬已經不再是政黨領袖，她仍聲明會持續支持緬甸的和平式政治革命。翁山蘇姬也展現與軍政府合作的意願，以求能讓緬甸從獨裁和平地轉向民主。

Exercise 解析

(D) 1. 第一段是民主運動領袖翁山蘇姬終於在 2010 年獲釋；第二段是談論翁山蘇姬替緬甸爭取民主所付出的努力；最後一段是翁山蘇姬獲釋後，仍努力尋求能讓緬甸從獨裁和平地轉向民主。故知本文主旨在討論翁山蘇姬努力替緬甸爭取民主，答案選(D)。

(B) 2. 本題問軍政府統治緬甸的時間，答案在第二段 ：...the military dictatorship that had ruled Myanmar since 1962...，得知大約五十年，故答案為(B)。

(C) 3. 答案線索在二、三段。NLD 成立於 1988 年，創始人為翁山蘇姬，故(A)為非；是軍政府將翁山蘇姬軟禁在家，故(B)為非；在軍政府的強力阻饒下，NLD 並未能在 1990 年大選勝利後成為執政黨，故(D)為非。

(D) 4. 推論此字有反義，故選(D)。

(B) 5. 文中並未提及翁山蘇姬是因為父親的遺願而參與政治，故(A)為非；根據第三段，可知(C)為非；文中並未提及翁山蘇姬成為執政黨的領袖，故(D)為非。

Pop Quiz 解答

1. care for	2. established	3. step down
4. coincidence	5. elections	

受困在地底兩個多月後，33 名智利礦工終於在 10 月 13 日從坍塌的礦坑中被救了出來。救援行動經由電視實況轉播，世界各地的人們都目睹了礦工一個個被密閉小艙載送到地表的過程。智利政府不僅因為這次救援的處置受到讚美，連帶也使得舉國歡騰、引以為傲。雖然礦工獲救後身體沒有太大的異狀，衛生官員仍警告說礦工所受到的煎熬可能會對心理狀態造成一段時間的影響。

這群礦工在 8 月 5 日當天因金銅礦坑塌陷而受困。接下來整整 17 天毫無音訊，直到探測孔鑽抵礦工，地面上的人們才經由他們捎來的一張紙條得知礦工全體平安。當局接著也利用這個管道運送食物、家屬的字條以及娛樂消遣給礦工。此外，來自全球的工程師、醫生和心理學家所組成的團隊則合力計畫如何鑽出一個更大的救生坑道及如何維持礦工在地底等待救援時的身心狀況。

在救援行動進行的同時，家屬、新聞記者、政府官員也與救難人員一起，在礦坑入口外搭建名為「希望營」的臨時居所。醫生們確保礦工的身體狀況能夠承受到他們回到地表，並讓他們戴上特製的太陽眼鏡來保護眼睛。智利總統薩巴斯提安‧皮涅拉也和家屬一同迎接從救生艙出來的礦工。在救援行動開始後，礦工們就達成協議要保密受困時的故事細節，直到他們取得可使所有人受益的出書與電影合約為止。

Exercise 解析

(B) 1. 此為關係子句的非限定用法，用來對專指的先行詞 (the operation) 進一步說明，故選(B)。

(A) 2. (A) 警告，告誡；(B) 證明；(C) 要求；(D) 希望。

(C) 3. where = in which。

(C) 4. 此為分詞片語，原句為：...they sent up a note which said that they were...，省略關代 which 後，將主動語態的動詞改成現在分詞，故選(C)。

(D) 5. 因為此句更進一步說明現場的救援情況，故選(D)。

(D) 6. (A) 向內地；(B) 直地，筆直地；(C) 無處，哪裡都沒有；(D) 在地下。此處問礦工的所處位置，故選(D)。

(B) 7. (A) 盯著 (某人)，注意 (某人的) 行動；(B) 發生；(C) 分發…；給予 (懲罰、建議等)；(D) 參與…。

(A) 8. 使役動詞 have 後加受詞和原形動詞，表示「使…去做…」，故答案選(A)。

(C) 9. 根據上下文意，故選(C)。

(D) 10. (A) 遺囑；(B) 輪班；(C) 選擇；(D) 祕密。

Pop Quiz 解答

1. ordeal	2. collapse	3. relatively
4. rescued	5. consequences	

　　很多人在幾個月前從來沒有聽過一家叫做富士康的公司。但當短短數月內，富士康出現十二名員工企圖自殺後，全世界的注意力便迅速轉移到自殺事件發生的富士康中國營運處。

　　第一位了結自己生命的富士康員工馬向前，是在 2010 年 1 月 23 日從高高聳立的公司宿舍跳樓身亡。馬向前 2009 年 11 月才剛進富士康科技集團工作，他每晚通常要輪值 11 小時的大夜班，死前一個月內工作了 286 小時，包括超時工作 110 小時以上。儘管如此，他的時薪只有 1 美元。

　　2010 年前五個月期間，總共有八名男性與四名女性在富士康位於深圳的兩處廠區自殺或者企圖自殺。其中絕大多數的年齡都介於 18 到 24 歲之間，而且進入富士康工作的時間都不長。

　　富士康是由臺商郭台銘所建立的，他在深圳的工廠替國際公司像蘋果和戴爾生產產品。為了因應自殺事件，富士康大幅度調漲薪資，有些還達到在中國的勞工基本薪資的雙倍之多。郭台銘本人則親自造訪深圳廠區並公開道歉。

　　有些專家指出這些自殺事件代表中國的一個潮流——當中國仍然普遍存在低薪與惡劣工作環境的狀況下，新一世代的工人，尤其是來自中國內陸省份的移民勞工，將不會再忍氣吞聲。有越來越多人就辭掉在這樣的工廠裡工作。其他的例子，像是在華南地區的本田汽車，就有員工罷工要求更高的薪資。

　　雖然有些人指出富士康的自殺率，其實還遠低於全中國的平均值——據信高達每十萬人中有二十到三十人自殺——但富士康自殺事件當然是一齣悲劇。只能期盼它會促使富士康以及中國其他地區的勞工，能獲得更好的工作環境與更高的薪資。

Exercise 解析

1. __E__　此格應填名詞，根據文意，故選(E)。
2. __I__　複合形容詞 high-rise 表示「高層的」。
3. __D__　此格應填動詞，根據後面提到薪資 (US$1)，常用的搭配動詞為(D)。
4. __A__　a total of 表示「總共…，共有…」，後接複數可數名詞。
5. __C__　此格應填動詞，前面名詞 (Foxconn) 為一間公司，常用搭配動詞為(C)。
6. __B__　此格應填形容詞，根據文意，故選(B)。
7. __F__　此格應填副詞，根據文意，故選(F)。
8. __J__　此格應填副詞，根據文意，故選(J)。
9. __H__　此格應填副詞，根據文意，故選(H)。
10. __G__　the rest of sth. 表示「其餘的…」。

Pop Quiz 解答

1. C	2. A	3. C	4. D	5. D

一篇名為《中國媽媽為何更勝一籌？》的文章，最近在網路上引起許多評論、轉貼及部落格文章討論。這篇以印刷及線上版本在《華爾街日報》發表的短文毫無疑問地在一月份時引發不少爭議。就連它的標題都讓人覺得反感，而其內容更讓許多人感到不快。

這篇文章的作者是蔡美兒，她是美國華人第二代，也是耶魯法學院教授。文中試圖解釋為何美國的中國媽媽能夠撫養出許多符合刻版印象成功標準的孩子。她一開始先列出許多大部分美國小孩在成長階段可以做、但她的兩個女兒不能做的事情：不許在外過夜、不准參加玩伴聚會、不可以看電視和玩電腦遊戲、學業成績不准低於 A。除此之外，兩人還得學一樣樂器，而且只能學鋼琴或小提琴。

蔡美兒的父母有華人血統，當初是從菲律賓移民到美國的。由於父母用嚴格的方式在美國養育她，蔡美兒在學業上表現傑出並在哈佛拿到學位。當她為人母時，她決心讓自己華人第三代的孩子，以跟其他美國小孩不同的方式長大成人。套一句她自己的話，她希望她以「中國媽媽」的方式養育她們——嚴格、要求、不讓步。

對於文章及蔡美兒育兒方式的反應不一。有人說她的部份舉動已經接近虐待兒童，包括罵其中一個女兒「垃圾」，還有不讓另一個女兒吃飯或上廁所直到練好一首鋼琴曲子等等。其他的則指出這篇文章是在蔡美兒的新書《虎媽戰歌》上市前幾天發表，是有意引發爭議來提昇銷售量。

可以確定的是：這篇文章確實在美國及全世界引發話題——到底什麼樣的育兒方式才是最好的。較寬容的西方方式比較好嗎？還是說要求嚴格的東方方式才是理想的？或是兩者應該綜合起來？

Exercise 解析

(A) 1. 第一段談及一篇題名為《中國媽媽為何更勝一籌》的文章引起各方廣泛爭議；第二段談及耶魯法學院教授蔡美兒嚴厲的育兒方式；第三段指出蔡美兒教授以「中國媽媽」的教養方式來養育女兒；第四段說明各方對其文章及育兒方式的反應不一；最後一段，作者以中立立場來做歸結。從以上重點可知，本文主旨在討論蔡美兒教授嚴厲的育兒方式，故選(A)。

(D) 2. 本題答案線索在第三段，可以知道她的女兒們應該在美國出生，故選(D)。

(A) 3. 本題問蔡美兒教授的女兒不能做的事，根據文章，答案為(A) 成績不准低於 A。

(C) 4. 根據後文 "...ended up with degrees from Harvard"，可以知道她在學業上表現傑出，故選(C)。

(B) 5. 本題問哪一個形容詞不是用來形容「中國媽媽」?，根據第三段，故選(B)。

Pop Quiz 解答				
1. B	2. D	3. D	4. C	5. B

UNIT 10

每年感恩節隔天，數百萬的美國人都會利用打折湧入商場搶便宜。這就是所謂的「黑色星期五」，這天不僅是美國一年之中最繁忙的採購日，同時也是耶誕檔期的非正式序幕。過去許多商家會在清晨六點開始營業，許多顧客則會提早數小時抵達以便在開門時拔得頭籌。2011 年時，部分連鎖零售商首次在午夜就開始營業，造成認為血拼活動不應當擾亂感恩佳節的人士極大的反彈。

「黑色星期五」這個措詞最早在 1960 年代中期的費城被用來描述漸漸成為常態的感恩節後塞車狀況。後來這個措詞傳到美國其他地區，有些人開始相信它代表著大多數商家在一年的這個時候開始賺錢，或是「呈現盈餘」的時候。今日的消費者必須事先計畫，才能在這場激烈的競賽中找到店面中最優惠的商品。許多人數週前就開始上網搜尋已上線的商家資訊，以便找到最優惠的商家。人們也會為了搶到好位置而提早十小時到店門口前排隊。

批評黑色星期五的人抱怨這樣的狀況促進揮霍無度的消費主義，且可能會引發動亂。2008 年時，一名沃爾瑪的員工就在顧客擠入店內時被踩死。今年，一名女子竟然用防狼噴霧對付與她競購同一款電玩遊戲機的其他顧客。由於近年來景氣低迷，黑色星期五的銷售比往年要低，但隨著人們在聖誕節禮物上的花費增加，今年商家回報的來客量還是相當可觀。

Exercise 解析

(C) 1. (A) 不是…而是；(B) 既不…也不；(C) 不但…而且；(D) 太…以致於不能。答案為對等連接詞，根據語意選(C)。

(C) 2. 此為分詞片語，原句為：...with shoppers who arrived hours earlier to be the first...，省略了關係代名詞，並將主動語態的動詞改成現在分詞，故選(C)。

(D) 3. 此為關係子句的非限定用法，用來對專指的先行詞 (some retail chains opened their stores at midnight for the first time) 進一步說明，故選(D)。

(B) 4. 說明特定的時間點時介系詞必須用 on，故選(B)。

(A) 5. (A) spread to 傳播到…；(B) take to sb/sth 開始喜歡…；(C) agree to sth 同意…；(D) flee to 逃到…。

(A) 6. (A) 提前，提早；(B) 在附近；(C) 向內；(D) 在旁邊。

(D) 7. (A) 關於；(B) 總共；(C) 不然；(D) 多達，高達。

(C) 8. (A) 受歡迎，流行；(B) 改革，變革；(C) 暴動，騷亂；(D) 和平。

(B) 9. 此題選連接詞，根據文意，故選(B)。

(B) 10. because 後須接子句，故不能選(A)；(C) in spite of 表示「儘管」。

Pop Quiz 解答

1. profit　　2. symbolizes　　3. fellow

4. compete　　5. in advance

毫無疑問地，全世界現正面臨著近代史上最嚴重的經濟衰退時期之一。由於這場危機，許多國家得想出創新的作法來解救國內的經濟，臺灣也不例外。1 月 18 日，臺灣的政府官員針對符合資格的居民，開始發放價值 3,600 元的消費券，希望藉此刺激國家經濟。

各界對消費券抱持高度期待，消費券才剛開放領取的星期天一早，引頸期盼的居民就開始在發放處外大排長龍，包括小孩和外籍配偶在內，總計有兩千三百多萬人有資格領到這筆錢。當天結束後，政府官員表示，有資格領消費券的人當中，已經有超過九成前來領取。

就在同一個禮拜天，「消費券狂熱」似乎席捲臺灣。雖然消費券的使用期限到九月份，但許多民眾當天馬上就把這「天上掉下來的錢」，拿去購物中心和超市花用。新聞報導中，看見消費者在傳統市場、餐廳和電器行使用消費券。然而，許多消費者表示他們會把消費券用來採買雜貨等日常用品。也有人說他們打算用消費券來為春節假期作準備。

許多想趁消費券風潮大賺一筆的店家，提供優惠活動給使用消費券的人。部分商家舉辦特別的抽獎活動，而其他店家則提供不等的折扣。包括長榮和華航在內的數家航空公司，也提供優惠給使用消費券來購買機票的消費者。一些大學甚至表示他們將准許學生用消費券來繳學費。

為了這次的消費券方案，政府挪出八百六十億元，希望能提升臺灣的經濟。然而，不是每個人都滿意，有人認為消費券是虛擲經費，也有一些批評者指出政府必須借錢才能資助這次計畫。

但有件事是明確的——不管他們喜不喜歡消費券，臺灣的居民已經領了他們的消費券，而且的確也在使用當中。不過，這些消費券對經濟能產生多少的效果仍有待觀察。

Exercise 解析

1. ___I___　此格應填原形動詞，後有 economy，根據常搭配動詞，故選(I)。
2. ___E___　此格應填形容詞，根據文意選(E)。
3. ___B___　此格後接名詞，根據文意選(B)。according to 表示「據…所說」。
4. ___H___　此格應填形容詞，根據文意選(H)。very 在此表示「(特指人或事物) 正是的」，有強調的作用。
5. ___D___　此格應填副詞，根據文意選(D)。
6. ___A___　此格應填 (代) 名詞，根據文意選(A)。此為分詞片語，原句為：...many businesses offered special deals for those who use vouchers.。
7. ___J___　此格應填動詞 (片語)，根據文意選(J)。
8. ___C___　此格應填原形動詞，allow sb. to do sth. 表示「允許某人去做某事」。
9. ___F___　此格應填名詞，後有 money，根據常搭配用法，故選(F)。
10. ___G___　此格應填名詞，根據不定冠詞 an，可知是母音開頭的名詞，故選(G)。

Pop Quiz 解答

1. B	2. A	3. D	4. D	5. C

9 月份剛開始還只是個組織鬆散、對抗企業貪婪的抗議活動，目前已經發展成為美國爭取經濟平等的全國性活動。雖然佔領華爾街活動始於紐約市的金融區，類似的佔領示威行動已擴及到國內各大城市。示威者將怒火對準他們稱為「百分之一」的人，也就是掌控國家大部分財富的企業主管和金融家。而示威者則自稱是「百分之九十九」的人，也就是在經濟衰退中深受其害的大多數美國人。

示威者從 9 月 17 日開始在鄰近紐約市華爾街的祖科蒂公園紮營，展開示威活動。在接下來的幾個星期裡，類似的示威行動在其他城市展開，越來越多對經濟上的高失業率以及逐漸攀升的企業獲利表示失望的一般民眾加入這個運動中。該項抗議行動得到部分民主黨人的謹慎支持，而共和黨人多半批評此示威活動。隨著有組織的領導產生、人們開始捐錢贊助，活動籌辦人開始得要努力應付日益倍增的示威人數。

這項示威活動中最有野心的一次嘗試行動 11 月 2 日發生在加州的奧克蘭。示威者組織了一次大型的街頭遊行，他們得到當地教師和碼頭工人的支持，在美國第五大港口發動一次真正的罷工。到目前為止，抗議行動還算和平，不過一位前海軍陸戰隊成員先前在奧克蘭遭警方催淚彈罐擊中，促使更多退休老兵加入示威行列。當地政府開始抱怨隨著佔領行動擴大，影響到地方公共設施及交通。但部分運動領袖擔心，當冬天越來越冷之後，支持者可能會隨之減少。

Exercise 解析

(B) 1. 本題問主旨，故須整合各段重點才能答題：第一段在敘述佔領華爾街活動源起的原因──爭取經濟平等；第二段談及此活動也在其他城市展開，有越來越多人加入；第三段是發生在奧克蘭的大型街頭遊行，活動影響所及和可能的後續發展。從以上重點可知，本文主旨在討論「佔領華爾街」活動所要對抗的不平等，故選(B)。

(D) 2. 根據後接的 the current economic downturn，可推論此片語應是跟負面的事物有關，故選(D)。

(A) 3. 本題線索在第一段，答案選(A)。

(C) 4. 從第一段可知此活動一開始並非組織嚴謹，故(A)為非；文中並未提及因為鬆散的組織，所以越來越少人參與，故(B)為非；根據第三段可以知道抗議行動還算和平，故(D)為非。

(B) 5. 本題線索在第三段，答案選(A)。

Pop Quiz 解答

1. cautious	2. occupied	3. greed
4. endeavor	5. set in	

經過數年的籌備及宣傳，2010 臺北國際花卉博覽會終於登場了。博覽會於 11 月 6 日正式開幕，展期預計會持續到 2011 年 4 月 25 日。

這是臺灣首度獲得國際園藝家協會認可主辦的大型博覽會，因此臺北市卯足了勁來籌備花博。籌辦時間歷時四年，估計已耗資臺幣 138 億 (折合美金 4 億 5695 萬)。這次花博以「彩花·流水·新視界」為主題，展區總面積 91.8 公頃，包含 4 大園區、14 座展館，共展出 3 千 2 百萬株植栽。官方估計參觀人次將超過 8 百萬，其中包含 40 萬以上的外國遊客。

然而，臺北花博並非毫無爭議。有人說政府在這件事上花太多錢，還有人質疑為何要在多雨的臺北秋冬季舉辦花卉展。事實上，雨水已經為花博的開幕煙火帶來問題，同時也使得花博第一週的參觀人潮低於預期。

儘管遇到這些難題，花博仍獲得大多數參觀者的好評。國際園藝家協會會長費伯便表示：「在我看來，臺北花博是近 50 年來花博辦得最好的一次。」其他遊客也多半持相同看法。許多人讚許這次花博讓他們有機會見識到新的環保科技，尤其是夢想館和由 150 萬支回收寶特瓶所建的流行館 (遠東環生方舟)。

無庸置疑地，臺北花博是臺灣近年來所主辦最重大的國際盛事之一。花博有這麼多好看、好玩之處，當然值得大家在接下來幾個月中一逛再逛。

Exercise 解析

1. __B__　(A) 大部分地；(B) 必定，一定；(C) 相對地；(D) 不久。

2. __D__　「as + adj. + as」為形容詞原級比較的用法，故選(D)。

3. __C__　介系詞 with 在此表示「以，用」。

4. __D__　此為分詞片語的用法，原句為：...with more than 400,000 foreign tourists who plan to visit the expo. ，省略了關係代名詞，並將主動語態的動詞改為現在分詞。

5. __C__　語氣上有所轉折，故選(C)。

6. __A__　others 是 other 的複數形，表示「另外幾個，其餘的」，是代名詞所以可以當主詞。

7. __A__　cause sb./sth. to V 表示「使…發生，造成…」，故選(A)。

8. __B__　根據下文，可以推論此格應填正面性質的形容詞，故選(B)。

9. __D__　此為關係子句的非限定用法，用來對專指的先行詞 (the Pavilion of New Fashion) 進一步說明，故選(D)。

10. __B__　此為分裂句型：It is/was + N(P) + that-clause，將要強調的部份放在 be 動詞之後，that 之前，表示「就是…」之意。

Pop Quiz 解答

1. on display	2. ceremony	3. recycled
4. appreciate	5. horizons	

就在不到一年之前，臺灣對中國的觀光客敞開大門。2008 年 7 月 4 日，第一批中國旅遊團抵達臺灣，之後中國遊客的人數便持續上升，特別是臺灣和中國之間在 12 月 15 日展開平日包機後更是如此。事實上，到了 2009 年 4 月初，每天造訪臺灣的中國觀光客就超過 4,000 名，這促使臺灣移民署將每日准許進入臺灣的中國觀光客限額提高到 7,200 人。

縱然有越來越多的中國觀光客造訪臺灣，但很遺憾的，近來和這些遊客有關的意外事件似乎也逐漸增加。4 月 24 日，一輛載著廣東觀光客的遊覽車，在前往臺北 101 參觀途中，遭從 37 層樓高處掉落的起重機吊臂壓垮。在這起事件中，三名乘客喪生、另有三名受傷。接著在 4 月 30 日，來自福州的某旅遊團中，有兩名中國觀光客在太魯閣國家公園遭掉落的石塊擊中而受到重傷，其中一名被砸中後昏迷，而另一名則有割傷和骨折，兩者都需要手術治療。接著在 5 月 1 日，一名來自廣東的觀光客從旅館 12 樓房間的陽臺墜樓身亡。這起意外發生在南投縣埔里鎮，67 歲的死者是中國長青觀光團訪臺 5 日遊的一員。

儘管在這麼短的時間內就發生這三起嚴重事件，但中國旅遊團仍不斷造訪臺灣，且造訪人數似乎還持續增加。政府官員表示，他們希望有朝一日能達到每天有一萬名中國觀光客造訪的目標，因為這將有助於提振臺灣的觀光業。然而，對於這些選擇造訪臺灣的觀光客，他們的安全也應列為優先目標。

中國觀光客變多，問題也變多？

Exercise 解析

1. **C** 此格應填副詞來修飾副詞子句，根據文意，故選(C)。
2. **F** 此格應填形容詞，且跟時間有關，故選(F)。
3. **H** 此格應填形容詞，根據文意，故選(H)。
4. **D** 此格應填複數名詞，根據文意，故選(D)。
5. **B** 此格應填副詞，動詞 injure 常與 seriously 搭配使用，故選(B)。
6. **A** 此句時態為被動式，故此格應填分詞，故選(A)。
7. **E** 此格應填動詞 (片語)，根據文意，故選(E)。
8. **J** 此格應填形容詞，根據前文知道這位觀光客已經 67 歲，故選(J)。
9. **I** 此格應填原形動詞，故選(I)。
10. **G** 此格應填單數名詞，根據文意，故選(G)。

Pop Quiz 解答

1. D	2. C	3. D	4. A	5. B

它是近幾年來臺灣最具爭議性的議題之一，甚至在最近一次選舉中也扮演重要的角色。而現在這個案子會不會開始進行似乎還是個未知數。當然，它就是蘇澳花蓮高速公路計劃，也就是大家所熟知的「蘇花高」。

對於這條提議中的新道路，人們分成兩派不同的意見。有些人是蘇花高建案的強烈支持者，包括很多政治家和大部分的東臺灣居民。他們主張往來蘇澳鎮和花蓮市的新路線是迫切需要的，因為不僅可以取代原本彎曲破碎的道路，也可以提振這個區域的經濟。由於這個地區大部分是由農村聚落所組成，因此相對來說仍處於低度開發的狀態，與臺灣其他地區比較尤其如此。此外，新的高速公路肯定有助於節省往來蘇澳與花蓮的時間——從幾近三小時縮減至只要約一小時。

然而，許多環保人士指出，建造新的高速公路可能會對東臺灣環境造成極大的傷害，而這裡正是以其非凡的自然美景而著名。蘇花高工程會破壞本地區許多特有動植物的重要棲息地。許多專家也表示，這條新道路包含四十公里以上的隧道和三十七公里的橋樑，由於其建造工程及路線離地震斷層線極近，因此可能更加危險。而最重要的問題是：我們真的需要建造一條極度昂貴又耗時的新高速公路來保證東臺灣未來的繁榮嗎？

雖然交通部已經審查過此建案，並在最近決定採用另外的提案來改善現有的蘇花公路，但蘇花高的命運仍懸而未決，因為這並非最後定案，一切仍有賴臺灣人民及政治家共同想出解決辦法，在對東臺灣有最大助益的情況下，同時也能保存這個地區獨特的美麗及環境。

Exercise 解析

(D) 1. 本題問主旨，故須整合各段重點才能答題：第一段談及興建蘇花高與否是近年來臺灣最具爭議性的議題之一；第二段是探討贊成興建蘇花高的原因；第三段是探討反對興建蘇花高的原因；第四段則指出因為太具爭議性，蘇花高興建與否仍在評估中。故答案選(D)。

(C) 2. 根據第三段，故答案為(C)。

(A) 3. 根據第二段：… not only to replace the original crooked and fragile road …，可以知道蘇澳和花蓮間並非沒有路可到，故(A)為非。

(C) 4. 根據第三段：… include more than 40 kilometers of tunnels …，知道(A)為非；根據文章，知道蘇花高是節省從蘇澳到花蓮間的行車時間，故(B)為非；根據第三段，蘇花高的興建會導致動植物棲息地遭到破壞，故(D)為非。

(A) 5. 根據最後一段，可以知道至今尚未決定是否興建蘇花高，故選(A)。

Pop Quiz 解答				
1. B	2. B	3. D	4. A	5. C

五十年來泰國最嚴重的水災

淹水對泰國來說並不是新鮮事。事實上，該國的雨季就常常會有小淹水。但今年泰國遭遇到 50 年來最嚴重的水災，連續數月的豪雨不只替泰國帶來危機，也影響了全世界。

麻煩早在今年三月就開始了，當時泰國北部某些區域的降雨量，比平常的降雨量還多出驚人的 344%。破紀錄的降雨持續了整個夏季，導致水庫漲滿、雨水匯聚於泰國北部及中部地區。過去這些水會慢慢向南流入泰國灣，造成最小程度的損害。然而，今年泰國破表的雨量卻造成大規模氾濫的洪流從北部開始，一路蔓延到南方。

七月下旬，大水開始流向泰國首都曼谷，這些洪水淹沒了數千英畝的農地。十月初，歷史古都大城府遭到淹沒，泰國中部有部分地區已經開始進行撤離，而在更南方，900 萬的曼谷居民也開始準備面對即將到來的洪水。

隨著洪水南下，泰國中部上百家工廠也慘遭淹沒。近年來，泰國已經成為全球汽車及電腦零件的製造中心，但 2011 年的洪災打斷了這些廠房的生產活動。目前專家預估，外接式硬碟的價格將因此次天災而上漲。

到目前為止，曼谷僅有少數地區因備有大規模排水系統及其他防災措施，故未受洪災波及。但救援機構警告，因洪水導致環境不潔、疾病感染的威脅依舊存在。在泰國政府部分，則承諾將進行大規模的清掃，同時也會對今年洪患的災區提供援助方案。

迄今，2011 年的洪災已造成泰國 800 人以上的死亡以及 59 億美元的損失。同時也對全球的汽車及電腦供應鏈造成嚴重破壞。顯然，2011 的泰國水災在未來的許多年中，都不會被人們所遺忘。

Exercise 解析

(B) 1. 本題選連接詞，根據文意，故選(B)。

(C) 2. record-breaking 為「N + V-ing」所組成的複合形容詞，表示「破紀錄的」。

(C) 3. 此為分詞構句，原句為：..., and it caused minimum damage.，省略連接詞和相同主詞，並將主動語態的動詞改成現在分詞，故選(C)。

(D) 4. 文意上有所轉折，故選(D)。

(A) 5. 介系詞 by 表示「在…之前」。

(A) 6. (A) 生產；(B) 娛樂；(C) 反對；(D) 爭議。

(B) 7. 後接名詞 (片語)，所以答案為(B)。選項(C)後接子句，故不選。

(D) 8. 連綴動詞 remain 後接形容詞，表示「維持、保持某種狀態」。

(D) 9. 此為分詞片語，原句為：...the areas which were affected by this year's floods.，省略關係代名詞，並將被動語態的動詞改成過去分詞，故選(D)。

(C) 10. 此為用副詞來修飾整個句子，根據文意，故選(C)。

Pop Quiz 解答				
1. C	2. D	3. B	4. D	5. A

日本於當地時間 3 月 11 日星期五下午 2 時 46 分發生強烈大地震。震央位於仙台以東 130 公里處，部分報導指出該次地震規模高達芮氏 9.0 級，是日本有史以來遭遇到最大的強震。

雖然地震造成相當大的損害，但真正重創日本許多地區的是隨之而來的海嘯。在地震發生後，日本政府立刻發布海嘯警報。接著約 1 小時之後，仙台機場便遭海嘯淹沒，新聞播放了當海嘯水牆往內陸移動時，海浪將飛機及其他交通工具全部捲走的畫面。令人遺憾的是，據報導，海嘯摧毀了日本沿岸幾個小鎮，家園、房屋都被沖走，城鎮變成殘破的瓦礫堆。

更糟的是，這次天災也對日本數座核能發電廠造成影響。雖然這些核電廠在地震發生後自動停止運轉，海嘯卻襲捲福島第一、第二核電站，破壞該地的緊急發電機，造成冷卻系統供電中斷並導致爆炸及輻射外洩。週邊逾 20 萬人撤離，而核電廠員工則急忙處理反應爐核心可能熔毀的問題。

有些人稱這次天災為「東日本大地震」，而這次的震災在網路上被充份報導，當地人幾乎即時上傳地震及海嘯的影像畫面。或許正是因為如此，來自世界各地的捐款及救援幾乎在災難發生後隨即蜂擁而至。許多國家迅速加入救援行列，包括臺灣捐出 1 億元臺幣，並派遣搜救隊到日本。

震災後數天，日本首相菅直人發表評論：「這是日本自二次大戰以後的 65 年以來遭遇到最嚴峻的危機。」無庸置疑地，日本人正歷經重建家園的困境。然而，來自世界各地的援助與祈禱，必然在這段時間裡，對他們大有助益。

Exercise 解析

1. **B**　此格應填被動語態的動詞，根據語意，故選(B)。

2. **E**　此為分詞構句，原句為：..., and made it the most powerful...，省略連接詞 (and)，動詞為主動語態，所以改為現在分詞，故選(E)。

3. **A**　此格應填副詞，根據語意，故選(A)。

4. **J**　此格應填副詞，根據語意，故選(J)。

5. **C**　此格應填名詞，根據後面的 the tsunami，故選(C)。

6. **D**　此格應填動詞，根據文意，故選(D)。

7. **F**　此格應填名詞，根據文意，故選(F)。

8. **I**　此格應填名詞，根據前面的 donations，可以推論此格應填(I)。

9. **G**　此格應填形容詞，根據文意，故選(G)。

10. **H**　此格應填形容詞，根據後文 the most difficult，可以推論此格應為最高級用法，故選(H)。

Pop Quiz 解答				
1. D	2. D	3. C	4. A	5. B

2010 年 3 月 20 日，當位於冰島南部的艾雅法拉冰河下的火山第一次噴發的時候，它僅僅造成當地一些麻煩而已。但 4 月 14 日第二次火山爆發時，瞬間將一大團火山灰雲霧送上天空。這團火山灰噴發的高度在兩天內便超過 8 公里，同時向北歐地區的天空飄散，造成航空交通自 4 月 15 日開始停擺，連帶迫使來自全球各地的旅客滯留機場。

當火山灰飄向歐洲時，由於它所含的矽酸鹽顆粒會嚴重損害引擎，官方決定取消飛機航班。在 1980 年代曾經發生過的兩起事件中，客機在不知情的狀況下飛經火山灰雲霧，造成引擎停止運轉。在這兩起案例中，雖然機組人員最終都還是能夠重新啟動引擎，但當時飛機早已下降數千公尺之多。

在火山灰往東方和南方飄散的時候，即使遙遠如羅馬的機場都被迫關閉。假期或出差的旅客努力尋找返國的替代方案。幾百名訓練數月的運動員原本計畫要從歐洲飛往美國參加 4 月 19 日的波士頓馬拉松比賽，也因此錯過了。大體上而言，估計禁飛的每一天約有 120 萬人次受到影響。

禁飛數天後，航空公司開始抱怨政府對於火山灰的處置反應過度。當航班終於在六天後恢復，航空公司從火山爆發開始算起的損失已將近 20 億。部份航空公司更要求政府賠償，但官方仍堅持寧可過於謹慎也不要出差錯。這次火山爆發在全球造成的影響，突顯出政府與企業需要發展危機應變計畫，以面對天災造成的問題。

Exercise 解析

(B) 1. 本題問主旨，故須整合各段重點才能答題：第一段談及冰島的火山爆發，大量的火山灰造成歐洲航空交通停擺；第二段舉出發生在 1980 年代的兩起事件，發現火山灰會造成飛機引擎停止運轉，所以官方決定取消飛機航班；第三段是火山灰造成的影響；第四段指出政府與企業都需要發展危機應變計畫。從以上重點可知，本文主旨在討論火山灰所造成的影響，故選(B)。

(A) 2. 根據第一段，可以知道航空交通自 4 月 15 日開始停擺，故答案為選項 (A)。

(C) 3. 根據前句：...governments were being too cautious about the ash...，可以推論出政府的做法比較積極、謹慎，故選(C)。

(B) 4. 根據第四段，可以知道損失金額為 20 億，故(B)為非。

(D) 5. 線索在第二段，故知答案為選項 (D)。

Pop Quiz 解答

1. means
2. shut down
3. highlighted
4. compensate
5. resume

　　針對「牛肉」這個不太可能的議題，在臺灣引發重大爭議。確切地說，來自美國的進口牛肉商品已經造成全國性騷動，有政治人物的反對，和 11 月 14 日臺北街頭數千人的遊行抗議。對於政府重新開放多種美國牛肉商品的進口，這些政治人物和抗議者都表達反對。

　　在 2003 年，臺灣政府禁止所有美國牛肉的進口。這是在美國傳出牛隻感染牛腦海綿狀病變，較為人熟知的名稱是「狂牛症」，之後所採取的措施。在當時，這個禁令被認為是很合理的，因為根據一些科學家研究顯示，如果食用感染狂牛症動物的腦和脊髓，會導致人得到嚴重、甚至致命的疾病。

　　這個禁令曾在 2005 年有條件放寬，不過當美國發現第二起狂牛症病例之後，很快就又恢復禁令。到了 2006 年，臺灣的衛生署決定允許一定年齡牛隻身上的不帶骨肉進口。接下來的三年，臺灣面對來自美國不斷增加的壓力，要求開放更多美國牛肉進口。最後，在 2009 年 10 月，臺灣終於解除了三十個月齡以下牛隻的帶骨肉、絞肉、內臟的進口禁令。

　　雖然這個政策受到美國牛肉出口商和政府官員的歡迎，但在臺灣可不一樣。兩大主要政黨的政治人物都表達了他們對這個措施的擔憂，而對於健康風險和狂牛症可能散播至臺灣，許多臺灣民眾也有所恐懼。有些人還指責現在的政府屈服於美方的壓力，置臺灣公共衛生安全於不顧。很多人都呼籲政府重新商討這項協議。

　　就衛生署而言，其官員已強調會採取嚴格的檢查措施以確保公共安全。但目前看來，關於美國牛肉進口與否——或甚至是要不要吃——的爭議，可能還會持續下去。

Exercise 解析

(A) 1. 從文意上可以推論此格的動作應是「從過去開始持續到現在，且仍在進行中的動作」，時態用現在完成進行式，故選(A)。

(D) 2. 與 step 常用的搭配動詞為 take，故選(D)。

(A) 3. 根據文意，故選(A)。

(C) 4. 介系詞 with 在此表示「具有，帶有」之意。

(C) 5. (A) bring down 減少；(B) bring up 撫養，養育；(C) bring back 恢復；(D) bring out 表現出。

(B) 6. (A) 增進的；(B) 增加的；(C) 減少的；(D) 發展中的。此為現在分詞作形容詞的用法。

(D) 7. 根據文意，故選(D)。in spite of 後接名詞 (片語) 或接「the fact that + 子句」，故不能選(C)。

(B) 8. (A) 暴動，騷亂；(B) 恐懼；(C) 方法，手段；(D) 視野，眼界。

(C) 9. (A) 照顧；(B) 湧入至、逃竄至 (某地)；(C) 公開呼籲；(D) (壞天氣、壞事等) 開始、到來。

(A) 10. 根據文意，故選(A)。

Pop Quiz 解答				
1. C	2. A	3. D	4. C	5. B

一切都是從 2011 年 3 月悄悄開始的。當時大眾對此事件還一無所知，臺灣食品藥物管理局在 16 種運動飲料及軟性飲料中發現有毒物質鄰苯二甲酸二 (2- 乙基己基) 酯的蹤跡，一般將這種化學物質稱為 DEHP。這種塑化劑常用來製造 PVC 塑膠管，已經證實食用後會造成癌症和其他健康問題。

接下來的幾個星期，食品藥物管理局進行了數次檢測來判斷其他食品或飲料是否也遭到 DEHP 污染。接著，食品藥物管理局在 5 月 23 日向大眾宣布部份產品已經受到該塑化劑的毒害。其後許多產品被下架，政府也開始要求五大類食品和飲料——運動飲料、果汁、茶飲料、果醬、果漿或果凍類，以及膠囊錠狀粉末類的廠商必須證明其產品不含有害的化學物質。

調查人員認為這次危機的罪魁禍首是昱伸香料公司。該公司是臺灣最大的乳化劑供應商，涉嫌在過去 15 年期間將 DEHP 作為食品添加物來販售。乳化劑常作為部份食品及飲料的起雲劑。不幸的是，昱伸香料公司在乳化劑中使用 DEHP 來取代棕櫚油；傳統上常將棕櫚油用於乳化劑成份當中，價格較 DEHP 來得昂貴。此外，另一家賓漢香料公司也被發現使用 DEHP 作為起雲劑。

這次食品恐慌對臺灣會有多長遠的影響還有待觀察。目前許多人感到害怕且困惑，不曉得哪些食品和飲料才能安心食用，製造及販售食品的公司紛紛向大眾擔保其產品安全無虞、絕不含 DEHP。由於業者預估營收將因此事件減少一到兩成，經濟部長施顏祥估計 DEHP 風波將使臺灣食品產業損失超過一百億元。

隨著 DEHP 風暴程度的擴大，大眾對於臺灣食品的信心可能需要好一陣子才能恢復。不過，也有人希望這次的食品恐慌能使政府對飲食產品的把關更加嚴格。這次事件也許能讓更多民眾注意到食品安全的重要性。

Exercise 解析

1. __B__ know sb./sth. as sth. 表示「將…稱為…」。
2. __D__ 根據前面提到 cancer，可以知道會有其他「健康」問題，故選(D)。
3. __J__ 此格應填動詞 (片語)，根據 test 的常用搭配語，故選(J)
4. __H__ 從文意上推論，此格應填人物對象，故選(H)。
5. __I__ 此格應填副詞來修飾句子，故選(I)。
6. __E__ 此格應填副詞，可以知道賓漢香料公司是另一家違法公司，故選(E)。
7. __A__ 此格應填形容詞，且根據介系詞 about，故選(A)。
8. __F__ 此格應填形容詞，根據後面的 free of DEHP，故選(F)。
9. __C__ 此格應填形容詞，根據文意，故選(C)。
10. __G__ 此格應填名詞，根據文意，故選(G)。

Pop Quiz 解答

1. D	2. C	3. C	4. A	5. B

全美的民眾都在密切注意蟲蟲危機。床蝨與臭蟲入侵住宅且危害全國作物。雖然床蝨在二次大戰後幾乎消失了，牠們在 1990 年代又捲土重來。 臭蟲則是亞洲原生種， 約 1998 年第一次出現在美國。這兩種蟲的繁殖速度驚人，使人們擔憂要如何除掉牠們。

床蝨的體型很小，會從房子門窗的縫隙鑽進去。牠們只要一進到屋內，便會想辦法躲在陰暗的地方，像是公事包、衣櫥抽屜等。牠們特別會躲在床墊底下，這樣一來，晚上就可以爬出來咬床墊上那些毫不知情的人們。一旦床墊受到感染，趕走床蝨的唯一方法就是丟掉床墊。

比起床蝨，雖然臭蟲的體型較大，牠們並不會咬人。臭蟲得其名是因為牠們被壓扁時會散發出臭味。牠們以蔬果為食，因此農夫對其感到頭疼。這些蟲子會在開門時自動鑽進屋內，接著就往所有東西一擁而上。

在亞洲，臭蟲能受到控制是因為黃蜂會吃掉臭蟲的卵。但在沒有天敵的美國，要擺脫臭蟲或床蝨真是難上加難。專家建議人們盡量密封住家，但蟲子仍能趁人不注意的時候潛入。消除臭蟲的研究包括誘捕牠們的幼蟲，而對付床蝨的手段則是出動嗅探犬來找出牠們的藏身之處。

Exercise 解析

(A) 1. 本題問主旨，故須整合各段重點才能答題：第一段在談論床蝨與臭蟲入侵美國境內，影響到住宅並危害作物；第二段是談論床蝨的習性；第三段是談論臭蟲的習性；第四段是討論如何才能消滅在美國境內沒有天敵的床蝨與臭蟲。從以上重點可知，本文主旨在討論美國人煩惱的床蝨與臭蟲問題，故選(A)。

(D) 2. 線索在第二段， 故知答案為選項(D)。

(B) 3. 本題問「make their way」的意思？根據後面是接地點，推論此片語跟移動位置有關，故選(B)。

(C) 4. 根據第四段，故知答案為選項(C)。

(D) 5. 第一段提到：Both bugs reproduce rapidly, and their large numbers... ，可以知道床蝨的繁殖力驚人，且其繁殖力與夜行性的習性無關，故(D)為非。

Pop Quiz 解答
1. C   2. A   3. B   4. D   5. C

這聽起來像是電影情節。一名銀髮澳大利亞籍的男子利用網路披露不僅足以使世界強權蒙羞,並改變國際事務走向的機密資訊。之後,這名男子遭到英國警方拘留,因為他被指控在瑞典涉及性犯罪,但隨即獲釋。同時,所謂的思想駭客為了表達對這個揭密網站的支持,對特定的公司展開網路攻擊。然而,上述的故事並不是好萊塢驚悚片的情節,而是當今的頭條新聞。近幾個月以來,維基解密及其神祕的發言人朱利安‧阿桑奇已經成為國際間的熱門話題。

維基解密創辦於 2006 年。它的目標是要讓人們重視一些平常可能未受注意的、來自走漏的新聞以及匿名提供的文件。往後的幾年,維基解密在世界各地變得較為知名,而阿桑奇則被視為其發言人。2010 年 4 月,維基解密公布了一段據說是 2007 年美軍殺害伊拉克平民及記者的影片。接著在 2010 年 7 月,維基解密發布了超過 76,900 份文件,記錄了美國在阿富汗的軍事行動。

維基解密立即遭到美國軍方的譴責,他們宣稱這樣的舉動是置在阿富汗及伊拉克的美國大兵於險境。然而,許多人卻予以支持,包括許多記者和新聞機構在內,他們認為這個網站只不過是行使言論自由權。

接下來,還有更具爆炸性的事件:維基解密開始將美國國務院外交電報公諸於世,其中有些祕密通訊讓美國政府官員感到十分難堪,但也有人說這些機密文件只是顯示出政府官員有在做事罷了。

維基解密是不是做過頭了呢?它到底是在揭發真相還是在製造混亂呢?唯一能確定的是:有時候現實生活比電影情節更加有趣,也更加詭異。

Exercise 解析

(B) 1. 此格填對等連接詞,後接文法作用相同的單字、片語或子句。根據文意,故選(B)。

(B) 2. (A) 突然地;(B) 同時;(C) 首先;(D) 最後。

(A) 3. 「for + 過去一段時間」的時態常用現在完成式,表示「從過去開始並一直持續到現在的動作」,故選(A)。

(D) 4. (A) 促進;(B) 吃,喝;(C) 散發 (光、熱、聲音、氣味等);(D) 開始從事。

(C) 5. be seen as sth. 表示「被視為⋯」。

(C) 6. (A) 狂熱;(B) 主題,題目;(C) 危險;(D) 議題。

(D) 7. 介系詞 to 用來表示「所屬關係,關於」。

(D) 8. 使役動詞 make 後接受詞,可接形容詞作為受詞補語。

(A) 9. 上下句文意有所轉折,故選(A)。

(B) 10. (A) 過度的,過多的;(B) 確定,確實;(C) 極端的,激進的;(D) 大規模的,嚴重的。

Pop Quiz 解答

1. altered	2. chaos	3. Normally
4. revealed	5. dedicated	

期盼數月之後，在 2010 年 6 月 24 日，蘋果最新一代的 iPhone 4 終於在五個國家上市了。雖然甫上市就因供貨短缺及天線問題而受到注目，iPhone 4 的視訊通話及高畫質影像等新特色達到廣告宣傳的功效。蘋果宣佈 7 月 30 日當天 iPhone 4 會在另外 17 個國家開始上市。

第一代 iPhone 在 2007 年 1 月問世時，就因為創新的觸控式螢幕、高機動性的網路連線能力及時髦的設計而成為全球熱銷的智慧型手機。此外，就像蘋果另一項熱門產品 iPod 一樣，iPhone 也可以播放影片和音樂。

蘋果在 6 月 15 日開始接受 iPhone 4 的預購，但大量的訂單迫使蘋果公司在數小時內停止預售。即使在 6 月 24 日 iPhone 4 送抵門市之後，需求量太過龐大，以致於持續一個月以上出現顧客在店裡無法直接購得手機的情況。

iPhone 4 最大的爭議在於它的天線問題。上市後不久，使用者發現在講電話時若握住手機邊緣，就會因為遮蓋到部分的天線而造成斷訊。在 7 月 16 日的記者會上，蘋果創始人史提夫‧賈伯斯宣布將會免費提供改善收訊問題的保護套給在 9 月 30 日前購買 iPhone 4 的客戶。他也指出其他智慧型手機也有類似的問題，並否認蘋果公司生產一款設計不良的產品。

除了天線問題之外，iPhone 4 的生產問題也連帶影響到白色款 iPhone 4 的上市時間。蘋果宣佈直到 2010 年稍晚才能買到白色款的 iPhone 4，顧客目前暫時只能購買黑色款式。儘管 iPhone 4 上市的爭議不斷，它依舊十分熱賣，在推出首週就賣出 170 萬支。

Exercise 解析

1. **D** 根據後文提到：...such as video calling and high-definition video，可知此格應填複數名詞，故選(D)。
2. **E** 此格應填形容詞，根據文意，故選(E)。
3. **G** 此格應填副詞來引導句子，因為後繼續談到 iPhone 的功能，故選(G)。
4. **I** 此格應填名詞，根據文意，故選(I)。
5. **A** 此格應填形容詞，根據文意，故選(A)。
6. **C** 此格應填名詞，根據後文提到 problems with its antenna，故選(C)。
7. **F** 此格應填過去式動詞，根據文意，故選(F)。
8. **B** 此格應填原形動詞，根據介系詞 for，故選(B)。
9. **H** 此格應填副詞，根據文意，故選(H)。
10. **J** despite 後接名詞 (片語) 和 despite the fact that-clause 都是表示「即使，儘管」。

Pop Quiz 解答

1. C	2. C	3. B	4. D	5. A

在人類對上機器的戰爭中，人類可能還得向其創造物學點東西。一個取名為華森的人工智慧電腦系統打敗了美國流行電視益智問答節目《危險邊緣》中兩名最厲害的參賽者。在兩天的聯賽中，華森輕鬆擊敗兩位人類對手——曾創下連續 74 場不敗紀錄的肯‧杰寧斯及節目中的獎金王布萊德‧洛特。這場勝利替華森的創造者 IBM 公司贏得 100 萬元獎金，也讓人不禁開始思考華森的意義。

為了增強系統的整體效能，華森實際上是由許多 IBM 伺服器連結而成。這臺「思考機器」使用的特殊軟體讓它不僅可以理解人類語言，更能夠以合成的聲音回答問題。當被問問題時，華森迅速在其庫存的大批知識當中搜尋，像是百科全書、字典、文學作品還有維基百科的全文。它每秒鐘可以處理 100 萬筆書目資料，接著以其資料庫內找到的三個最有可能的答案回答。

《危險邊緣》節目的比賽過程中，華森在人類參賽者身旁是由螢幕上的虛擬化身作為代表。不同於人類的是：它無法離開在 IBM 的房間，也不能在沒有電力的情況下運作。不過，電腦在按鈴答題時有極大的速度優勢。先按鈴的參賽者 (人或是機器) 可以先回答問題，而華森可以比人類更快按鈴搶答。

確定落敗之後，肯‧杰寧斯在他的螢幕上寫下一段幽默的話：「我，代表全體，歡迎我們新的電腦霸主。」然而，大部分的分析師承認華森的勝利對人類來說是正面的。它的成功證明了人工智慧系統能以精細複雜的模式為基礎，分析錯綜複雜的問題並建議解決方法，人們可以利用這樣的技術去解決例如保全、保健、金融等不同領域的挑戰。

Exercise 解析

(C) 1. 本題問主旨，可以知道是人工智慧電腦系統 (華森) 如何擊敗人類對手、贏得電視益智問答比賽，故選 (C)。

(D) 2. 線索在第一段，故知答案為選項 (D)。

(B) 3. 前文提到：...held a record of winning 74 games...，可以推測此片語應該有「連續」之意，故選(B)。

(A) 4. 根據第三段，可以知道人工智慧電腦系統 (華森) 不能離開 IBM 伺服器，故知(A)為非。

(C) 5. 根據第三段：...Watson can buzz in much quicker than humans.，可知(A)為非；根據第一段，可知應該是 Brad Rutter，故(B)為非；根據第一段，可以知道華森輕鬆擊敗人類對手，故(D)為非。

Pop Quiz 解答

1. B	2. A	3. A	4. C	5. D

2009 年夏季聽障奧運於九月十五日落幕。數以千計的聽障運動員，連同他們的教練、家人以及朋友，在這為期十一天的賽會期間，都受到身為東道主的臺灣人親切且殷勤的招待。在先前的預報中指出，降雨可能讓賽會大為掃興，但很幸運地，比賽期間的天氣一直都很好，這更成了一個令人愉快的驚喜。

九月五日於臺北市立體育場，一場絢麗的開幕典禮為今年的聽障奧運拉開序幕。絢爛煙火照亮夜空，同時張惠妹以特殊鋼索懸吊飛越天際，並高唱著聽障奧運的主題曲「聽得見的夢想」。為了向莫拉克風災的罹難者表示哀悼，還舉辦了一場特別的燭光晚禱。接著，高聳的聽障奧運聖火點燃，比賽也隨之展開。

今年大會共舉辦 20 種運動項目，其中包含羽球、足球、網球以及游泳，這些比賽於臺北各地的場館中舉行。在這些比賽中，臺灣表現傑出，總計獲得 11 面金牌、11 面銀牌以及 11 面銅牌，這讓臺灣在獎牌的總排行上名列第 5，是臺灣在聽障奧運中所得到過最好的名次。

大會舉辦期間，臺北的街道上，尤其是臺北市立體育場附近，總是擠滿了外國運動員及觀光客。同時也可以看到許多參賽者在當地公園裡跑步，或是在臺北各地的體育中心裡接受訓練。對於工作人員能將每件事都安排得如此妥善順利，參與本次賽會的運動員都讚譽有加。尤其是數千名志工更是不斷受到讚揚，他們其中有許多已經學會基本手語，並總是面帶微笑來提供協助。

2009 年夏季聽障奧運以傳統的臺式「辦桌」收場。超過 350 張圓桌擺設整齊，運動員和賓客均被饗以臺灣特產，其中包括蒸餃、甜不辣、牛肉麵、芒果剉冰和珍珠奶茶。聽障奧運聖火及會旗隨後便傳遞給雅典，該市將負責主辦 2013 年下屆的聽障奧運。

Exercise 解析

(D) 1. 根據文意，故選(D)。

(A) 2. (A) 進展，進程；(B) 浪費；廢 (棄) 物；(C) 邏輯；(D) 混合。

(B) 3. 根據文意，選表達時間的連接詞 as。

(C) 4. 介系詞 with 表示「有」之意。

(C) 5. (A) 幾乎，差不多；(B) 不幸地；(C) 尤其，特別；(D) 相對地，相當地。

(B) 6. 根據文意，故選(B)。

(D) 7. 此為分詞片語，省略了關係代名詞 (who)，並將主動語態的動詞改成現在分詞，故選(D)。

(A) 8. 因為這些義工早已學會基本手語，是更早之前就發生的動作，所以時態用過去完成式，故選(A)。

(A) 9. 根據文意，故選(A)。

(C) 10. (A) 提高，增加；(B) 開始有 (感覺或意見)；(C) 設立，設置；(D) 導致。

Pop Quiz 解答

1. are blessed with	2. hospitality
3. spectacular	4. medal 5. indicates

2010 的世界盃將會因為許多的「第一」而名留青史——這是非洲國家首次舉辦世足賽，也是西班牙首度贏得各方垂涎的冠軍頭銜。

南非是今年世界盃的主辦國，舉國為了球賽卯足全力，在全國各地蓋了幾座壯觀的體育館，包括位於索維托的足球城體育館。不幸的是，部份遊客、甚至球員都抱怨比賽期間南非的天氣寒冷，其他人則是對當地的大眾運輸不太滿意。

然而在球場上，2010 的世界盃絕對不乏精彩刺激的鏡頭，荷蘭對西班牙的冠軍賽也不例外。這場精采的決賽全程緊張刺激，甚至踢進延長賽，直到西班牙的安德烈斯・伊涅斯塔進球，西班牙才以一比零抱走世足金盃。這場勝利讓西班牙初嘗世界盃冠軍頭銜的滋味，而荷蘭則吞下歷來世界盃決賽的第三敗。

這次世界盃的另一個「第一」則是巫巫茲拉，這種南非傳統的「體育場號角」成了比賽的必備道具。有人很愛這些響亮的號角，有人則深惡痛絕。對收看電視轉播的觀眾來說，巫巫茲拉的聲音聽起來就像一大群憤怒的蜜蜂。

最後一個 2010 世界盃的「第一」就是神算章魚保羅的出現。這隻兩歲的章魚連八次命中本屆賽事的贏家。保羅當時預測西班牙會在決賽擊敗荷蘭，而德國則會打敗烏拉圭贏得季軍。當地準確地預測出德國隊將吃敗仗之後，某些憤怒的德國球迷甚至揚言要把保羅做成壽司來吃。

無疑地，2010 的世界盃會被全世界球迷記上好一段時間。這是首次在非洲舉辦的世界盃，還有巫巫茲拉、神算章魚跟西班牙隊的首度奪冠。

Exercise 解析

1. __E__ 此格應填名詞，根據文意，故選(E)。

2. __A__ 此格應填副詞以修飾整個句子，後面談及在比賽期間南非的寒冷天氣，推論應是負面，故選(A)。

3. __J__ 此格應填形容詞，public transportation 為搭配用法，意思為「大眾運輸」。

4. __H__ 此格應填形容詞，根據文意，故選(H)。

5. __B__ 此格應填名詞，be no exception 意思為「…不例外」。

6. __C__ 此格應填連接詞，前後句文意上有所轉折，故選(C)。

7. __G__ 此格應填形容詞來形容樂器 (號角)，故選(G)。

8. __D__ 此格應填動詞，sound like 意思為「聽起來像…」。

9. __I__ 此格應填名詞，推論應與比賽有關，故選(I)。

10. __F__ 此格應填副詞以修飾整個句子，根據文意，故選(F)。

Pop Quiz 解答				
1. B	2. C	3. A	4. B	5. D

在 2009 年 2 月 1 日的第 43 屆超級盃比賽中，匹茲堡鋼人隊在最後剩 35 秒時達陣得分，以 27 比 23 擊敗亞利桑那紅雀隊。在 8 次進攻就前進 78 碼的長傳後，接球手荷姆斯從四分衛班‧羅斯里伯格手中接過致勝傳球。鋼人隊第六度勇奪超級盃冠軍，而荷姆斯也因為個人的優異表現，榮獲最有價值球員。

第一屆超級盃是在 1967 年 1 月 15 日開打，比賽原本是由國家美式足球聯盟 (NFL) 的冠軍隊伍，對上美國美式足球聯盟 (AFL) 的冠軍。兩個聯盟於 1970 年合併後，超級盃便成為新的國家美式足球聯盟冠軍賽事。隨著時間的演進，超級盃已經成為美國最多人收看的電視節目，而今年比賽約有 9,870 萬人觀賞，更是刷新記錄。

美國大多數的民眾把超級盃的星期日當成國定假日來看待。除了比賽本身，也有許多的宣傳活動集中在超級盃的電視廣告上。諸如蘋果電腦和可口可樂等公司就砸下數百萬美元購買 30 秒的廣告，而這些廣告所受到的分析研究可不少於比賽。此外，中場休息時間也往往吸引大牌明星前來表演，例如保羅‧麥卡尼、滾石合唱團和布魯斯‧史普林斯汀。

老美熱愛美式足球的原因在於它是一種講求速度的肉搏戰。一整個賽季，球迷大力支持自己喜歡的球隊挺進超級盃。開賽之前，人們提早抵達體育場開起後車廂派對，一邊大吃，一邊慶祝有趣的傳統活動。舉例來說，綠灣包裝工隊球迷會戴起狀似起司的造形帽，並且自稱「起司頭」。許多球迷超級熱愛美式足球，甚至到了超級盃結束後會難過的地步，不過，他們也只能倒數日子，期待新球季的開始。

Exercise 解析

(C) 1. 本題問主旨，可以知道超級盃比賽是美國最受歡迎的運動賽事，故選(C)。

(D) 2. 答案線索在第一段，故選(D)。

(A) 3. 從下文可以知道球迷如何幫他們喜歡的球隊加油，可推論此片語應有正面的涵義，故選(A)。

(B) 4. 根據第一段可以知道鋼人隊是第六度勇奪超級盃冠軍，意即在 2009 年之前有拿過五次超級盃冠軍，所以(B)為正確；根據第二段可知超級盃原本是國家美式足球聯盟 (NFL) 對上美國美式足球聯盟 (AFL) 的冠軍比賽，故(A)為非；從第三段可知廣告和比賽一樣受到歡迎，故(C)為非；根據第二段，約有 9,870 萬人觀賽，故(D)為非。

(B) 5. 根據第二段，可以知道國家美式足球聯盟 (NFL) 和美國美式足球聯盟 (AFL) 是在 1970 年合併，並非在第一屆超級盃後，故(B)為非。

Pop Quiz 解答

1. merge	2. revolves around	3. regularly
4. stadium	5. valuable	

在全球享有「流行音樂之王」美名的麥克‧傑克森，6 月 25 日於加州洛杉磯逝世，享年五十歲。擁有 *Thrillers*、*Bad*、*Black or White* 及 *Heal the World* 等金曲的傑克森，以動聽的歌曲和絕妙的舞步，在全球廣獲千千萬萬歌迷愛戴。雖然傑克森在 2005 年遭人指控性侵男童以致名聲下滑，但後來陪審團宣判他無罪，而就在死前數個月，他還宣布將在倫敦舉辦一系列的復出演唱會。

麥克‧傑克森出生於 1958 年 8 月 29 日，擔任傑克森兄弟合唱團 (由他和四個兄弟組成的歌唱團體) 主唱的他，在 11 歲時一舉成名。1970 年代晚期，麥可已經是很成功的男歌手，而在 1982 年發行《顫慄》專輯後，他的名氣更上層樓，當中的 *Beat It*、*Billie Jean* 等知名歌曲，贏得破記錄的 8 座葛萊美獎，並成為史上最暢銷專輯。

雖然之後麥克‧傑克森又發行了幾張暢銷唱片，但他的私生活開始讓歌唱事業籠罩陰影。從 1980 年代初，傑克森的容貌便明顯改變，他的膚色愈來愈白，臉上也出現多次整容痕跡。傑克森有 3 名子女，但他是否為生父的疑雲卻始終揮之不去。

在 7 月 7 日的追思會上，有超過 1 萬 7 千位民眾到場為傑克森送行，會中歌頌傑克森對世人的貢獻，瑪莉亞‧凱莉、萊諾‧李奇、史提夫‧汪達等巨星也到場致哀。典禮最終，傑克森 11 歲的女兒芭莉絲緬懷父親的談話令人動容，她強忍著淚水表示，他是「你能想像出最棒的父親」。

Exercise 解析

(D) 1. (A) 而不是；(B) 導致；(C) 取代，代替；(D) 例如。

(A) 2. (A) 遭受，承受；(B) 佔領，佔據；(C) 宣布，公布；(D) 停止。

(A) 3. 介系詞 as 意思為「作為，當作」。

(C) 4. (A) (國家經濟) 部門，領域；(B) 措施；(C) (唱片、電影) 發行；(D) 首次亮相。

(B) 5. 《顫慄》專輯為專有名詞，所以用非限定用法的關係子句，故選(B)。

(C) 6. 此為「adv. + V-ing」所組成的複合形容詞，best-selling 表示「暢銷的」。

(D) 7. 上下語意有所轉折，故連接詞選(D)。

(A) 8. (A) 外表，外貌；(B) 醜聞；(C) 威脅，恐嚇；(D) 藥片，藥丸。

(B) 9. (A) 好像，似乎；(B) 關於，至於；(C) 若非，要不是；(D) 多達。

(C) 10. 此為分詞構句，原句為：..., and held back tears to declare that...，省略了連接詞，並將主動語態的動詞改成現在分詞。

Pop Quiz 解答

1. acquitted	2. noticeably	3. career
4. reputation	5. touching	

許多人使用臉書來和朋友及家人保持聯繫。現在,這些使用者中,有很多都不只將它當作分享照片與張貼最新近況的工具。《黑幫戰爭》及《農場鄉村》這些遊戲讓使用者在虛擬世界中團結一致,共同執行黑手黨任務或是看顧田地。這些遊戲不但讓玩家日以繼夜地守在電腦前,還為遊戲設計者帶來數百萬美元的利潤。

臉書的遊戲大多有個標準模式。在《黑幫戰爭》中,玩家成為虛擬黑幫家族的老大,賺取虛擬金錢來購買武器和地產。玩家可以利用完成工作的方式或是與其他黑幫家族打鬥來獲取經驗值並升級。此外,他們也可以利用每日樂透來得到一些隨機的收集品或更好的獎品。在此同時,《農場鄉村》則提供玩家一片虛擬農田,讓他們耕種作物和飼養家畜以賺取更多的虛擬金錢。農場玩家們獲得經驗值後,可進階到更高的等級,也可藉由擁有更多鄰居、金幣或現鈔來擴充農場的面積。這些遊戲不斷鼓舞玩家,要他們向朋友宣告自己的成就,並提供免費的每日虛擬禮物,讓玩家可以送給自己的好友,以邀請更多的潛在玩家來加入遊戲的行列。到最後,許多玩家不自覺完全沉迷在線上社交遊戲裡。

在這些遊戲裡,如果玩家花光虛擬金錢,他們還可以選擇用「現金」來兌換,5 美金在《黑幫戰爭》裡可以買到 21 個「教父回饋點數」,這樣的交易對玩家來說很划算,對遊戲開發公司 Zynga 來說也是棵搖錢樹。Zynga 在 2009 年預計獲利近 2 億 5 千萬美元,其中大多來自《黑幫戰爭》及《農場鄉村》這類遊戲中的小額交易。

諸如此類的臉書遊戲因為簡單易玩而大受歡迎,也讓玩家更容易沈迷在虛擬成就之中。在這些遊戲裡,雖然沒有人是輸家,但真正的贏家只有那些賺到真實現金的人。

Exercise 解析

1. __J__ 此格應填形容詞,可以知道與遊戲《黑幫戰爭》及《農場鄉村》有關,故選(J)。

2. __C__ 此格應填名詞,根據文意,故選(C)。

3. __D__ 此格應填副詞,根據後面有 or,故選(D)。either...or... 表示「不是…就是」。

4. __H__ 此格應填形容詞,根據文意,故選(H)。

5. __I__ 此格應填形容詞,根據文意,故選(I)。

6. __B__ 此格應填副詞,根據文意,故選(B)。

7. __E__ 此格應填名詞,根據文意,故選(E)。

8. __A__ 此格應填動詞 (片語),根據後接動名詞,故選(A)。

9. __G__ 此格應填原形動詞,後有提到金額,故選(G)。

10. __F__ 此格應填複數名詞,根據文意,故選(F)。

Pop Quiz 解答

1. D	2. C	3. C	4. A	5. B

阿凡達的精彩：未來趨勢電影

《阿凡達》不僅是史上製作成本最高的電影，可能還會改變觀眾看電影的方式。《阿凡達》的導演是詹姆士‧卡麥隆，曾拍過《魔鬼終結者》以及《鐵達尼號》兩部熱門鉅片，此次號稱砸下近三億美金以 3D 科技拍攝的《阿凡達》，讓觀眾不只觀賞這部電影，更能身歷其境。

《阿凡達》故事發生在西元 2154 年遙遠的潘朵拉衛星上，人類企圖支配此星球上的某種礦產，以解決地球的毀滅危機。一群科學家將受傷的退役海軍陸戰隊士兵傑克與名為阿凡達的混血生物進行連結，此生物的外貌與舉止都和潘朵拉原住民納美人一模一樣。然而，傑克並未達成臥底、偷取納美人祕密的任務，反而和納美族公主墜入愛河，並且一同抵抗人類入侵、使潘朵拉不受佔領。

雖然這只是個有趣的科幻故事，但是有些人還是會因為視覺特效而一次又一次地進戲院觀賞《阿凡達》。除了令人印象深刻的 3D 科技之外，潘朵拉星球的虛擬生物也為觀眾帶來視覺震撼，電腦以停格動畫技術將真人動作轉移到螢幕上的外星人身上，十呎高的納美人擁有藍色皮膚與貓一般的雙眼，讓這些虛擬人物簡直栩栩如生，擄獲不少觀眾的心。卡麥隆甚至還請了個語言學家創造獨特的納美語，讓這群外星人感覺更為真實。

《阿凡達》首映票房大約兩億七千八百萬美金，打破影史上首週票房最高的紀錄。本片勾勒出一段愛與冒險的史詩故事，還呈現出令人嘆為觀止的特效，相信會在未來幾週持續發燒。

Exercise 解析

(B) 1. 本題問主旨，可以知道是探討電影《阿凡達》成功的原因，故選 (B)。

(C) 2. 根據後文：...looks and acts like the Na'vi... ，可以推論不是真的納美人，故選(C)。

(D) 3. 根據第三段，可以知道所謂的「納美語」是導演卡麥隆請語言學家創造出來的，並非基於非洲語，故答案為(D)。

(B) 4. 根據第二段，可以知道答案為(B)。

(A) 5. 根據第一段和第三段 ，可以知道 3D 科技和停格動畫技術所呈現令人嘆為觀止的特效是電影 《阿凡達》的賣點。

Pop Quiz 解答

1. premiere 　　 2. breathtaking 　 3. on-screen
4. destruction 　 5. captivated

字彙翻譯HOW EASY

王隆興　編著

大考字彙與翻譯
一次搞定 HOW EASY！

1. 彙集歷屆大考精選單字500個，撰寫成情境豐富的文意字彙題，利用這些測驗，保證讓你不僅能記下單字，更能達到活用 HOW EASY！
2. 綜合多元且生活化的各類翻譯題目，讓你輕鬆做好翻譯練習、徹底厚植翻譯實力，保證面對大考翻譯感覺 HOW EASY！
3. 解析本收錄字彙題幹完整中譯、重點單字片語整理；翻譯部分則有重點句型及文法歸納，善用本書的豐富內容，保證讓你英文進步 HOW EASY！

三民網路書店　會員
獨享好康
大　放　送

書種最齊全
服務最迅速

通關密碼：A9599

憑通關密碼
登入就送100元e-coupon。
(使用方式請參閱三民網路書店之公告)

生日快樂
生日當月送購書禮金200元。
(使用方式請參閱三民網路書店之公告)

好康多多
購書享3%～6%紅利積點。
消費滿350元超商取書免運費。
電子報通知優惠及新書訊息。

超過百萬種繁、簡體書、原文書5折起　三民網路書店 www.sanmin.com.tw

新聞+英文+閱讀測驗+字彙　通通宅配到府

★ 特別聘請專業外籍作者為讀者量身打造30篇符合程度的文章。內容
　囊括國內外最熱門的新聞話題，讓你讀新聞學英文，立足臺灣，放
　眼國際。

★ 歸納整理文章中的關鍵單字與片語，讓你掌握新聞要點，迅速累
　積大量字彙。精心設計的Exercise與Pop Quiz，可立即診斷學習成
　效。每單元都有該新聞的相關資料補充，讓你了解其來龍去脈。

★ 解析本附詳盡中譯及解析，幫助你洞悉文章脈絡，強化理解能力。

三民網路書店
www.sanmin.com.tw

「新聞宅急通C」與
「翻譯與解析」不分售
80975G